The Kingdom Written in Sand and Time

Part 1

The Kingdom Written in Sand and Time

Part 1

Ashfaq Ahmad

GRADIAS
PUBLISHING HOUSE

Gradias Publishing House

448/843, Ghasmandi

Thakurganj, Lucknow— 226003

Ph. 9616066930, 9473926431

E-mail: *gradiaspublishinghouse@gmail.com*

Book: The Kingdom Written in Sand and Time Part 1

Genre: Fiction/Fantasy

Author: Ashfaq Ahmad

First Published by **Gradias Publishing House** 2026

Edition: 1

ISBN: 978-81-996162-9-5

To everyone who still believes that the ancient stories never died—
they only waited for someone to listen.

"Every empire falls.
But some empires learn to rise again."

—Ashfaq ahmad

Before the Journey Begins

This story is born from deserts older than memory, myths older than fire, and a question older than destiny itself:

What happens when the human world and the jinn world collide again?

Every page of 'The 'Kingdom Written in Sand and time' is an invitation— into a universe where legends breathe, choices burn, and love carries the weight of centuries. Step carefully… for once the journey begins, it does not forget its travellers.

— ***Ashfaq Ahmad***

Contents

Disclaimer— *All the characters and events in these stories are fictitious and have no relation with any person or event. If there is a resemblance to a person, then it will be called a mere coincidence. Real names of some places have been used to give authenticity to the story. The stories are written for entertainment purpose only.*

Introduction

The Journey Where Truth Refuses to Hide

This is an epic of a story forged between humans and jinn—one that may appear, on the surface, fragmented and unconnected, but whose threads are in truth deeply intertwined. The human narrative is rooted in Pakhtunkhwa, where you will encounter the social structure of the Pashtuns, their internal conflicts, and their interactions with the jinn. The jinn, on the other hand, trace their background across regions stretching from western Pakistan to Turkmenistan, Syria, and Oman—desert expanses and green yet desolate lands where four distinct sultanates once flourished. These realms were, in the distant past, part of a single great empire.

In broad terms, the Pashtuns are divided into four major groups: Sarbani, Gharghasht, Kharlani, and Baitani. Each group comprises anywhere from eighteen to thirty-eight tribes and sub-tribes.

At the heart of the narrative are four families belonging to the Sadazoi, Hamaar, Afridi, and Khasoor tribes, associated with the jagirs of Bagraat, Mahepora, Kaanwabeel, and Shahelaar. Each family comes from a different group, and all are settled between Swat and Upper–Lower Dir. Among them exists a fierce antagonism, where taking a life is considered trivial, and winning a woman is seen as a means to elevate one's honor and social standing.

Much like the humans, the jinn too exist in numerous scattered settlements. In the past, these were unified into a single sultanate known as Greater Altunia. Due to a curse, this realm fractured into four territories: Rakhaan, Aramin, Panjshir, and Qazaar. Each territory is now mired in internal strife, while all four continue to battle one another. Before proceeding, it is necessary to understand, in brief, who the jinn are and how their society is structured.

According to legend, the jinn are a distinct entity separate from humans. They generally inhabit desolate lands away from human settlements and are largely devoted to worship. Their concepts of life, death, and family may closely resemble our own. It is said that a human, one to eight thousand years after death, may become a jinn and dwell in a different dimension—one that coexists with ours, yet remains unseen by us. Many jinn are believed to live among humans in human form, though they remain unrecognized.

Broadly, jinn are divided into four primary categories. The principal race is the Ifrit. These jinn possess a social structure closely resembling that of humans, and most tales associated with jinn revolve around Ifrits. The central jinn characters in this story also belong to this category. Another race is the Mareed— exceptionally powerful and dangerous beings capable of flight, often found near water. Their conceptual similarity may be drawn to the mythological yaksha. There is also the Sila race, consisting solely of female jinn. They are extraordinarily beautiful, highly intelligent, and alluring, comparable to the yakshini. The fourth major race is the Ghoul—flesh-eating, perilous entities commonly associated with graveyards, comparable to what might be understood as vampires.

This entire concept is Arabic in origin and rooted in Islamic belief. Its truth or falsehood may be debated, and it may be dismissed as superstition. However, the purpose of storytelling is purely entertainment, and this narrative has been written with that intent alone. To truly enjoy the story, one must set aside demands for logic and scientific exactitude and engage with it solely as a work of imaginative fiction.

At its core, the story contains three love stories intertwined with a larger conflict whose foundation lies in a curse. One love story exists between two humans. One unfolds between two jinn. And one bridges a human and a jinn. The true fulcrum of the narrative lies in this final story, for it is bound to a prophecy—one that foretold that the violent struggle raging between these two worlds would reach its conclusion through this very union.

CHAPTER 1

He drove in silence— a muted heaviness pooling in his chest, tangled with a thread of irritation. Atif Aslam's "Sang-e-Mah" played inside the car, but the music failed to distract him; his gaze kept drifting toward the sky beyond the windshield, thick with dark clouds that looked ready to burst, the kind that would pour without mercy once they began. For him, a storm like this was no small inconvenience. Where he lived, the route lay far beyond treacherous mountain paths— and once the weather turned ugly, reaching home often became impossible.

He was returning from Peshawar; after Gul-abad he had left NH-45 and taken the Asbanr Road. Verdant slopes stretched along the mountainsides, and on his right flowed the Shewa-Khwar River, its waters running parallel to the road. A small army convoy moved ahead, accompanied by a few civilian vehicles heading toward Totano Bandai. Safir Khasoor had to reach the Shahélaar estate near Qalagay, and that required at least enough mercy from the clouds that the road did not collapse into oblivion. He himself was the son of Chaudhary Anas Khasoor, the jagirdar of Shahélaar, returning from a business errand in Peshawar— but under the worsening sky, frustration had begun to sting sharper than the rain.

He wanted to overtake the army convoy, step on the accelerator and be done with the crawl, but the road wasn't wide enough— and overtaking an army convoy was never a wise idea. So, he remained behind them, bound by circumstance.

His annoyance came from the weather. But his melancholy— that bruise was named Rimsha.

Rimsha, who had once studied with him in Islamabad. Rimsha, because of whom he had first understood what it meant to fall in love. Their story had once been warm and bright, but the harshest hurdle had always been her family. She was the daughter of a Baloch army officer who dreamed only of an army officer for his daughter. Under her father's pressure and fearing future turmoil, Rimsha had slowly stepped away… until one day she cut the story clean with a proper goodbye.

The blow had gutted Safir so deeply that he abandoned his studies mid-way and retreated to Shahélaar.

Today, in that very convoy ahead, he had caught a glimpse— just a fleeting reflection of Rimsha. His mind, reluctant yet helpless, slipped back into those painful corners of memory he had sealed away. It had been two years since he left the university. He had, over time, buried the ache. But that single accidental glimpse tore open what he had just barely stitched.

She probably hadn't seen him… But he had seen her. And that alone was enough to sour his breath.

The convoy had barely crossed Asbanr when the sky suddenly split open— the first burst of rain came down with a fury, as if crazed droplets had declared war on the earth. A frustrated curse escaped his mouth as he slapped the steering wheel. It was almost certain he would be stranded now, and he began calculating where he might spend the night if the roads closed.

Half an hour crawled by on the Swat Road— they hadn't even reached Totano Bandai when gunfire ripped through the storm, drowning the roar of the rain. Several cars and containers stood off the left side of the road, and the gunfire had erupted from there. The harsh rattle of bullets thundered across the valley, and every vehicle on the road lurched violently, drivers swerving to hide behind whatever shelter they could find. The first burst seemed aimed at the army convoy, but the ricochets struck other vehicles too.

One such stray bullet shattered Safir's windshield, and he ducked instantly, heart pounding. Another grazed a tyre, dropping the car heavily to one side. The sound of the shots told him they were firing with assault rifles. Whoever had been hit in the first volley, the remaining soldiers fired back, and soon the entire stretch echoed like doomsday had descended on the mountains. Curled up inside the car, Safir's ears rang painfully— and through the chaos, one fear carved itself into him—

What had happened to Rimsha?

His thoughts hadn't even steadied when, through the rain and gunfire, a sharp, terrified scream pierced the noise— unmistakably a woman's.

He lifted his head, anxious, and spotted a few Pashtun men dragging a girl out of one of the cars ahead. It was the same car in which he had seen Rimsha moments earlier; the girl had to be her, even if distance and chaos blurred his view. They pulled her in front of them, using her as a shield so the army wouldn't shoot. Their backs were toward Safir— if anyone had been on his side of the road, they could have fired at the kidnappers from behind… but there was no one left capable of fighting in this chaos.

They dragged her behind a container, vanishing from his sight.

The gunfire continued— and moments later a car shot out from behind that very container, speeding away toward the rear. Covering fire erupted instantly, the bullets raining harder to protect their escape.

Safir understood what was happening. They were abducting her. And the ambush, this entire eruption— had been staged for that.

Who could it be? The 'Tehreek' came to mind— natural candidates, always in conflict with the army. Perhaps they hoped to use Rimsha to pressure his father, Hafeez Shirani, for some advantage.

But logic aside— something primal stabbed Safir's chest. A Pashtun's honor could not tolerate watching an azeez taken helplessly before his eyes. Something inside him rose— a challenge, a fire, an obligation.

The engine of his own car was still running— he slammed it into reverse and pushed the accelerator down with everything he had.

The kidnappers spotted movement. Bullets raked across his car, drilling holes through the metal, shattering every remaining window. Safir stayed low, barely escaping the spray — by nothing but sheer luck.

With one tyre ruined, he couldn't escape far, but he could at least get out of the direct line of fire. He reversed hard until he reached a fallen motorcycle; its rider had abandoned it and fled into the chaos. Safir left his battered car parked at an angle, using it as a shield from the gunfire, grabbed the motorcycle, and mounted it. Someone shouted in the distance— probably its owner, but Safir ignored it.

This road veered off from the Swat Road into the interior— and he sped into it, chasing the kidnappers' car. Within minutes, he could see it ahead. They were armed; he wasn't. So he kept a careful distance, weaving the bike to avoid becoming an easy target. The downpour helped him— rain blurred visibility, softened the sound, but he was drenched, freezing, and the slippery road threatened to throw him off at any moment.

Still he rode, reckless, relentless, heart pounding against the storm— because Rimsha had once been his world. Breakup or not, she remained precious. He could not watch her meet a brutal fate before his eyes.

Whatever happened to him— whatever it cost… he would not let them take her.

●●

She didn't look a day older than twenty, yet her deep black eyes held an unusual sharpness— a mind far wiser than her age. At this moment, though, her face carried the unmistakable shadow of a deep, unrelenting unrest. Her lips were pressed tightly together; anyone could see the worry etched across her expression. She was driving, and the road she took had turned to mud— a rough dirt path that the rain had beaten into patches of swamp. Had there been any hope of the storm easing, she would have waited… but the rain had shown no such mercy; it had poured relentlessly for two hours straight.

By now, the sun must have set— almost everything around her was swallowed in darkness. And part of that was the storm's own doing; the path ahead looked deserted, stripped clean of human presence.

She was Zikra Waqar, daughter of Chaudhary Waqar Afridi of Kaanwabeel— returning home with a piece of news she wished she never carried. She had gone to Tazeekba to meet her closest friend, Tanaz, so she could receive her brother from there— but now she was returning alone.

Her brother, Rayyaan Afridi, Kaanwabeel's only heir— was coming home today after two years in London. The haveli had been decorated for his welcome, but the sudden turn of weather had destroyed everything… and worse— there had been an incident no one at home knew yet, but she did. And it was tearing her nerves apart.

The family had wanted to go all the way to Islamabad to receive him, but Rayyaan had insisted they not trouble themselves. They had sent only the driver; by now he should have returned safely with Rayyaan… but neither had arrived, nor was there any news.

Zikra had gone to Tazeekba only so she would be able to receive Rayyaan earlier, but he had never reached. She could imagine the state of panic her mother and father were drowning in back home, and that thought alone tightened her chest. This region and its endless conflicts were the kind where no possibility could ever be ruled out… they had already lost one son, Shameel. Losing Rayyaan was something they simply could not endure.

To make things worse, the area had terrible mobile connectivity, and the landline had been down for a month due to some government repair work. She had tried to reassure her parents over the phone, but the network was so poor that neither side understood the other.

For a girl to travel alone here was risky enough, but love for her brother outweighed fear. Now, on her way back, a dark thought gnawed at her— what if something even worse had happened? In her heart she prayed— Wherever Rayyaan is, may he be safe. And may I reach the haveli unharmed.

The road was so miserable that the ten-minute stretch took half an hour. But the moment the haveli came into view, a surge of relief warmed her chest.

The gatekeeper opened the gate the moment he recognized her car, and she drove inside.

The haveli, beautifully decorated earlier, now looked devastated. The rain had ruined everything— lights hung lifeless, soaked through, the electricity gone since the storm began. Though they had a generator, it would have been used only upon Rayyaan's arrival. Now Rayyaan was missing— and so had Zikra been, until this moment.

She left the car in the portico and hurried into the main hall, where several servants stood silently with lowered heads. Her mother, Amziya, sat on the sofa, pale with worry, while her father, Waqar Afridi, paced the hall restlessly. At the sound of her footsteps, every face turned toward her, and Waqar stopped mid-stride. She went straight to her mother; Amziya seized her hand as though bracing herself against some incoming storm.

"Ammi… nothing is clear. No one knows what exactly happened. Not only is Rayyaan missing, Elma and Safir are also missing— and no one knows what became of them." Her voice quivered as she spoke.

"Ya Allah!" Amziya clutched her chest.

"What happened— tell the whole thing." Waqar stepped forward, his voice grave.

"Baba— Tanaz's father found out that there was a major shootout on the Swat Road near Khan Market about two hours ago. They say Tehreek gunmen targeted an army convoy. Many were killed on both sides, and some civilians got caught in the crossfire. Several vehicles were hit. When I begged him to ask around, he sent one of his contacts there — and that's how we learned more. The army has sealed the entire area now; no one is allowed near it. But we did learn this much— Rayyaan's car was there during the shootout, and it moved away from the site, but… it never reached anywhere beyond that. Meaning, He must have been dropped off somewhere in the middle and taken another route. And you can see the weather… nobody can guess where they might be stuck."

"Ya Allah… have mercy on my child." Amziya swayed as though she might faint.

"Ammi— hold on. Nothing will happen to Rayyaan," Zikra said, trying to comfort her.

"And Daaud— that wretched boy isn't even picking up his phone!" Waqar clenched his fists.

"He was shot, Baba. They took him to the hospital. He was unconscious— no possibility of speaking. After Tanaz's father told me about the shootout, I called Daaud. A soldier answered his phone— said they found him lying there. But our car wasn't found at the spot, which means Rayyaan left before Daaud collapsed. He didn't reach ahead— that part Tanaz's father confirmed. So, he must have left the Swat Road somewhere in between, but where— no one knows."

"And Safir and Elma? How did you learn about them?" Waqar demanded.

"By coincidence— the contact Tanaz's father sent to the site learned from the soldiers that a car belonging to the Shahélaar family was badly shot up, but no one was found inside. They called Anas Sahib, and he told them the vehicle had been driven by Safir, who was returning from Peshawar. The soldiers tried his number— but the phone never connected."

"And Huzaifa's girl— how did she get trapped in this mess?" Waqar's voice hardened.

"There's a colonel in the army whose daughter is Elma's friend. She was traveling back with the convoy, so Elma decided to accompany her— hoping to reach home safely. But then the attack happened. They say the colonel's daughter was hit early in the crossfire and taken to the hospital, but she couldn't be saved. The attackers carried Elma away with them. Now no one knows whether they intended to abduct the colonel's daughter or Elma specifically… even the army has no clue."

"Then the kidnappers could be from Bagraat or Shahélaar— maybe this is one of Anas's boy's tricks!"

"Baba— they may be capable of spilling civilian blood for revenge, but they are nowhere near foolish enough to attack the army directly. These were Tehreek militants— that's what the army themselves believe."

"But why would Tehreek risk their lives for some girl from Mahepora's family?"

"That's what no one understands."

"Enough. Go inform Hamdoo and Changez to ready the weapons, the men, and the horses. We leave now to search for Rayyaan. Load the horses onto the trucks— where the vehicles fail, the horses will carry us through. We cannot leave our farzand alone in such danger." Waqar issued the command sharply, striding toward the door.

As he left, Amziya broke into sobs, and Zikra wrapped an arm around her, trying to hold together what little strength remained in the room.

●●

A light spray of rain had begun to lash the air, the gusts picking up speed, when the tall, broad-shouldered Pathan rode into the kahwa-khana on a black horse. The few people sheltering inside glanced up as he entered— all of them Pashtun, stout and weathered, but there was something about this newcomer that set him apart. He stood well over seven feet in stature, his breadth matching his height. His face was large, his eyes hawk-like, his lips thin; the sinews of his jaw stood out, a testament to a hard temperament. A black cloak hung from his shoulders down to his calves. He flicked water from his clothes with a single look, surveyed the room, and then strode over to the lone man sitting at a corner table.

The man at the table grew visibly nervous as the rider approached; he tried to rise, but the newcomer pushed him back down by the shoulder and seated himself opposite.

"Good," the rider said, peering calmly into the man's eyes— "You can smell me out, and I can see you— so let's skip ceremony. They call me Aghazir. If you prefer not to give your name, that's your right. But I'll ask two questions — answer them, and perhaps we both leave satisfied."

"You can't force me into anything," the man replied, attempting to sound fearless.

In the blink of an eye Aghazir's hand struck his cheek like lightning; the man flew off his bench and slammed into the floor by the next table. The slap snapped everyone alert — they all sprang up as if responsibility for what happened had fallen onto their shoulders. As they started toward Aghazir, the man who had been struck waved them back with a trembling hand, rose, shook his head, and sat back down across from Aghazir.

"This is not the right way to speak," he said, glaring.

"Perhaps," Aghazir said, easing himself back against the seat— "but sometimes a beginning like this gets people to take you seriously. Now that you seem to take me seriously, allow me to apologize for raising my hand." He inclined his head with deliberate courtesy.

"What do you want to know?" the man asked.

"Only two questions— no more. Look… I am of the sixth century, and you can imagine the distance I have traveled to come here. It's not as if I rode straight across time; I wandered through many centuries between. Yet now I feel I have come at the right moment— that here I will find answers."

"Are you Aaghazir, the ancestral retainer of Princess Alaina, remembered as the guardian of one of her hereditary legacies?" This time the man opposite spoke with visible surprise, quickly regaining his composure.

"Yes. Now you have understood correctly— I am the very one."

"Please command me, Huzoor. What service may I render you?" His tone had changed completely now.

"The truth is, if I put it in clear words, time moves along a straight line, and this itself is the divine order— that applies to everyone, humans and jinn alike. Still, by design there are rare exceptions— a few people, under special circumstances, can slip forward or back in time. Five reached the Alabar sultanate using that flaw, and because of them I carry a debt that will not let me die in peace. Of those five, four were human and one was our man… It was one of our own men who took them there, tempted by personal interest."

"Who was he?" the man asked.

"Hikmatyar Ghazavi."

"What?" the man stammered.

"Do not be surprised— it is the truth." Aghazir's voice was steady. "Now here's the catch— Hikmatyar himself belongs to the eighteenth century, while the people he brought were men of the twentieth. I cannot find them together, but at this point in the twenty-first century I hope to trace their news. From them I will know which direction my path must take."

"Hikmatyar disappeared sometime in the last century." the man said slowly— "We never heard from him. It's been over thirty years since— likely he is no longer among the living. After he vanished, such discord spread through Altunia that the entire sultanate fractured into four pieces. His only heir, Aryan Ghazavi, was still a child when Hikmatyar left, and a loyal servant named Nazaar spirited the boy away. We lost sight of them, though once there came word that Aryan had grown and was in Masrib."

"Masrib… under the care of the Silaas? Ah— if only I could go there. Still, I will find a way to reach him. Whoever hides Hikmatyar across the folds of time, Aryan will know. As for the four humans who went with him— they were Pashtun from these parts, as you know. My information says one was Sarbani— Abu-zar Sadazoi; another Gharghasht— Khudabaksh Hamaar; a third Kharlani— Hassaan Afridi; and the fourth Baitani— Araaz Khasoor. Do you know them? Have you heard of them?"

"Yes— I know all four. They are great jagirdars nearby. But I am surprised they'd ever act together. These tribes are longstanding enemies— they have fought for generations. They have kidnapped each other's women to keep honor high."

"The spread of unrest in Altunia is the punishment for the debt I owe because of them. Are they still alive?"

"Three have been killed by each other's descendants. Only Abu-zar Sadazoi of Bagraat remains alive— but he is very old now and seldom leaves his haveli. If you can go, you may meet him. Bagraat is not far— perhaps ten miles from here."

"All right— tell me the way."

A few moments later he was mounted on his black horse, riding east. The winds had strengthened and the rain grew heavier; under such weather, the chances of meeting anyone on the road were slim. These parts were thinly populated already; who would be out in a storm like this? The sky was a blanket of clouds, and the sun— sinking— could barely send any light through, so dusk fell early. By the time he reached Bagraat, it would likely be night.

The pelting rain, the lashing wind and the mud-slick trail would have slowed most men, but Aghazir seemed indifferent to all of it. If anything, his face had settled into a calm he wore like armor.

He arrived at Bagraat's principal settlement, where the famous mansion stood at one edge. The hillside ended behind it; beyond lay nothing. The villagers huddled inside their homes against the weather. The mansion's main gate was shut; the gatekeeper likely crouched inside a little room nearby. Aghazir paused a moment, considering tethering his horse to the gatepost, but he had no intention of making a fuss— so he rode on.

He circled the mansion and came up behind it. The muddy ground made his horse stumble, but it caught itself and surged toward the main building. At the rear veranda he dismounted.

He was thoroughly soaked from the journey, yet the moment he stepped into the veranda and shook himself, the water seemed to fall away as if he had never been wet; in an instant he was dry. From a room somewhere came the sound of someone coughing; he moved toward it.

A servant sat there, puffing a hookah. At the sight of Aghazir, he jumped to his feet in alarm. At first the man's face showed confusion and then a flicker of anger, but when Aghazir met his gaze the fellow trembled like a dried leaf.

"Lead me to Chaudhary Abu-zar Sadazoi— without attracting attention. I do not want a scene," Aghazir said, patting the man's shoulder.

Shaking, the servant moved mechanically and Aghazir followed. The servant led him upstairs to a rear room where an old, frail man lay in bed. Strangely, no one else crossed their path in the mansion— perhaps the storm had kept everyone indoors.

"All right— you may go rest now," Aghazir told the servant, who retreated. Aghazir closed the door behind him.

"Who are you?" the old Chaudhary growled from the bed.

"Try to remember. you saw me decades ago, in your youth— though for me it was only two or three months ago that you stood before me." Aghazir stepped closer.

The old man narrowed his eyes, searching for recognition. When it failed, his face hardened with irritation.

"I do not know you— get out of here."

"Try harder. Think of the But-e-Aswa and the Khanjar-e-Shamsi— that might jog your memory." Aghazir placed both hands on the old man's shoulders.

The Chaudhary's eyes widened; his face drained of color and collapsed into stunned horror. A trembling fear seized his body— Aghazir could feel it. The old man could not find words.

"See? You remember now. What did Ghazavi tell you— that you had fled so far back that even Aghazir, chasing you, would never find you? You believed him. You were wrong. You should have feared; you should not have sided with him."

From the old man's lips nothing came but whimpers.

"In which layer of time Hikmatyar Ghazavi lies hidden, I will find that out myself," Aghazir asked, "I have come to you only to ask where the Shamsi dagger is."

"I— I do not know… Hikmatyar never entrusted it to us to hide. He kept it with himself." The old man stammered.

"Surely you know where he hid it. He could not have kept it on him forever— otherwise his identity would have revealed itself and I would have found him. He had to hide it somewhere. Where?"

"In Afghanistan… perhaps Tora-Bora… I do not know exactly. He had a servant— Nazaar. Only Nazaar could tell you the precise place, if he is alive." The Chaudhary managed to answer.

"So, you have no more to tell me. Fine. Time has come to punish you for what you did. Your three companions were fortunate— they left before I arrived. But you, Sadazoi, were not so lucky." His voice sharpened.

"P-please… forgive me." The old man began to plead.

"There is no forgiveness in my dictionary," Aghazir said simply.

Then, without relish but with terrible precision, Aghazir seized the old Chaudhary and began to smash him against the wall as if he were a plaything— so swiftly that the man never had a moment to scream. The frail body did not hold long against the onslaught; it broke, and life slipped away quickly. Aghazir dropped the now-lifeless, bloodied form back onto the bed and stepped out, opening the door.

The noise had likely stirred some servants; those who met his gaze froze in place, trembling, unable to act. Without further obstruction, Aghazir mounted his horse waiting outside. In a single bound the animal cleared the mansion wall, and the two vanished into the rain.

●●

Rayyaan Afridi was a handsome, refined young man—the kind who carried both taste and temperament with disciplined grace. He was not someone who usually lost patience easily. Yet now he was unable to keep irritation from clawing up his spine. Whatever had happened earlier on the Swat Road had been bad enough; but losing the route afterward, getting trapped in this violent storm— it was turning the night unbearable. The rain hammered so fiercely that even the wipers had become useless; he could barely see inches ahead. The track beneath his wheels was muddy, broken, and so unpredictable that driving felt like wrestling with the dark.

There wasn't a sign of human habitation anywhere—nowhere to stop, nowhere to seek shelter.

For the past hour he had been wandering aimlessly, so exasperated he was tempted to somehow find his way back to the Swat Road. But even that now seemed impossible.

At the moment the army convoy came under attack, he had, by sheer coincidence, been ahead of them. The first volley had shattered his windshield; a stray bullet skimmed past his shoulder and buried itself in the shoulder of Daaud — who had been driving. Daaud screamed, lost control, and the car skidded sharply downhill, stopping squarely in the line of fire.

The attackers must have mistaken his vehicle for part of the convoy, because they kept shooting at it even after it had stopped.

Daaud, in agony, pushed the door open and fell out, urging Rayyaan to take the wheel— "I can't drive— get us out, now… staying here is suicide." The urgency made sense. Rayyaan slid into the driver's seat and sped in the same downward direction the car had veered. In the rear-view he saw an SUV jerk into motion, following him— and he knew they wouldn't let him go.

He drove blindly— any dirt path, any broken lane he saw, he took it. Eventually the Swat Road vanished behind him— and after some distance, the pursuing SUV vanished too.

But ten minutes later he realized he was lost. Completely. He had no idea where he was wandering.

Most of his life had been spent either in Kaanwabeel or London. He knew only one primary route back home, and that road was far behind him now. His phone was in his pocket, but the SIM was London-based— useless in these mountains. Normally, on short visits, he'd pick up a local SIM, or rely on whoever came to receive him. Today the lack of that simple detail had rendered him helpless.

An hour passed. The hills loomed like dark silhouettes; trees swayed violently in the wind; the rain showed no sign of mercy. The deepening darkness hinted that evening had fallen — which meant soon he wouldn't even be able to drive forward. His car didn't have enough petrol to wander all night.

And then, in the darkness— a faint thread of hope appeared.

Ahead on the roadside stood a figure— clothed in white, perhaps a raincoat. Lightning flashed just long enough for him to make out the shape, and that was all he needed. If there was a human, there might be a settlement. A refuge. A direction.

He accelerated, worried the person might disappear before he reached.

But the figure stayed where it was— as if waiting for him. When Rayyaan stopped the car, the stranger stepped toward him.

He switched on the dome light, rolled down the passenger window glass— and froze.

It was a girl.

A girl in a raincoat, breathtakingly beautiful— the kind of beauty that held the eyes captive. Rayyaan couldn't understand how someone like her could possibly be wandering this wilderness alone in such weather.

"How can I help you, mohtarma?" he asked politely.

"Could you drop me a little further down the road?" she asked softly— her voice had a magic the thunder could not drown.

"Of course— please," he said, opening the door.

She slipped inside with a gentle— "Thank you."

It felt as though a swirl of fragrance and silk had glided into the seat beside him. She removed her raincoat, tossed it behind, shook her wet hair lightly, and smiled at him— and the moment she did, it felt like lightning flashed inside the car. There was something hypnotic in her eyes.

Rayyaan found himself staring, helplessly— his mind scattering into memories, searching for the last time he'd seen a face that could disarm him like this. Every face he'd ever known flickered across his mind and dissolved— she stood above them all.

He wondered when he had ever seen eyes like hers— that seemed to speak. Or a smile so luminous that it unsettled a heartbeat. What spell was this beauty weaving that even someone as steady as he felt weakened, bent, claimed? For the first time, he realized that beauty did, in fact, possess a kind of sorcery— the power to take hold of one's senses.

"Hello?" she snapped her fingers before his face, and he startled back to awareness.

"Sorry!" he muttered awkwardly and began driving.

"What happened to you? Are you alright?" Her voice felt like music rising again in the car.

Ah, magician— unaware of her own spell.

He smiled helplessly, not daring to meet her eyes.

"Nothing… just a small paralysis attack, it passed," he said dryly.

"Paralysis?" she asked, confused.

"Hmm. The kind inflicted by beautiful women— it freezes the mind for a moment," he replied, still avoiding her gaze.

She burst into laughter— and the car suddenly felt alive.

"So this is a compliment? Not bad," she said, watching him with amused eyes.

"May I know your name?" he asked, a little hesitant.

"Ghazal," she replied with a smile.

"Well… I've heard many ghazals in life, but this is the first time I've seen one alive in front of me. Tell me— is the copyright still with your father or…?" he teased, leaving the sentence open.

"You think I'm married?" she raised a brow.

"I'd rather not imagine such a horrifying possibility. Anyway— I hope no one has claimed you yet." He chuckled softly, "But there's something I forgot to ask— something that came to mind the moment I saw you. I've been wandering for an hour and haven't seen a single human being or settlement. Seeing you gave me hope— perhaps there was a village nearby where I could shelter for the night. But it looks deserted. So… where did you appear from in this wilderness?"

"There are settlements— but not on the main track. You need to take one of the mud trails. The one I came from leads up to a small village. I saw your car lights from above and took the risk to come down— otherwise in weather like this, who expects a lift? But why are you lost? And why do you need shelter?"

"Well… I'm from Waadi-e-Karagal too, but I've lived in London for the last eight years, so I don't know these areas well. My childhood was limited to Kaanwabeel— that place I know, but nothing beyond. I was returning from London when I got caught in a shootout… my driver was hurt, left me midway, and I'm stuck with a mobile phone that doesn't work without a local SIM. I just need to reach the Swat Road again— or Kaanwabeel. Any help would be a blessing."

"Both are quite far— and judging by the weather, you won't reach anywhere before tomorrow. My village is a little ahead— Dera Jamal Khan. You can spend the night there… tomorrow someone can guide you. And yes— in Kaanwabeel, there's only one family of your standing. You must be Waqar Sahib's son?"

"Oh wow— you know me!" he exclaimed.

"Everyone around here knows a little. Of the four major jagirs, Kaanwabeel is the only one with a single young heir— and people say they sent him to London so he'd stay away from the feuds here. With that much information, guessing wasn't hard. Though I didn't recall your name."

"Rayyaan— Rayyaan Afridi. Do you have a phone? I should inform my family. They must be worried."

"No… no one uses mobile phones in our village."

"What— shocking!"

"Not really. We live far from cities; the network barely works, and people don't need connectivity much. Everyone is content in their own small worlds."

He nodded silently, and Ghazal too fell quiet. The road slipped by under the hush of rain.

"It feels like I've stepped into a time machine— like I'm wandering centuries back, in barren lands where no human seems to exist," Rayyaan murmured.

"Why alone? I'm here with you." she said softly.

"Hunh… meeting you in this storm, in this desolate place— it feels like a beautiful spirit has crossed my path. A spirit who'll lead me to some hidden lair, pounce, and drink my blood while laughing."

"You believe spirits exist?" she asked.

"When I lived in Swat— yes. Then London broadened my mind. I don't think such things exist… but who knows? There are many things we don't understand. Paranormal events recorded across the world— they must have some explanation."

"Then answer something… can you see with your eyes closed? Hear me with your ears covered? Reply to me without moving your lips? Or drive this car without moving your hands or feet?"

"Of course not. What's the point?"

"That for speech, hearing, seeing, thought, and action— we depend on this body, these organs. After death, these remain behind as dust. So how would a spirit act without them? And if a spirit does have these organs— then with your eyes closed, you should still see through the spirit's eyes; with your mouth shut, you should still speak; with your ears covered, still hear; and with your body frozen, still move."

"Then what is the concept of a spirit? Our faith speaks of it too," Rayyaan asked.

"Yes— but not the way most imagine. Think of it like a radio, a TV, or a mobile… as long as the device and the power source work together, they transmit the world. If the connection breaks, both become useless. A battery alone is nothing, nor can the device function without it.

The device is our body; the energy is the ruh. One without the other does nothing. Our faith says this energy is moved to another dimension— Aalam-e-Barzakh. There it is given a virtual body and remains until the Day of Resurrection, where it will be judged and sent to either Jahannum or Jannat."

"So you can't possibly be a spirit?" Rayyaan joked lightly.

Ghazal extended her hand. Understanding, Rayyaan took it— soft as butter, warm with life, trembling with a strange electricity. A cold shiver ran through him as he let go.

"Could a dead body hold this warmth?" she asked quietly, eyes locked with his.

He had no answer. His silence was the answer.

A little later she pointed out that her village Dera Jamal Khan— was now in sight. The village lay off the main track, down a sloping mud trail. From above, its faint outline could be seen whenever lightning cracked across the sky. Though night had barely begun, the storm made it feel like midnight.

As Rayyaan turned the car down the narrow path, the world vanished into darkness again. The trail was thin, muddy, flanked by dense brush and tall trees swaying like shadows.

They were nearing the outskirts of the settlement when suddenly a cat darted across the road— from right to left. A large black cat.

But how large?

The sight jolted Rayyaan's mind violently. In the split-second flash of lightning, he felt as if the cat's front half had leaped across the road— but its hind half seemed stuck on the right side for a moment. For one impossible second, the cat's body appeared to stretch across the entire width of the trail— nearly ten feet.

Then the hind portion snapped forward— like a rubber band released, and the creature vanished into the bushes.

●●

CHAPTER 2

Keeping the fleeing SUV in sight without getting too close was nearly impossible for Safir— especially in this weather, on these treacherous slopes carved with twisting mountain paths. He couldn't afford to close in; the moment he did, they would fire. And surviving those bullets would be far more difficult. All through the chase, Rimsha's face kept flashing before his eyes. Whatever happened, he could not watch her be dragged into hell.

The rain refused to soften. The icy gusts slicing across his face made the ride even more punishing.

Then came the moment he dreaded— the car vanished.

He skidded his bike to a halt, stunned. The road ahead split into three— one straight, one climbing upward, and the third snaking downward. And, as though fate mocked him, each path was lined with boulders big enough for a car to hide behind.

Completely rattled, he decided to choose the straight path first. At least he could reach the nearest boulder and scan ahead.

But the moment he reached it— a figure stepped out of the darkness and swung something like a stick, or perhaps the butt of a rifle, straight into his chest. The blow was so brutal that he was flung off the bike, crashing onto the muddy ground. For a second, he felt his breath stop inside him— frozen in his ribs.

He barely caught his breath when two more men burst out from behind the rock and lunged at him.

It wasn't that Safir was weak— he was anything but. Under normal circumstances he'd have taken all three apart. But that first strike had locked half his chest, and in that tiny window of weakness they overwhelmed him. Even as blows landed, one after the other, a part of him wondered—

Why weren't they shooting him?

They had every chance.

When they finally felt he'd stopped resisting, two men grabbed him by the arms and the third crouched before him.

"You're Anas Khasoor's son, aren't you?" the man asked coldly, lifting Safir's chin with the butt of his rifle.

Safir didn't answer.

The response came as a rifle-butt cracking against his skull— and darkness swallowed him whole.

When he regained consciousness, he couldn't move. His hands and feet were bound, his mouth gagged, and he was lying inside a cramped, shaking space. It took a few seconds for the realization to hit him—

The car's trunk.

The rattling confirmed it— they were still driving, and the road was rough. From the muffled sounds outside, the rain had grown lighter, but it hadn't stopped.

Another thirty minutes passed before the car halted. He felt bodies dragging someone out first— Rimsha, it had to be Rimsha. He waited for his turn, heart sinking with each second.

Was this what he had risked his life for— running blindly into death for someone who had already left him long ago? Would she even acknowledge the madness he'd thrown himself into for her?

And then another thought crept in— They knew him.

They had recognized him before knocking him out.

Perhaps that alone was the reason he wasn't dead yet.

Footsteps approached. The trunk opened, his legs were cut loose, and he was hauled out.

Night had already fallen thick and heavy. They had brought him to the edge of a tiny settlement— just a handful of houses. The building before him was a large wooden house surrounded by a courtyard. The three gunmen forced him inside.

A dimly lit verandah greeted them, a hurricane lamp casting just enough light to shape the outlines. On a chair sat a tall Pathan with a long goat-style beard, wrapped in a turban — around forty, perhaps. He studied Safir carefully as they dragged him forward.

"This really is Anas Khasoor's boy?" he asked in Hindko instead of Pashto— but Safir understood it well enough.

"Yes— when these people attacked Bagraat and abducted Nabam Sadaazoi's daughter, they had taken Ameer's side, and I was one of Ameer's companions as well. I have known him since then," the man said— the same one who had questioned Safir before rendering him unconscious.

Safir stared at him, trying to place him— three years had blurred too many memories.

"Fine," the bearded man said. "We can't reach our commanders— our phones aren't working. We'll take them to Shazoom. Nabi will decide what to do with them. Lock him with the girl."

They dragged Safir down a narrow hallway to a room at the far end. They shoved him inside and locked the door.

The room was pitch-black— he couldn't see his own hand. He reached reflexively for his phone, but it had already been taken.

Since they'd said "lock him with her," Rimsha should have been inside.

"Rimsha," he whispered.

"h-h-who is there?" a frightened voice responded from a corner.

He followed the sound and found a faint shadow huddled against the wall. He sat beside her.

"It's me… Safir."

"S-Safir who?" the girl asked nervously— and right then he realized it wasn't Rimsha's voice.

"What do you mean— who? If you're not Rimsha, then who are you?" he asked, startled.

The girl didn't answer.

Safir felt his gut twist. If this wasn't Rimsha… then what in God's name had he risked everything for? Had he thrown himself into death for nothing?

"If you're not Rimsha, why did they take you?" he snapped.

"I… I don't know… I don't recognize these men." Her voice trembled.

"They're militants— a Tehreek faction. But what enmity do they have with you? Are you someone important? And the car they dragged you from— Rimsha was in it. I saw her myself. I chased them thinking they were taking her."

"I'm her friend," the girl whispered— "She was traveling to a friend's wedding. I joined her so I'd be safer with the convoy… I didn't know this would happen."

"But Rimsha— what about her? They didn't touch her when they dragged you out."

"When the shooting began… s-suddenly a bullet hit her neck. She collapsed instantly. I… I don't know what happened after." Her voice broke into a sob.

"What?" The world swayed around Safir.

Rimsha. Bullet. Neck.

His own breath shuddered as memories clawed at him. The love he'd buried, the wounds he had stitched— ripped fresh again. He leaned back against the wall, tears burning behind his eyes.

"Who are you?" the girl asked softly.

He didn't answer. Words felt pointless.

Silence stretched. Safir sunk deeper into memories— of Rimsha's laughter, her touch, her presence. Everything that once made him whole.

"Were you related to her?" the girl asked after a long pause.

"No."

"Then… did you love her?"

He could only let out a quiet sigh— what answer could he possibly give her? If she was her friend, she would surely know that Rimsha had left him, and yet today he had once again run to save her like a madman. What would she think of him now? What kind of shameless lover was he— unable to let go of his devotion even after being rejected? He did not have the heart to say anything more. On one hand, a fierce anger was rising within him at his own foolishness; on the other, grief weighed heavily on him as he thought of Rimsha's fate.

The girl fell silent too.

An hour later, they were given food along with a lantern. They were forced to eat— clearly their captors wanted them alive. They were given a chance to use the washroom one by one, and then were marched outside.

The rain had stopped— but the sky was still thick with clouds; without electricity, darkness swallowed everything around.

This time an SUV waited for them. They were shoved into the back. Two men sat in the front, two behind them, and one right beside the captives. Their eyes were blindfolded.

The SUV sped away.

The journey was long— the early part on mud paths and washed-out tracks. Neither Safir nor the girl could see anything, but they could sense the direction— westward, toward the Afghan border. The routes were too smooth, too uninterrupted to be random. These men knew every hidden path, every gap in the military's presence.

Somewhere along the better roads both captives dozed off— exhausted.

Later the SUV rumbled over harsh terrain again, making it clear they were crossing the border through unmarked, forbidden routes.

By the time the vehicle stopped, dawn was about to break.

They were dragged into a house and thrown inside a room. Weak, aching, freezing— they collapsed onto the floor mattresses and slept under coarse blankets.

They weren't allowed to sleep long, but the few hours were enough to clear their minds slightly.

New faces woke them. They were escorted outside into an open courtyard— sunless morning light illuminating everything.

The moment the girl saw Safir's face clearly, she gasped in shock.

And Safir— he felt a flicker of recognition too, but couldn't recall where he'd seen her before.

Armed men surrounded the courtyard. In the center, a large woven cot stood— on it sat a heavy-set older Afghan, the one clearly in command. Beside him stood the goat-bearded man from earlier, and the three who had captured them.

As soon as the older man saw girl, he erupted—

"Oy khonche— this isn't Sheerani's daughter!"

The armed men stiffened nervously. This had to be Nabi, the one meant to decide their fate.

"W-what? Then who is he?" the goat-beard stammered.

"You tell me— who is he?" Nabi thundered.

The goat-beard turned toward the three abductors— and they looked ready to collapse.

"There was another girl in the vehicle as well, but she had been shot. From the clothes of this girl, we assumed that she must be the colonel's daughter. The other girl, however, was dressed like she wore everyday clothes, so we thought she was a maid," one of them explained haltingly.

"O khonche… atleast ask!" Nabi slapped his thigh in rage. Then he shifted to the girl, "Who are you? And why were you with the colonel's daughter?"

"I-I'm her friend… she was coming for a wedding… I just came along… I didn't know this would happen."

"Our entire effort wasted… seven of our Mujahids dead… Allah!" Nabi sighed, grief flickering for a moment. Then his gaze locked onto Safir.

"And him? Why bring him?"

"He chased us," one of the three explained, "We almost shot him, but Haroon recognized him, so we captured him instead. Killing him would've caused trouble. Keeping him alive might give us leverage."

"What leverage? Who is he?"

"From the Khasoor family of Shahelár. Youngest son of Anas Chowdhary."

"Oh! Anas's boy. Then you did right." Nabi nodded— "No point mourning now. The mission failed. We'll deal with Sheerani later. Today was cursed enough."

"What do we do with the girl?" the goat-beard asked.

"Keep her as a laundi— a slave. Killing her brings us nothing. Let her repay what our fighters lost… that's all I have to say for now. Hameed— contact the Khasoors. See what the boy is worth."

At this, the girl's face drained of color. She screamed, struggled— panic exploding out of her— but the gunmen grabbed both captives and dragged them back toward the house.

●●

Though the rain had stopped sometime during the night, its traces clung to the morning. Green slopes gleamed freshly washed; streams and rivulets had swollen. The problem was the roads— most of the dirt tracks had turned to mud, and driving across them had become a treacherous business.

Chaudhary Huzaifa Hamaar of the Mahepora jagir rode hard with a dozen men— his nephews Owais, Hanzla, and Rushan among them— rifles slung in their hands, AK-47 visible even from a distance. It was early; most people in the village were still waking. Furious and impatient, Huzaifa's party thundered up to a small settlement on the hillside.

The hamlet had only a handful of houses. The moment Huzaifa's men opened fire into the air on arrival, everyone woke alert— people scrambled, unsure whether to defend or surrender. The intent was obvious— their target was the two-storey house in the middle of the cluster. Huzaifa's men had made their message clear with bullets through the doors and windows— this was between them and the house's inhabitants; outsiders should not interfere.

From inside, those at the house were on edge— bewildered by the sudden assault and reluctant to start the fight. Still, the warning shots had let them know they were not to be underestimated.

"Come out, Dabir— we want to speak with you," Chaudhary Huzaifa roared from outside.

"What sort of talking is this, Chaudhary Sahib— you could have asked politely." a voice called back. It was Dabir, speaking in the same rough cadence.

"This is our politeness— we are asking you to come out to speak, otherwise we bring people to us; we do not go to their doorstep. Come out, scoundrel— we will not repeat ourselves."

The threat worked. A man of perhaps thirty, stepped out, rifle in hand.

"What has forced your noble self to come knocking?" he said with a hint of sarcasm.

"Where is your brother Musa?" Huzaifa demanded, fists clenched.

"He hasn't been seen for three days— he comes and goes. He doesn't live here all the time, Chaudhary Sahib."

"We know that, which is why we gave you a chance to answer. If he had been here, we would have levelled this house first. Yesterday there was an attack on the army convoy, and witnesses spotted Musa among the attackers. We know Musa is seen with Shahélaar people— we need confirmation whether Shahélaar had a hand in this attack. Then we will deal with Shahélaar."

"Do you think Shahélaar carried out the attack? But why would they attack army men— what would they gain?" Dabir sounded genuinely confused.

"Because our daughter was in that convoy. They would have wanted to abduct her. One of their boys was there too, who went with the abductors— we will not let Shahélaar carry him away alive."

"Chaudhary Sahib— I truly don't know where Musa is. I don't think this attack was Shahélaar's doing. Musa does live among them sometimes, but he's also tied with TTP's Lakwal group. I've heard that the attack may have been by the TTP."

Huzaifa's temper flared.

"What would TTP want with our daughter? We have no enmity with any of their factions— why would they abduct her?" he snapped.

Dabir was momentarily silenced.

"Tell us where Musa might be." Huzaifa pressed.

"He has a Dashta in Naushera— Habiba. He spends nights there often; perhaps he's there. But Chaudhary Sahib, please— speak with him first. I don't believe this is as simple as it looks."

Huzaifa said nothing more. He signaled his nephews and the convoy moved on. Dabir watched them go, worry etched into his face.

They rode toward the place mentioned. Half an hour later they reached a crossroad— and fate placed them there at the same moment as three other parties. On one approach arrived Anas Khasoor's convoy— his son Farrukh and nephew Sohail among twelve armed Pathans, rifles ready. From another way Waqar Afridi's party pulled up— Waqar himself in an open jeep, the rest mounted on horses, all armed. Tension tightened like a wire as all parties came to a stand.

"Where is our daughter?" Huzaifa's eyes burned toward Anas Khasoor.

"How should I know where your daughter is— my own son is missing and I'm searching for him," Anas replied bluntly.

"Anas— this cannot be repeated… our daughter is our heartbeat and we will not let her be taken. If your boy has her, Shahélaar will not reach her alive— this is my promise,"

Chaudhary Huzaifa spoke as though chewing on burning embers.

"If he is even scratched, the consequences will be very bad. He went to Peshawar on business and was returning alone— he has nothing to do with that attack or with taking your daughter." Anas shot back in the same tone.

"But my son— how did he vanish in all this? I had sent him away to study; he should not have been caught in such a chaos. Where has he gone?" Waqar asked, stepping in.

"It is possible that seeing Safir succeed in taking Elma, Rayyaan too decided to try his own luck," Rushan offered. He was Huzaifa's nephew but also Waqar Afridi's son-in-law by marriage and had a history of similar rash deeds in youth.

"Nonsense— we did not send him to London to have him stuck in feuds. The question is why would Shahélaar attack an army convoy at all? If Anas's son was supposed to abduct her, he'd have done it when she was separated from the convoy— not while the army was present."

"You're assuming too much, Waqar. He went to Peshawar on a business trip; the attack was by a large group — many killed on both sides. Where does Safir fit into this? Why do you insist our son is involved?" Anas addressed Chaudhary Huzaifa.

"Because Musa was reported present at the attack— and Musa is known to Sohail here, and Musa had ties that led to Ameer Kharotai of the TTP. If Musa and Safir were both seen, perhaps Shahélaar had a role in this," Huzaifa countered.

"That's not true— Musa's association with Ameer doesn't make us jump into war with the army. And Safir barely knows Musa— he wouldn't know Ameer. This theory holds little weight," Sohail protested quickly.

At that moment a military convoy appeared on the fourth road— vehicles, mounted troops— they halted among the assembled jagirdar parties. The officer in the open jeep stepped forward, surveying them.

"What is this dispute?" he asked, addressing all of them.

"During yesterday's attack my son and others were present— Anas's son and Huzaifa's daughter were with your convoy, and since then these three are missing. I don't know where Rayyaan is, but Huzaifa believes Anas's boy instigated the assault to abduct their daughter," Waqar explained.

"It wasn't the Shahélaar lads," the officer said, "We detained Shazaib Barkazai of the Lakwal group a few days ago. His people may have tried to free him by attacking— they targeted the colonel's daughter traveling with the convoy; she was hit and later died. Your daughter was among the convoy as well and likely taken by mistake. Your boy chased after the abductors and may have been lost in the scramble— we found the motorbike used to chase them, but not him. And your son… He probably veered off the main road to escape and may have sought shelter; he'll likely be found and brought back."

"And where are you heading now?" Anas asked the officer.

"We're going after Musa— the reports say he was at the scene. Last night, Chaudhary Abu-zar Sadazoi was brutally killed— Bagraat suspects are pointing fingers at your lot. So be cautious." The officer returned to his convoy.

Their convoy pulled away in the direction Huzaifa had been heading. Knowing now that Anas's son likely wasn't the abductor, there was little point in further confrontation— so Huzaifa's party silently withdrew. Anas's men turned back too, but Waqar would not return— his son were missing, and they would press on searching, while Rayyaan's fate still had room for hope.

••

"Did you see that?" Rayyaan asked, wide-eyed, turning to Ghazal.

"What?" she asked, directing her face toward him.

"That cat— it was so big it spanned the entire width of the track, then vanished."

"You must've been imagining it— cats don't haunt lanes, and none are that big. Perhaps we were deep in conversation and your mind played tricks," Ghazal said.

He fell silent. Could that have been possible? The flash was so sudden— a single second that bent perception. The path narrowed and worsened; Rayyaan stopped the car.

"Leave the car here— it won't go further. The path can't bear it; you'll get stuck and ruin your morning's departure." Ghazal put on her raincoat from the back seat.

"But it's still raining— I'll get wet," he protested.

"No matter— I can lend you dry clothes, and yours will dry by morning."

Reluctantly he stepped out. A cold wind cut through him. Though not winter, the highlands had a chill, and the storm had turned the air January-cold. Rain still fell thinly— enough to soak.

Rayyaan breathed out a small, rueful sound.

"What's wrong?" Ghazal's voice brushed his ear.

"Nothing… just spoke my fate in a single word," he said.

She smiled. Ahead the path reduced to a two-and-a-half-foot gravel track, flanked by waterlogged ground— a muddy corridor. As they drew closer, the village's broad track came into view. At its start stood a small round platform with a circular pillar supporting an eight-foot domed canopy— like a tiny shrine and a lamp affixed above. A statue crouched on the platform, head bowed.

"Salam, Darain Chacha," Ghazal called, her voice carrying across the open air.

The statue stirred— not only that, its bound hands and feet loosened and it rose as if powered by an unseen electric circuit flipped on. Rayyaan's surprise doubled.

"Salam, Ghazal beta— you came. I didn't expect you in such foul weather." a gravel voice boomed.

"Yes— think of it as fate. If not for his mercy, I mightn't have made it," she replied.

The man turned to look at Rayyaan— his black-and-white eyes seemed to pierce right through his spine. Rayyaan lowered his gaze instantly.

"The wind eases, Chacha— light the lamp," Ghazal said.

"All right, child." The man's voice carried in the wind.

They passed the platform. Rayyaan couldn't shake a prickling unease, but ten-twelve steps on he glanced back— was the figure looking at him?

No— the figure had returned to its statue-like pose. The lamp was lit. Rayyaan felt his throat tighten and did not move. Ghazal looked back, reading his unease.

"What is it?" she asked softly.

"H-he— he lit the lamp himself— but how? The lamp hangs twelve feet up— there's no stool, no ladder, and no one to hang it up. And we had only passed that spot a minute ago. He did it and was back to a statue in a blink. For a moment I thought he wasn't a man at all."

"Darain Chacha is like that— his work happens in microseconds. For him sitting is an art."

"Still— how did he light a lamp so high?"

"Oh,forget it— some techniques belong to city folks, some to villagers. Wait here."

Ghazal knocked on the nearby house's door. After a moment the door opened, but no one appeared— only a lantern swung in the interior, and Rayyaan's head spun.

"Here, take your medicine." Ghazal produced a small bundle from her garments and pushed it inside the doorway — it vanished into the house, but no hand reached out to receive it.

Rayyaan thought of stepping forward to look— but the moment Ghazal's lips tightened, the door slid shut again and he followed her without a second thought.

"Was someone really inside? It looked to me like the lantern just hung there," he said, curiosity prickling.

"Come on— lanterns are always hung up, and the interior above is dark. The lamp didn't catch in its light because someone stood in the doorway's shadow. In this village modest women don't step out into view unless they know the person," Ghazal's explanation made sense, and he had no answer to offer.

Their steps halted before the house that held the status of a small palace among the cluster—the grandest residence in the village. She knocked— and the door opened without delay.

But as he entered, he felt another jolt of surprise— between the outer gate and the inner door there was a courtyard of at least fifteen paces— and no one had been standing there to open it. Who had opened the door?

"Surprised again?" Ghazal smiled— "Many of our people know tricks— we depend on small magics here. This door is one of them. Come in."

He didn't agree with the idea, yet had no answer to offer. The main door swung wide again and this time a maid appeared to welcome them. She was pretty— but beside

Ghazal she seemed like a pale star against the moon. She looked at Rayyaan with more interest than he understood.

In a few minutes he was introduced to the household— eight beautiful women servants in all. No family members were present; Ghazal explained that only her father existed there, and he was away. Two male servants worked the outer courtyards but did not enter the inner house.

"Come," Ghazal took his hand and led him to a door— "This is the hammam. Hot water is ready. Bathe; it will be a relief. The maid will bring you other clothes. I'll freshen up too— then let's meet at the dining table."

He stepped inside.

Every corner of the house glowed with wax candles and lamps— even the hammam. A tub held pleasantly warm water. He stripped and slipped into the bath, luxuriating until a maid knocked on the door.

She brought him a warm cloak— a fabric he had never seen or touched before. His wet clothes were taken away with the promise they would be dry in the morning.

Wrapped in the cloak he emerged to find the maids waiting. They guided him through corridors into a dining hall where a long table groaned under food— some dishes he recognized, many he did not. Ghazal sat at the head; at her signal Rayyaan took his place.

"Please eat," she gestured.

He ate— hunger having found him fierce. In fifteen minutes' time he tasted twenty different flavors he had never known. The maids served attentively so he would not need to lift a finger.

After the meal his hands were washed and dried. Ghazal led him to a sitting room where the next hour slipped by in conversation. She revealed little about herself but learned everything about him.

"You may rest now," she said finally, signaling to a maid.

"Thanks," he replied, though words felt inadequate. He gave a brief, grateful smile the meaning of which he did not fully grasp, and the maid escorted him to an upper-room with a soft bed. Coals glowed in the brazier, warming the space. A thick curtain covered the windows; lightning still flashed from time to time.

He stood at the window. Drawing the curtain back, he saw the village asleep— or so he thought. Wind had slackened and the rain had stopped. Lights began to appear in houses; with no electricity these were lanterns, lamps, and candles. Doors opened and people emerged; in moments the streets filled as if evening had arrived. He checked his watch — it read eleven at night.

A maid appeared with a silver tray and a glass of some drink.

"Do people here stay awake at night?"

"Yes," she replied briefly and slid the glass toward him.

He drank; the maid stood motionless like a statue and, when he finished, took the glass away and closed the door.

The drink brought a strange warmth and a sleepy calm. He wrapped himself in the quilt and sank into sleep.

Sometime in the night that sleep was broken.

He felt something crawling over his legs— soft, feather-like fingers, a velvet touch. His mind stirred, groggy. He opened his eyes.

She was there— Ghazal— dressed like a bride. Her outfit was a rich red embroidered with zari; henna decorated her hands, gold bracelets chimed at her wrists, a jeweled necklace rested on her throat, earrings swung, and a tika crowned her brow. Her lips were painted deep; her eyes downcast with the lovely modesty of a newlywed. For a moment he wondered if he still slept.

He blinked several times, shook his head as if to clear a dream, but the sight would not melt. Ghazal's fingers pressed tenderly against his feet, and every nerve unraveled with the sweetness of that touch. She looked at him— and in her gaze something entered his chest and stirred.

"How do you find me?" she asked, her red lips parting.

"No words fit to describe my feelings," he stammered— "There is something in you I have never seen or heard before." His phrases came disordered— he had no control over words.

"Do you like me?" she asked.

"Certainly— I've lived by rules, but looking at you I feel every rule could be broken. Anything could be set aside." The confession slipped out as if his will had dissolved.

"Do you want to make me your wife?" Her voice trembled.

"Of course— it would be like finding paradise after death," he said in a fever.

"Would you accept me before your family?" she asked, voice small.

"I do not think my choice will trouble them," he said, and for a moment a smile lit Ghazal's lips— a smile he had wanted to see.

He had no real control. Something invisible pulled him like a thread— his own principles, once solid, crumbled like sand beneath his feet.

"Come with me." Ghazal stood.

He rose and followed, as if drawn by an unseen cord. She led him into a large chamber where many men sat— white-robed elders, white-bearded, but Ghazal stood alone among them. He was the only stranger and only woman present.

"Sit." a comparatively younger elder gestured.

There were cushions on the floor and a velvet cloth spread above them. Rayyaan complied and seated himself.

"Will you marry Ghazal?" the younger elder asked.

"Yes," he heard himself say— refusal was unthinkable.

"Do you assure that your decision will not cause strife among your people and that they will accept our daughter as their daughter-in-law?"

"Yes— I give my full assurance that Ghazal shall have her rightful status," he replied.

They spoke among themselves in a tongue foreign to Rayyaan, then they made him cover his head and a man performed marriage rites. He repeated phrases, then Ghazal and he both affirmed the nikah. They wrote the contract and signed; two men signed as his guardians, two as hers. He learned then that Ghazal's father, Safdar Hayat, was the younger elder, who had spoken to him earlier.

The ceremony was complete and the maids led Ghazal away.

Then in the men's chamber a potent drink was passed. He drank and felt his remaining sleep evaporate— a bright wakefulness filled his limbs, and he felt alive, alert, whole.

When the gathering dispersed Ghazal's father signaled the maids and the bridal chamber was readied. Rayyaan took his leave with a bowed head and followed the maids.

They led him to a bed chamber arranged like a bridal room— flowers, a modestly shy Ghazal perched upon the bed. The whole experience felt like a dream he feared might break at any sound. After the maids left, his feet moved toward the bed on their own.

"Sit." Ghazal crooned.

What followed was slow and gentle— an embrace, then kisses, conversation, and the tenderness of first union. Rayyaan experienced a pleasure he had never known before

— not even in the embraces of the women he had known in London, which he had once considered unmatched. Night deepened, and his body, mind, and will all surrendered to the intimacy until, utterly exhausted, he finally slept.

He awoke late— the sun high, a bright warmth filtering the house. When he opened his eyes, he realized his world had rearranged itself.

Not merely because he was married— because the fear that had shadowed the night had, in truth, dissolved.

But the bed was empty. The bridal room was bare. He lay shivering and naked on a low divan; his clothes, taken by the maid the night before, lay nearby. The room looked unused, untouched, as if it had been waiting for an occupant for years.

Cold filled him; he dressed hurriedly and called for Ghazal. He searched the house like a madman, calling until his throat ached— but no reply came. The household looked strangely deserted, as if it had been uninhabited for decades.

He tumbled into a state of panic.

●●

CHAPTER 3

They were led back to a room and treated with a surprising gentleness— at least they were given the use of a bathroom and a little food and drink. They had eaten well the previous afternoon, so this was not a small courtesy.

Now they sat, each leaning against opposite walls and staring at one another. Safir tried to puzzle out what advantage these men hoped to gain by keeping him alive, and who the girl actually was— she looked spent, her face hollowed by worry. From the way she sat one could tell she had the bearings of someone from a good, educated household— almost like a princess. The thought of such a girl reduced to a captive "laundi" felt like punishment that had already fallen. Hearing about Rimsha's fate the night before had drained him of any appetite for personal interest in the girl, but now, looking at her, pity rose in him.

After a while Safir rose and sat down near the girl.

"Does no one fight on your side? Who are you, after all? Where have I seen you before— you look strangely familiar," he asked— part sympathy, part curiosity.

"It would have been better if you had taken me instead," she said in a broken voice and turned her face away.

For a moment he did not understand her meaning. He thought on it, puzzled, but the clue did not come. Then, like a flash, the girl's face snapped into place in his memory— and with that memory he understood her words.

"Y-You're Elma?" he said, not sure if he was asking or stating.

"Yes." She nodded, putting her hands on her knees and lowering her face.

He found himself smiling despite everything. Elma did not respond with surprise; she only looked at him as if she understood the state of his mind.

Although their jagirs were rival households, the lines between these great families were tangled; relations leaked into one another. He must have seen Elma four or five years before— then he'd made a teasing, half-wicked gesture as if to "take" her away. Not that he had any honest intention; at that time, he was with Rimsha, and Rimsha was the only woman he cared about. He had been young— about fourteen and Elma perhaps eleven, at a wedding where the big families had gathered. On that day he'd taunted her and claimed he would take her away in keeping with their conventions; she'd scolded him and run off.

It had been a temporary fancy— she lingered in his mind for a day or two, then vanished. Four years later, at a signal in Islamabad, his memory of that childish prank had returned; on impulse he jeered the old line. Elma had retorted, and that had been that.

He had not seen her much since; when he glimpsed her with security a few times, no thought deeper than a passing recognition emerged. That was why, when she stared at him now with the shock of immediate recognition, he knew she had known him from the first glance.

"Truth is, I had no such intention. I only said it to tease," he said, taking a breath.

"That outcome my mind might have accepted," she said with a tone of grief, "but this outcome…!" Her sentence trailed off.

"If I had not chased after you thinking you were Rimsha, maybe no one would have known where you were taken. If I survive, at least I can tell your family what happened."

"You'd be glad at my misfortune?" she hissed.

"What? Why would I be glad at your misfortune?"

"We belong to enemy households."

"Our enmity is among men— not with women. You should have told them who you were… Mahepora has enough standing that no man would take their daughter and treat her however he pleases. We too take women to raise our own honor, but we keep their dignity— at least we claim to. These ones… what can I say— they're Pashtun by blood, but they seem to have no Pashtunawli."

"What benefit do they hope to gain through you, that they are letting you stay alive? Even if they had killed you, what would the people of Shahélaar ever have known about what happened to you?" she asked.

"I have no idea. I've been thinking the same since yesterday— what do they hope to gain through me?"

"They took me thinking I was Rimsha— but why take Rimsha? What grudge did they hold against her? What advantage did they hope for?"

"She was the colonel's daughter— maybe they meant to use her to put pressure on him. But you weren't part of their plan so everything went wrong. What was it about the clothes that caused them to be mistaken."

"I left home carefully dressed, because when we reached Totano Bandai she was supposed to get ready for the wedding and I thought it best to be presentable. Rimsha was in casual clothes and they mistook me for her, thinking I was a maid. If they'd just asked, I would have said I'm not Rimsha."

"I'm sorry about Rimsha. When I left university two years ago you weren't yet on her friend list."

"I joined Islamabad College after you left. Rimsha was a senior, but we became friends quickly."

"Did she ever talk about me?" he felt his old hurt rise up.

"Did you really love her enough to drop university for her?" Elma asked, looking into his eyes.

"How can I say? I barely held myself together afterward," he answered.

"Then she was not right for you. You're emotional— like a Farhad or Ranjha… whereas she was too practical. She didn't want life decided by someone else; love was a part of her life, not the whole. She wanted to live life on her terms. The Laila-Majnu type of romance— she didn't agree with that. She did love you, but love wasn't everything for her. She had a boy before you— perhaps you know already. He was possessive, like you. That relationship tangled her; she broke it off. Then you came into her life, and in time you resembled the old pattern, which unsettled her. She wanted freedom, not the oppression of some macho ego deciding for her."

"If there is no desire to achieve something, then what is love?" he muttered.

"You won't understand— love isn't something to win or lose. It's something to live, not a property to be claimed. A woman is a person who decides for herself, not a property whose life is decided by others."

"In our world such things happen."

"Yes. And your tribal pride drove you away from her. You both might have married, but not with the same understanding. You two were never suited for the same horizon."

"You're not on her mind— if you speak for her like this…"

"I am— but our worlds differ. She was a modern Baloch; I am a tribal Pashtun. I know my limits. If I had lived her life, it would have been hell for me. But what use are these words now? These people have decided my future."

They were quiet for a long moment, each feeling the scratch of old pain and new fear. Safir's ego smarted; Elma's face clouded with the thought of a future being set by others.

"After you left, a Baloch boy came into Rimsha's life who planned to join the army. He believed, like you didn't, that a woman should have freedom. They were happy together." Elma's voice softened.

That stung. Safir felt humiliated— as if public opinion had declared him unworthy and Rimsha had moved on to someone better... someone who matched her. It hurt to think she had found someone she deserved and that he had been a fool risking his life for a love that had already expired.

"I was doing it out of duty and old ties," he said, trying to soften his humiliation. "If she was happy, I am too."

"You're not. But maybe you'll be happy now," Elma said sympathetically.

"Have you ever loved someone?" he asked.

"No. What good would it do? Our will counts for nothing; our fate is uncertain. Who knows when some hot-headed enemy might seize a girl and turn her life into servitude? You thought marriage would give me security, but fate denied even that."

"Was your security detail with the convoy?"

"No. They were sent on ahead to meet us at a drop point where Rimsha would leave and they would take me on, but we never reached that point."

They fell silent. The shock of Rimsha's injury and the new details had eased the edge of his fury. Whatever love Elma described, he lacked the capacity to measure it— and perhaps that knowledge eased him— if Rimsha had chosen differently, he could accept it.

After half an hour, steps sounded and the door opened. Two Pathans entered, rifles ready.

"Let's go," one ordered.

Elma's face crumpled. She looked at Safir with a plea in her eyes, but he had none left to give. They were forced up and led out— past the house, through the courtyard, into the open where three closed vehicles waited. Neither the man with the goat-like beard nor their leader, Nabi, was among them.

They were shoved into the middle vehicle and the convoy set off.

The road was rough; the cars jostled wildly. The bouncing threw Safir into Elma, sometimes she against him, sometimes he against her. They were bound together by captivity, but for the first time Safir noticed a heady scent rising from Elma— a faint intoxicating perfume that made him restless. He shook his head, trying to shrug the sensation away, but the scent clung like a shadow.

He tried to gauge their whereabouts from the passing landscape but could not. Hills rose on either side— some dry and brown, some green with tall trees. A thought crept into his mind that they might have crossed the border and entered the Nuristan region, but he couldn't trust the guess.

Elma's scent began to agitate one of the Pathans. She tried to keep distance on the cramped seat, but there was barely room. Ten minutes into the drive they reached a stretch where the road narrowed into cliffs, gullies, and small rock outcrops. There the tempers snapped.

The SUV stopped. Everyone dismounted and an argument began.

Everyone was aware of what the elders had decided about Elma— she was to be kept as a "laundi." Now the younger men, driven by lust, argued they had the right to first take their pleasure with her before the older men decided what to do next— while the older four urged restraint in the name of Pashtunwali and honor. They also argued that Elma's being could placate their leader Zargam if handled, so some called for self-control.

Their talk made Elma tremble; she clung to Safir's hand as if pleading to be saved, but what could he do? They were all armed, and he had nothing.

In the end the younger men prevailed and the elders had to step back.

The moment the decision was made, they stormed toward the vehicle and dragged Safir out. Elma tried hard not to let go of his hand, but that wasn't possible— and she broke down crying. Why would her tears matter to these men anyway…?

Now the person who had caused this commotion entered inside and tried to pull Elma down with his strength, making her helpless.

Safir's honor would never allow him to witness this, but the situation was combustible. Every pair of hawk-like eyes stood fixed on him— waiting, almost inviting him to make one wrong move so they could blow his head off. If he tried saving Elma now, he would die instantly… and Elma would still face the same fate. Intelligence demanded restraint; rage demanded patience. He had already sworn in that moment that if he survived, he would settle this blood-debt.

The Pathan who had mounted Elma had just opened his shalwar when a shot was fired from somewhere and One of their companions fell down there bleeding.

The shot cracked sharply through the barren valley. A second man collapsed in the dust— his skull shattered before he understood he'd been targeted at all.

All hell broke loose.

The captors dove toward cover, abandoning their positions. Safir dropped instantly, crouching low. The man atop Elma scrambled off, horrified, only to be struck by another precise shot that flung him lifeless beside Safir.

"Elma— don't move. Stay down," Safir whispered urgently.

He pulled the fallen attacker's body half over the doorway and slammed the car door shut, shielding her as best he could. Bullets rained toward the vehicles. Their enemies were positioned higher, hidden behind rocks— snipers, not amateurs. Meanwhile the captors fired wildly, blind into the slopes. Two more of them collapsed under clean headshots.

Realizing their disadvantage, the remaining men used the vhicles as cover and rushed downhill.

Safir used the brief distraction to move. He crawled toward the SUV's passenger door, judging angles the way hunters measure the movement of prey. He pushed the door open and peeked toward the snipers' direction— ready to pull back if they objected. No warning came.

Climbing over the corpse outside, he dragged himself in.

"You, okay?" he whispered.

"H-hmm," Elma's fragile voice replied.

Safir gently pulled the door shut. Their captors already knew they were inside— but the unknown shooters didn't. Best not to draw their attention.

He slid into the driver's seat, keeping his head low. Carefully, inch by inch, he raised his eyes just enough to read the terrain ahead.

There was danger everywhere… yet also the first sliver of hope.

If he dared.

He inhaled deeply— Bismillah, he murmured under his breath and twisted the ignition.

The SUV roared to life. Gunfire erupted instantly from both sides. Bullets shattered the windows, punched into the body, ricocheted off metal, clattered in the dashboard. Safir floored the accelerator, weaving wildly so no one could shoot out the tires. The SUV leapt forward like a maddened bull.

Miraculously, the wheels held.

Behind them the hillside dipped, shielding them from direct fire. Safir finally raised his head fully and sped through the ravines, leaving both factions behind.

"Elma— are you okay?"

"Yes," she answered faintly.

"Sit up. We're clear for now."

"He has snapped the drawstring of my shalwar."

"Hold it with your hand for now— we'll find a safe place and fix it. For the moment, we just need to keep moving."

"Where are we, even?"

"No clue. Somewhere between Kaga, Garga or Lar Sholtan… I've never crossed these valleys."

"Who were those people who saved us?"

"No idea. Could be Taliban, Pakistan Rangers, Northern Alliance… or even another TTP faction. Anyone."

Elma peered out anxiously— "Move toward the sunrise — if we can reach our own side of the border, the army might help."

"I'm trying, but the terrain isn't straight. These aren't roads— they're scars on the mountains. Just let me think."

She fell silent as Safir tried to judge bearings through broken terrain— valleys ruled by dozens of factions. Even the army couldn't fully claim this region.

After half an hour on pitted mud-tracks, a checkpoint appeared ahead. Safir braked sharply. The structure was crude

— sandbags, a roofless hut, a hanging torn flag whose color he couldn't identify.

It could belong to anyone.

Or… no one.

"Why did you stop?" Elma asked anxiously.

Safir explained the problem. One wrong move, and the freedom they had risked their lives for would be snatched back instantly.

"What do we do now?" she whispered.

Safir had no answer.

••

Rayyaan's mind had stopped working. The rich feast from last night churned inside him and he desperately needed a washroom. As he wandered through the house, he realized something was terribly wrong.

The home that had been alive with lanterns, candles, servants, voices…

…was now a corpse.

Every door creaked open to empty rooms. The bathing pool he had soaked in was dry— so dry that the stone at its base had dusty cracks. No trace of steam, no scent of warmth. Where dozens of lanterns had glowed, there was not a whiff of soot.

He ran from room to room— no furniture, no rugs, no utensils. The chamber where his nikah had taken place looked untouched for decades. The dining hall was bare. And the bridal chamber, where he had spent the night with Ghazal— held nothing but a decaying wooden cot.

Not a single object proved that last night had ever occurred.

A hallucination?

A dream?

But the intensity of Ghazal's touch, the taste of her breath, the fever in her eyes— that was no dream. His mind refused to accept it.

He found the abandoned outhouse behind the house. Rainwater collected in a trough gave him enough to wash up. Feeling marginally more sane, he stepped outside.

The entire village was dead.

His watch read noon. Sun high. Yet the streets lay cold and abandoned. Yesterday at 11 p.m., the whole village had been awake, alive, moving. Now it looked centuries deserted.

Panic stung his chest.

He knocked on the nearest door. No reply. He shoved it open. The house was hollow, dust-ridden, long forsaken. Exactly like Ghazal's.

He staggered through every house— one after another… calling, shouting, pleading…

Nothing.

As if an entire population had vanished in a blink.

Fear— real fear… crawled up his spine. The same spirits and shadows he had scoffed at… now they felt plausible. His heartbeat pounded in his ears. He imagined unseen eyes staring from rooftops, malicious laughter echoing in the empty lanes.

He ran.

Ran as if hell chased him.

Houses whirled past. The laughter in his mind grew shrill. He didn't know where the path led— only that he had to escape. Somewhere along the way, he tripped over rubble and fell into the remnants of a ruined structure— half-sunken walls, a shattered mulberry tree, stones swallowed by earth.

He pressed his face to the dirt, trying to breathe.

Minutes passed before his lungs settled. He lifted his head, trembling.

Fear. Pure fear.

He had never known it like this.

Then—

Grr—rr—rr—rr…

A guttural growl sliced the silence.

He turned.

Behind him stood a massive wild wolf— jaws open, fangs bared, drool threading down to the dust.

Ice flooded his veins.

His body, already damp with sweat, began to sweat anew as terror set in. The animal was far too large to fight bare-handed, and there was no weapon to be found. If this was how it ended, then it was to end now.

Rayyaan pushed himself up into a half-sitting posture as the wolf leapt at him with a throat-shuddering snarl.

Death danced in his eyes.

Then something else blurred into view— another wolf hurtled at the first one. The charging beast struck and the attacker buckled, spilling to Rayyaan's right. The impact made the ground shudder.

Both wolves hit earth; then, jawing and snarling, they sprang apart and slunk off a little distance. Whatever had been their focus just moments before, Rayyaan no longer existed to them. They regarded one another like sworn rivals — fangs bared, breath rasping, slobber stringing from their mouths.

And then Rayyaan saw what even a hard-hearted man would call terror.

Before his very eyes the two wolves grew— greatening not merely in size but in shape— until they were no longer simply wolves. They swelled into hulking, elephantine forms that nevertheless retained a lupine anatomy; their teeth lengthened into monstrous tusks. Rayyaan felt himself shrink inside his skin— the courage he thought he owned reduced to a frightened kid's.

His body went limp with fear; his legs trembled so badly he could not stand. His head hummed and his lungs forgot how to draw breath. Heat and haze fogged his vision.

The two titanic wolf-beasts crashed into one another with a roar that made the earth ring like an upraised drum. The ruined house around him shook as if struck by an earthquake. Trees and shrubs caught between those crushing bodies were flattened as if they were mere reeds.

This was a battle Rayyaan had never seen nor could have imagined— a fight whose outcome would settle his fate.

Amid the thunder of it all, he sensed another presence behind him.

He craned his neck, and his breath froze.

A wooden club was swinging in the air— suspended without a hand to wield it, a stick moving as if animated. Before Rayyaan could understand what he saw, the club arced down and struck his skull.

The blow was so violent that darkness spread through his mind. He felt the back of his head meet the earth, and then he had no more consciousness.

When he came to, he was somewhere else.

A mountain stream ran close by; the tinkling water met his ears. He lay on a mossy bank among stones and slick earth, the soil still damp from the recent rains. A cool wind drifted. His clothes were intact; his belongings lay with him — small mercies.

He closed his eyes and breathed, slow and deep.

The feeling of not being alone returned— an impression that someone's gaze rested on him. The memory of how he had gone under a short while ago crawled back and a cold shiver ran through his body.

He opened his eyes and found someone standing very near— someone who stepped back when he blinked awake. He adjusted his focus and saw a girl in tribal dress. Relief flooded him; there were no other people in sight.

He sat up and dusted himself off. She looked twenty-one or so— healthy, fair in the way girls from these parts often are. Her clothes marked her as tribal, but in manner and bearing she did not seem out of place in decent company.

"Who are you?" he asked in Pashto.

"Actually, I should have asked this question," she replied, a small edge in her tone.

"Ask," he said, glancing around.

She started slightly— "What?"

"The question you should have asked— and strange that I asked it first by mistake."

She smiled, and her deep black eyes smiled with her. Rayyaan's mind jerked— there was a flash of Ghazal's face in those features, but this was not Ghazal. Still, the resemblance in the eyes hit him.

"All right. I'll tell you. My name is Rayyaan Afridi. I'm the only son, Chashmochirag, of Chaudhry Waqar Afridi of the Kaanwabeel jagir. I'd been caught in last night's storm and, trying to find shelter, fell into the wrong company. I was knocked out and left here. If you don't mind, think of me as a trouble-ridden guest— take pity, trust me, believe me that I mean you no harm. Can we sit and talk? Or walk toward your place— whichever is easier for you."

She smiled again and stepped off. Rayyaan followed.

"You were sleeping here?" she asked, studying him.

"Do you think I'm mad, that I'd sleep here."

"You mean unconscious?"

"Completely— just came to. I have no idea how I got here." He looked up; the sun was already dipping toward the ridge. He must have been out for four or five hours. He was hungry; he hadn't eaten since yesterday.

"You were somewhere else before waking up, then."

"Obviously. There's nothing around here— where I took shelter last night there was a settlement. What is this place?"

"This is the Karagal valley."

"Karagal… where exactly in Karagal? Which jagir, which area?"

"I don't know."

"Do you have a name?"

"Yes— people call me Saarah."

"Who calls you that? Where are they from?"

"See this forest?" she said, pointing— "Across from it is Gulzar Shah's dyodhi. People there call me Saarah because I'm of their village."

"Why are you alone in the forest?"

"I herd goats. A lamb went missing while I was grazing. I sent the rest of the flock back with my little brother and set off to find the lamb. It didn't turn up— then you did."

"And the lamb? You gave up?"

"I accepted it. In the wild there are jackals, wolves, even pythons— anything can happen."

"My stomach's been empty since yesterday," he said.

"There are two mulberry trees and some pomegranates over there. They'll help a little. The village might have more."

He felt his insides protest less vocally now. They walked toward the trees Saarah had indicated. Rayyaan crashed into the mulberries like a starving man; Saarah tore down a dozen ripe pomegranates and handed them to him. The sweet, astringent fruits eased his hunger and thirst; the sugar in them gave him some strength.

The sun was already leaning toward the hilltop— they needed to move fast.

"Do you know how to get to Kaanwabeel?" Rayyaan asked as they walked.

"I don't. I've never been beyond these parts. I've only heard its name."

"A young, pretty girl wandering alone in the forest— aren't you afraid?"

"Afraid of what?" she said.

"Well, if I were a worthless man right now, I could—" he broke off, embarrassed by the thought— "What if I took you? What then?"

"Nothing more than this— it is not within my power to stop you. But it is possible that some man from our village may be nearby, and if he happens to see this, he will be driven to take your life. Here, in such a situation, nothing less than killing is considered acceptable. A woman is the shared honor of the entire tribe."

"And what if no one saw?" he pressed.

"Then fate," she shrugged— "Besides, in a man's world a woman's value is seldom high. But you won't get far with me. If you want to reach a settlement, you'll have to find one."

"Don't worry. I'm from a family that keeps distance from such foolery," he said— "Which side is Dera Jamal Khan?"

"There's no village by that name around here," she answered, shrugging.

Rayyaan's head spun— "What? But that's where I slept last night... people there knocked me out and left me here. Whoever drops someone unconscious would leave them not far off— maybe ten, twenty kilometres at most. If I was left here, the village must be close."

"Maybe not. I don't know of any village by that name nearby." Saarah shrugged again.

He felt the world tilt. What he had experienced could not be dismissed as illusion— Ghazal's touch, the bridal bed— those had been too real. And yet here was a girl who did not even know the village name. Was he still half-out of his mind? Was she real? He gripped her hand impulsively; her palm was warm. He concentrated until the trembling in his head steadied. He closed his eyes, focused, and then opened them — the blue sky through leaves, the drifting clouds, the bird returning to a branch— everything was as it should be.

"Are you all right?" Saarah asked, worried.

"Actually... what happened to me last night is so strange I wonder if I'd been poisoned. Some drugs make one hallucinate in such precise ways that you cannot deny them even when they're false."

"Don't stop; keep walking. Tell me while we go— what happened?"

They picked up their pace and he related the events— the convoy, the shooting, the kidnapping, the chaos, the capture, the escape. Saarah listened with astonishment.

"It's possible you were drugged during the lift," she said — "If so, the effect may have worn off now. There's an elder here— Abba Ji... very wise; he might help you."

He thought further. If Ghazal had indeed dosed him, why would she lead him here? Perhaps she herself misled him. The sunlight sank and the forest grew dimmer.

Suddenly Saarah was gone.

Panic seized him. He spun and called her name. No answer. The hush that settled around him felt suddenly oppressive; his heart hammered.

A rustle in the bushes snapped his head around. A "myaaow" broke the silence and a cat sprang between the shrubs— its body seemed to stretch in the flicker of fading light, then snapped back as if some elastic had released.

His throat tightened.

One by one, several "myaaows" sounded and a dozen lithe cats leapt and bounded, their cries slicing through the dusk. He called Saarah again but there was no reply.

As the cats mewed, a low growl began answering them — first one, then another— until it sounded like dogs answering the felines. Though the dim light kept him from seeing clearly, the rustling bracken suggested a fearsome skirmish was beginning among the undergrowth.

His nerves frayed. He felt a hair-raising prickling from head to heel. Then he felt something brush the crown of his head and looked up.

Above him, coiled on a branch, a great python had dropped, its bulk falling straight down— then looped itself around him. Before he could move, the serpent had wrapped its coils and opened its mouth.

Rayyaan's world narrowed to a single, cold point— the inside of that open mouth. The python snapped its powerful jaws over his skull and began to draw him in. The pressure at his temples was excruciating. He felt his skull being gripped — and then everything went black.

••

The sun was tipping toward west— soft breezes were moving. In three directions the desert shimmered— high and low dunes of sand whose shapes and sizes the drifting wind kept reshaping. To one side a town rose in an old-fashioned pattern; its palaces and the minarets of its enclosures could be seen from afar. A road led to it through the heart of the desert. On that road there was a small green patch— solid earth amid the sand, a few date-palms, some grass and a little spring. It was a kind of resting place where passing caravans paused to catch their breath and freshen up.

There, under the shade of a date-palm, lay a young man with a dozen donkeys grazing about him; he watched the sun redden and spoke to it as if talking to an old friend. He wore a jubba and a safa; by looks and bearing he seemed Arab— broad-shouldered and striking, with a clear complexion and deep black eyes.

"Lower your pace, Hazrat, and we'll move on— by sight Rakh'aan is ahead, but there's so much ground between that darkness will fall before we reach it. Rakh'aan's folk won't be out to welcome us with spread cushions; we must make our own arrangements— for ourselves and for our brothers." He waved his hand toward the sun as he spoke.

One of the donkeys brayed in agreement and the young man nodded, thanking the donkey.

The sun, of course, answered nothing; he continued in a low chant, singing a nazm in praise of the Sun.

Before he could finish, two caravans came into view and his voice fell silent.

The caravans approached from different directions. One rode camels; the other, horses. The camel caravan emerged from behind a high dune and was quite near; the horsemen were farther off, coming along the road from the opposite side, riding toward the town. The camel group's track suggested they were passing by Rakh'aan's right side to go left — they seemed to have no interest in the road. The young man sat up— his gaze fixed on the horsemen.

The donkeys continued grazing, unconcerned. The camel train drew close quickly. Seven camels carried seven riders, their faces burnt and weary from sun and wind; they looked at the young man and his donkeys as if neither patch of green nor the man or animals mattered to them. Indeed, some of the camels trampled the grazing donkeys and even the young man, but the beasts' padded feet seemed to pass as if the man and donkeys were nothing but air— images that neither the camels nor their riders could truly see. The uneven ground was smooth for them; they crossed puddles as if the water had turned to firm ground beneath them. The young man and perhaps his donkeys could see the caravan, yet they showed no reaction— while for the riders it was as if there were nothing there at all. The camel caravan passed between the dunes and vanished behind the next rise before the horsemen drew near.

The horsemen numbered seven. They wore shalwar-kameez and safas that wrapped most of their faces; as they came closer, they fixed their gaze on the young man, who was now standing. They reined their horses and halted.

"Who are you?" the leader asked.

"A— Aryan," the young man answered, hesitating.

"What are you doing here?" another demanded.

"Tired, janab… I was resting," Aryan replied.

"Are you headed to Rakh'aan or coming from there?"

"I'm going to Rakh'aan, janab... I've come to sell my donkeys."

"Good— come with us. We're merchants as well; we're bound for Rakh'aan on business," The leader said.

Aryan hesitated. They certainly did not look like traders, but what choice had he? He nodded, tied the remaining donkeys with a thin rope and mounted the last one himself. If the donkeys matched pace, the horses found it easier to walk than run, and so they all set off toward the distant town.

The horsemen peppered him with questions— who he was, where he lived, whether he had been to Rakh'aan before. Aryan answered in a way that reassured them; the leader told him that they'd come from Aramin and were simply on a long journey. The leader's name was Elman.

It took them perhaps an hour to reach the town; by then the sun had sunk into the sandball of the horizon and the outlying date-palms were turning dark.

Rakh'aan was a fine, sizeable town ringed by a ten-foot wall and entered through ornate, Babylon-like gates— decorative portals that looked like the work of a royal mason, guarded with strict security. When they reached the gate Elman warned Aryan to keep his mouth shut and to simply agree with whatever was said. Aryan understood why when Elman presented him at the gate as their servant and slave who had come to sell donkeys. He decided not to argue and went in with them.

The city was beautiful, planned in a Babylonian style. In the center stood the royal palace; gardens like hanging terraces spread around it. Fountains and pools played water; stone towers and houses with tall turrets rose around them— visible even from the desert. Lanterns began to light as evening fell and the town grew lively. Elman left Aryan with his men and went on business; Aryan lingered in the market, where the bustle intensified and his donkeys sold one after another.

In an hour four donkeys were sold. With the money in his hand Aryan ate and drank, then settled near his stall. Then a trumpeter's cry announced the arrival of Princess Manaal— the crowd hushed and everyone lowered their eyes. Manaal's fame had reached Aryan beforehand; he longed to see her but did not want to risk rudeness. He searched for a place to view from without being noticed and found a corner to hide in.

When the procession entered, most bowed their heads; women, by custom, had a little more liberty but remained respectful. The escort included footmen and horsemen; in the center rode a royal carriage bearing the princess and her attendant. While others behaved like automata, the princess and her maid looked at the wares in the market— if something pleased her, she took it and one of the escort paid.

When the procession passed near Aryan, he could not help looking up— and a lightning struck his senses. He stood transfixed.

Manaal was truly breathtaking— a masterpiece whose every part was beautiful. Black silk hair fell like thunder-clouds, her deep eyes resembled a lake, her lips like rosebuds, her face matched the moon in beauty, her long neck, carved shoulders, rising chest and slender waist— all wrapped in royal garments that revealed more than they concealed. Her beauty made eyes go dazed; anyone who saw her risked losing composure. In Aryan's chest a soft, involuntary sigh escaped.

Manaal had not been looking toward him; she and her attendant were examining goods at a stall. But Aryan's audible breath reached her ears. She turned— caught him staring and for a moment he froze. Then her face tightened into displeasure. Such blatant staring was impertinent.

"Jalal," she said sharply.

The man leading her escort signaled at once. Footmen grabbed Aryan, forced him to his knees and bowed his head so he could not see the princess. When he still did not stop, a handkerchief was wrapped over his eyes. The commander sentenced him to ten lashes and two footmen began to strike him.

After the lashes, the procession prepared to move on— but a commotion arose at one end of the bazaar. People paused and turned. Breathless riders arrived and reported in haste— Vizier Alesar had been killed— there had been a band of seven assassins, one was captured and six had escaped.

The mention of seven assassins pricked Aryan's ears, and one of the arriving soldiers recognized him.

"Hey! This is one of those men's servant— when they entered the southern gate with them, I was there... they presented him as their slave," one of the soldiers called out.

"Wait-wait— don't be hasty, brother. I am no one's slave — when I met them, I was resting in the green patch; they frightened me into silence. Then they told me thcy were merchants and I thought they travelled on business. I had no idea of what they would do," Aryan protested, his eyes freed from the blindfold— love's fever drained away in the face of danger.

"You lie— if that were true why didn't you deny them at the time?" the commander snapped.

"S-sir— I was afraid... They told me to keep quiet. Later they called themselves traders; I took them at their word. How could I have known they meant murder?" Aryan stammered.

"Arrest him," the commander ordered.

"Brothers— please. Show mercy. I'm a stranger here. Ask around— I have been selling donkeys for an hour. What business would I have with a Vizier? I'm a humble donkey-trader— how could I know theVizier?" he begged, but nobody would listen. They hauled him toward the palace.

He cried out his innocence; he begged for justice, but his pleas fell on deaf ears. Manaal watched him dragged away in silence, but no compassion showed on her face.

●●

CHAPTER 4

Safir had no answer to Elma's question. He simply stared around silently, as if a single sign would reveal the way. He had no weapon in his hand— and the thought of confronting people with AK-47s while unarmed, was foolish.

"Guessing won't help… I'll have to check myself. Stay here— and if you sense danger, run. Quietly."

He glanced back toward Elma.

"My shalwar's naada is broken…" she whispered, on the verge of tears.

"I know… but if danger comes, you'll still have to run. If you can drive, come forward a little. If anything goes wrong, push the vehicle back and hide. Listen— without taking risks, nothing will work. If we walk straight in, they might shoot us on sight. Empty-handed, at worst they'll detain us."

"Fine. Go."

He exhaled hard, stepped out of the vehicle, and began walking toward the small cabin of the check-post. For a moment he turned back— Elma had already driven forward a little, and that sight steadied him.

As he closed the distance, a faint echo of music drifted through the warm air— scattered by the wind, but growing clearer with each step. Someone was inside… humming along to Pashto music. That single detail made it impossible to judge whether they were friend or foe. The slopes on both sides were forested, perfect for ambush. If there had been danger, men should have shown themselves already— but none had. That meant perhaps only one or two were inside.

If they turned out to be enemies, he'd simply have to fight his way through.

He reached the cabin— nothing unexpected happened.

He peeked inside. Two Pashtun men swayed to a tune playing on a mobile phone. Their rifles lay right beside them — which meant they were some kind of border guards… but their plain clothes revealed nothing beyond that. They were certainly not Pakistan-side forces.

Now what?

They hadn't yet noticed his presence. He could quietly turn back. Or try speaking to them— Kabul had changed hands, a new government had settled in, and these men might even be Taliban, who had a standing enmity with TTP and might help him.

But if they were TTP…

Then the escape they had risked everything for would be wasted. He was still weighing possibilities when the air shifted — silently, sharply.

He whirled around.

From both slopes, men emerged— rifles in hand, muzzles pointed— eight people. Enough that resistance was meaningless. Safir instinctively raised both hands.

An involuntary "Ah…" escaped him. The very thing he'd feared— happened exactly so.

Behind him, Elma had already understood. She saw Safir lift his hands and saw armed men rising from the trees— and in the same breath she threw the SUV into reverse. Her only chance was to run— and she was not one to surrender without trying. The bend behind her was close; if she reached it, she'd get cover.

Gunfire erupted— the men had spotted the jeep. But Elma had already swung behind the curve, vanishing from their line of fire.

The armed group shouted among themselves— words Safir understood, but meanings he could not grasp. They split immediately— one cluster surrounded Safir, while the other ran downhill toward the spot where an SUV had been hidden behind a rock embankment. Bullets had drawn out the two guards from the cabin as well; they stumbled outside, rifles raised— and seeing Safir, confusion flashed across their faces.

The second group reached the SUV and drove it after Elma.

"Who are you?" one of the men asked.

"A traveler… Safir Khasoor. From the Valley of Karagal. I lost my way. Some men tried to loot us— we ran, saw the check-post, and hoped for help. But I also sensed danger… so I came on foot to see."

"Who was in the jeep?"

"My companion— Elma Hamaar. We're to be married soon… I told her that if anything happened to me, she should run and try to find her way across the border."

"This jeep belongs to Nabiullah's men. How did you get it?"

Safir froze for a heartbeat. That one line was enough— they weren't from the group who had kidnapped them. But whether that made them friends or another enemy… impossible to assume.

"There was a fight… men killing one another. Many died. The survivors fled. We took what was left behind— the jeep was abandoned."

"Hmm. Who knows how much of that is true. But if you are a lost traveler, we'll escort you across the border with honor. Until we're sure… consider yourself a prisoner."

Safir had no choice— he walked where they led.

They ascended a ridge. The two men stationed at the cabin stayed behind. Those who had gone after Elma were still out of sight. One of the guards carried a satellite phone and exchanged coded messages— impossible for Safir to decipher.

When they reached the top, he saw rugged brown hills rolling endlessly in every direction— barely a trace of greenery. A cluster of mud-built structures stood below, ancient and abandoned in appearance. A few young women moved between them— their dress and manner revealed they were not relatives of the fighters. They were captives.

Safir was locked into a mud room— door latched from outside. A single barred window opened to the slope.

He was worried sick about Elma.

Better these men than the others… but only if they truly were enemies of Nabiullah's group. If Elma had escaped in the opposite direction and fallen into another trap… then God alone knew what awaited her.

Hours passed. No one came.

Near afternoon, a young woman entered— holding a plate of food and a glass of water. She set them down before him and sat across from him. Her Pashto carried a faint, unfamiliar accent— she was not a Pashtun.

"Eat. At least hunger won't trouble you when they kill you."

He stared at her. "So, death is certain, then?"

"Of course. What else would they do with a man? If you were a woman, they'd keep you as a laundi… but a man?" Her tone was edged with a tired bitterness.

"Who are these people? At least let me know whose hands I'm dying in."

"Taliban border Guards… who else, but you— who are you? And how did you fall into their hands?"

Safir ate while speaking— not much harm in telling her the basics.

"I'm Pakistani. TTP picked us up— by mistake. We escaped somehow… wandered here… and your people caught us."

"Was there a girl with you? Sounds like it."

"Yes. She escaped when they caught me. I don't know what happened to her."

"That's why they kept you alive. If she falls into their hands, they'll decide what to do. Whether they keep her like us… or something else. Are you people Pashtun?"

"Yes— I am Khasoor, and she is Hamaar."

"Then it is hard to say what they might do. Their conduct toward us is different, and different again with the Pashtuns… even so, there is no guarantee what decision they will take. There is no main route here that the authorities keep an eye on. Only government personnel or supplies pass through occasionally, and that is why one of their units is stationed here. If they are in the mood, they might let you go — otherwise, who knows… Is the girl very beautiful, or just ordinary?"

"She is beautiful, but what do you mean by 'us'? Who are you, and who were the other women seen here?"

"We are Hazaras. A long time ago we fell into their hands, when the reins of government were not yet with them. They kept us as slaves— to satisfy their physical needs and for other services. Generally, their behavior with Pashtuns remains one of parity, but if your companion is beautiful, their intentions may well stray, and then they will not spare you either."

Safir's face darkened.

"And why did you let me come here like this?"

"There's no one here right now," she said, pointing at a sharp rock-ledge high on the slope— "There. Two men are watching from that ridge. Anyone tries to run— they shoot. Even at night. They have night-vision scopes."

"How many total?"

"Dozen men. Two at the check-post, two at the ridge, rest around here. Four women— we used to be six. Two died trying to escape."

Safir exhaled slowly.

Hope looked worse than death.

"Then what will you do?" she asked softly.

"I don't know. But I won't sit waiting for luck— not for myself, not for Elma."

She gathered the empty plate and glass.

"If you have to do anything… let the night get very dark," she said before leaving the room.

The room he was in had a window that opened outward, fitted with iron bars, and a door that could be locked from the outside… though for now it had not been shut. He stood by the window and looked out. In front of him stretched an uneven, rocky slope, and a little higher up on it, a ledge jutted out like a projecting awning. Two bearded Pashtuns were seated there, scanning the surroundings. Rifles rested across their laps, and a few other items lay placed nearby. This was on the exact opposite side of the slope from where he had been brought in— where the checkpoint lay.

He stood there for a while, thinking, then lay down and began to weigh his options… what should he do now? It was not absolutely necessary that those two would prove to be enemies— but what if they did? For the moment, before they reached any decision, he still had a window to act. Once they came to a decision— and if that decision went against him— there would be no chance left to do anything at all. Better than taking that risk later was to take a risk now… to try and get out of here while there was still time. But what about Elma? Where would he go looking for her? If she fell into their hands, then there would be no option left but to fight them directly.

He had barely been lying on his back for a short while when the harsh crack of gunfire tore through the silence, and he jolted upright in shock.

Safir leapt to the window.

The two guards on the ridge jerked violently— like puppets cut loose and tumbled down the slope, rolling lifelessly across the khud, that rocky protrusion jutting out of the hillside.

He had no way of knowing where the shot had come from. The narrow window didn't allow him to see far left or right, but one thing was clear— this was his moment.

Without wasting another second, Safir slipped out through the door. A few faces appeared behind nearby windows— women, the same Hazaras he had seen earlier. Among them was the one who had brought him food. They watched him in utter silence… with eyes that resembled caged birds watching a companion suddenly break free.

He wished he could do something for them too, but survival came first. He crouched low, keeping to whatever cover he could find, and began climbing toward the ledge where the two sentries had collapsed.

It didn't take long to reach them.

One was already cold; the other was breathing his last. Safir pulled the rifle out of his limp hand, pressed himself against the rocky ledge, and peered from behind it— toward the direction where the shot might have come from.

It was guesswork at best. The bullet could have come from behind as well. But considering that during his climb he had crossed several exposed angles and no one had fired at him, his instinct insisted the attacker belonged to the opposite side.

Still… he saw nothing. No movement. No shadows.

He turned to look toward the opposite slope— the one facing the road and the checkpoint. Even there, nothing stirred. Which meant only one thing— the men stationed there hadn't realized what had happened yet. And they could arrive any moment.

He had no time.

A strange tug of instinct made him turn— and there she was, far above on a jutting rock, waving at him. Elma. Even from that height he could see the rifle in her hand.

So, she had pulled the trigger.

His shock froze for barely a heartbeat. This wasn't the time to stand around marvelling. He sprinted upward toward her— the same direction from where the checkpoint men could appear without warning.

By the time he reached Elma, still no one else had shown up.

Which meant the eight men still unaccounted for were likely split— four had chased her earlier, and the other four must have gone looking for them. The two guards at the checkpoint couldn't abandon their post.

So, they had a small window. A thin breath of time.

"You know how to fire a rifle?" he asked, breathless and astonished.

"My father taught all of us sisters," she replied with quiet pride, "To protect ourselves. To fight if we ever had to."

"Then why were you trembling earlier? They were dragging you away— turning you into a slave. You could've fought back and put an end to them."

"That's not how it works!" she snapped— "Training is training— real life is different. When everything happened at once, my mind went blank. I reacted on instinct. But when it finally came down to survival… courage shows up too. Anyway— do you think we can find something to eat? I'm starving."

"There's food down there," he said— "But going back would mean walking straight into them. For now, move. And keep watching every angle. This place is crawling with people hunting us— Taliban on one side, TTP on the other."

Elma made a face but followed him as they moved to the other side of the ridge, both alert, scanning the terrain.

"How did you get here? And how did you know where to find me?" he asked.

"I guessed they must've kept you near the checkpoint," she said, "So once I got a rifle, I headed this way. When I reached the post, it was too quiet. No guards. No movement. So, I scouted around. A checkpoint isn't big enough to house so many men— so their real base had to be nearby. Then I spotted this place… and the two guards watching from this rock. Just then, I saw you through the window. That confirmed it. Those two weren't much trouble." she added— "After that, I waited for the others to appear— but instead, you walked out. There was no one else up there?"

"Not a single person. There are four Hazara girls," Safir said quietly— "Kept as slaves. No guards inside. The twelve men… two here, two at the post, and eight who roam around. Four went after you. The remaining four dropped me here and must have gone after them. You didn't see them on your way back?"

"No."

"So, they must be close," he muttered— "How did you escape the four chasing you?"

"Do you think I'd outrun them on the road? I drove into a slope full of rocks and trees— let the vehicle crash, and slipped out. They reached the jeep but didn't find me. Then they split up looking for me… and I got a chance to smash one of their heads. Took his rifle. But I can't fight all three. So I slipped back, thinking if anyone can be saved… it's you."

Safir let out a low laugh.

"All that training your father gave to keep you safe from men… and you've used it all to save me. He'd be thrilled."

Elma pouted but said nothing.

"And your shalwar? I thought the drawstring was torn."

"It was a complete nuisance," she muttered. "I had to take it off when I hid. After hiting that man, I found the courage to fix it. Tied a knot, tightened it over my waist. If I ever get a peaceful moment, I'll fix it properly."

Safir smiled.

"Looks fine for now."

He paused, remembering the Hazara girl's warning.

"By the way… those men might not have been enemies at first. They're Taliban border guards. For us, not exactly enemies. But the girl warned me— your beauty could've turned their intentions in seconds. That's why I didn't want to trust them."

"Because of me?" Elma raised an eyebrow.

"Have you seen yourself? Don't you know what you are? You're trouble. Pure trouble," he said— "The man who went crazy sniffing around you? He wasn't entirely to blame. If he hadn't lost control, those attackers wouldn't have gotten the perfect moment to shoot."

"Oh, so he was innocent— and I'm the cursed one?" she snapped.

"That's not what I meant—"

"Sounds exactly like that."

"Okay, sorry! I was trying to compliment you, idiotically. My mistake."

"Is this how you sweet-talked Rimsha too? Shame on you, Safir," she shot back. Then, narrowing her eyes— "And that smell you keep talking about—what if you get tempted one day?"

"I swear I won't," he said instantly, "I was just… trying to explain a point. Besides, I promise— once we reach home, I'll drop you at Mahepora, not Shahelār."

"Oh? Won't you honour the tribal custom? The mighty Khasoor taking home a Mahepora girl? Your people would be thrilled."

"Let them talk. I don't care. I'll live my life on my own terms."

"Funny. You followed tradition quite nicely when you kidnapped Raika."

"That was revenge," he shot back. "They'd taken Inaya first. We couldn't let that slide. But I never liked this kind of heroism."

She exhaled— "Where do we go now? I can't make sense of anything."

"That checkpoint means the border is near. The sun's position says East is that way. If we circle around from the side instead of walking straight across, we can reach our territory or at least the no-man's-land. But you… you're the real danger. A stunning girl wandering here? Every man's ego will chase you."

"And how is that my fault?" she muttered— "What about those Hazara girls? Can't we help them?"

Safir's face darkened.

"I see everyone as human, Elma. But this place… if you get caught again, both of us die. They have night scopes, roaming patrols, vantage points. Saving you already feels like a miracle. Saving them is beyond what we can do. I hate it… but we leave them because we must— not because they're beneath us."

Elma fell silent, her eyes damp with helplessness.

They circled the hill for a long while, descended, then climbed another ridge. Ahead lay endless small hills— some barren, some green. No paths, no houses, nothing man-made — just wild nature.

"Nothing seems possible from here— this much we can at least walk," Elma said, but the sight before her drained her resolve. "My throat is parched with thirst, and my stomach is growling with hunger."

"What other option do we have except to keep moving? If we stay put here, who will come to help us? There is greenery in that direction— we might even come across some Gujjars wandering in search of pasture. Think of it this way; we can fight hunger and thirst again, but we do not have the strength to fight the cold of the night. Come— before the sun sets."

With a heavy heart, Elma had no choice but to follow behind him.

After about an hour, they did come upon a mountain stream, clear water flowing through it, and they quenched their thirst there. Food or not— taking the water itself as a blessing. Elma drank so much that it became difficult for her to walk any further. Eventually, she sat down at one spot.

"I can't go on anymore… let's stop here," she said in a defeated tone.

"Think about it— there isn't even a shred of shelter here to hide under. By morning, we will be found as two bodies stiffened by the cold."

"There is no hope anyway."

"Look over there— at least let us walk as far as that greenery. There is a good spread of vegetation there. It is possible we might find something there to take shelter and ease our hunger. Here, we will find nothing at all."

"I have no strength left, Safir. You go on. Let me die here— just make sure a message reaches my family that I am dead."

Safir stood there, helpless, watching her crumble.

He understood her exhaustion— she had been starving since morning, running for her life. Anyone's strength would break.

"Fine," he said softly— "Then climb onto my back. I'll carry you."

"What?" She stared at him.

"Come on— how heavy can you be? Forty-five kilos, maybe."

"That's not the point! It's… its weird!"

"When life is on the line, forget weird," he said. "Imagine I'm a horse. Just climb."

She hesitated… then slowly wrapped her arms around his neck and climbed onto his back. A strange shiver rippled through both of them— an involuntary spark. Then they steadied themselves. Safir tightened his grip around her legs, slid the rifle across his chest, and she placed hers on her back.

He walked on. She was a weight, but not unbearable.

"Not a stranger," she whispered under her breath.

"What?"

"Nothing… Does my smell still bother you?"

"Terribly," he confessed with a half-laugh— "I think once you leave, I'll spend days smelling nothing else but you. Never knew some girls had a scent that addictive. Good for you, though— after marriage, your husband won't need much convincing."

"Shut up or I'll get off!"

"Sorry."

"And why are you taking me home? You could take me to Shahelār, boost your tribe's pride."

"I told you— I don't like forced marriages. If I marry someday, it'll be by my own choice."

"And the girl you loved? She's gone. Will you fall in love again?"

"Who knows… love before marriage isn't a rule. If it happens, it happens. If not, marriage itself creates love later."

Elma said nothing. She just rested her cheek lightly against his shoulder.

••

Rayyaan was awake.

Through half-opened eyes, he saw a figure leaning over him— his head resting gently in her lap. There was almost no light around. He searched for the source— and spotted a tiny firefly flickering nearby.

The hand stroking his hair left his head— stretched toward the firefly… pinched it by the ear, so to speak… and brought it back.

The firefly morphed into a lantern— glowing softly, illuminating the space around him.

Rayyaan finally saw the face above him.

It was Ghazal.

He closed his eyes again and tried to think… who was this Ghazal? The sluggish fog that had crept into his mind lifted as soon as he tried to focus. A sharp shock jolted him awake and he sat up with a start.

"Ghazal!" the name escaped him.

She was no dream; she sat there in the lantern light. The room was small and shut— lantern-glow pooling against bare walls. He pinched himself, shook his head, and tried to force every sense back into service— was he still half-unconscious or drugged, or was this solid reality?

Nothing in him answered yes. Still, it was possible that everything he felt real was only imagination— he could not rule that out.

He said her name again. She did not speak; she only watched him in silence. Rayyaan touched her cheek— warm flesh met his fingertip. She was real.

Instead of more words, Rayyaan took stock of the place. It was a sealed cell with no window and no visible door— only two small ventilator slits high up. Small holes pierced the walls into darkness beyond. A shallow alcove had been carved into one wall and in it burned the single lantern that lit the room. The word lantern tugged something in his mind.

"You— What are you, madam... you had convinced me that you are human like me, but you had just increased the flame of that lantern while sitting right here," he said, peering into Ghazal's eyes— "And when you did it your hand stretched so far it almost reached eight feet—how can a human arm do that?"

"You must be dreaming— the lantern is just burning," she answered.

"No… I saw it with my own eyes."

"Were you fully conscious?" she asked, looking straight at him and he hesitated— "No, you have just woken. The earlier things you saw were your mind's imaginings. Or maybe you are not yet fit to make sense of things."

"But how did I get here— an enormous serpent swallowed me!"

"Possibly this cell is the serpent's belly," she said.

"You are mocking me."

"You speak like that— would anyone survive being swallowed by a huge snake?"

"My point is… when the serpent coiled around me to swallow, I lost consciousness. Was I rescued?"

"Your mind does not seem well."

"Perhaps you're right… I feel nervous and stupid in a way I never have before." He gripped his head with both hands. "If someone saved me, who was it— and whose prisoners are we?"

At that moment Ghazal startled; a sound and movement behind him. Before he could turn, a pair of strong hands seized his neck.

The man was not much taller than Rayyaan— perhaps a foot, but his strength made Rayyaan feel null. He hoisted Rayyaan by the throat a foot into the air. The man's face was ordinary enough, but his eyes burned and his spotless clothes gleamed strangely.

"You are in my captivity, wretched human— my captive… and you will remain so. Until the last breath in this body. Did you think you stole her from me? No— you have committed a mistake whose punishment will be worse than death. Understood?"

His voice struck like a thunderclap. The words hit Rayyaan as physical blows; hair stood up on his arms, his heart thudded, his body shivered. Mercifully, the sentence was short; the man tossed Rayyaan against a wall. He crashed down and groaned, fighting to keep consciousness.

The man loomed before Ghazal and spoke again— his voice echoing as if through a great hall, every syllable ringing in Rayyaan's skull.

"You thought by marrying him you could escape me, Ghazal? Wait— soon Chaudhry Safdar Hayat will kneel before me. After that you will be mine."

Ghazal answered— Rayyaan could not catch her words, but the man slapped her, and she collapsed. Rayyaan struggled to rise; the man turned and strode toward him, his boots thudding. He crouched over Rayyaan, slipped his hands under Rayyaan's ribs, and lifted him like a toy.

"You will divorce her at your own will," he hissed, "and then you will witness— until your dying breath… my every union with her." He looked toward Ghazal, turning Rayyaan's head so he would see— "You bestowed your first companionship upon this worthless man— this shall be his recompense."

He slammed Rayyaan again into the wall. This time Rayyaan blacked out.

When he recovered, the room was unchanged. Ghazal still sat against the wall, watching him. Silence had fallen; the lantern flame stood motionless.

Rayyaan, drawing breath with a small sound, moved closer.

"Who was he?" he asked, meeting her gaze.

"Shah Alam," she answered with the barest movement of her lovely lips.

"Your suitor— the man you escaped by marrying me? Did the events of last night actually happen?"

She gave no reply.

"Can you tell me— how did he come into this sealed cell and leave? How can there be a door if I can't find it?"

"The door is where you and I were brought in from," she said.

"But I cannot see that door— are these walls a figment of my imagination?" He looked into her eyes again. She did not speak; he pushed on— "Did you drug me? Did you use something that altered my thinking?"

"No."

"Then explain. I cannot make sense— first I get lost on the road, then in some ghostly village you appear alone. You take me to a strange settlement called Dera Jamal Khan where things don't make sense— people who were alive and social by night, evaporate by morning. We married; we consummated; in the morning the village is empty. A monstrous wolf chases me, another wolf saves me; both swell to the size of elephants; a flying stick knocks me out. When I regain consciousness, a girl is hovering over me. She tells me that there is no village here by the name of Dera Jamal Khan. She wants to take me to her tribe, but she vanishes midway, and right there dozens of dogs and cats start fighting among themselves. At that very moment, a python coils around me and tries to swallow me, and I pass out. When I come to again, I find myself imprisoned in this strange place— where I see no door at all, yet you keep saying there is one. Tell me, how much of this is real, and how much is my imagination?"

Ghazal only looked back at him. Her eyes held an answer — yes, it had been true— but she would not say it out loud.

"Maybe some of it was imagination," he went on. "But why would I imagine such things? Am I ill?"

"Perhaps." Her reply was quiet.

"If you hadn't been real, I might have blamed everything on my mind. But if you are real and our marriage is real, then the rest should be true, too."

She faced away and said nothing.

"So, this is truth… astonishing. It feels as if I've been trapped in a world of spirits— things I never believed in."

"Do spirits need transportation? Do they marry? Do they imprison others?" she teased lightly.

"This is exactly what I still can't figure out—how any of this is possible. Are you people masters of magic—like those

Harry Potter college types? Because this is beyond human capability."

"Perhaps." She gave a strange smile.

"This Safdar Hayat—he is your father, the one you expect to bring to his knees, isn't he?"

She only nodded in quiet affirmation.

He frowned, then gave a short, bitter laugh. Why am I even thinking this way? he scolded himself. He was a learned man; superstition had never been his habit. And yet… his mind drifted to those television magicians who performed the impossible— walking on water, defying gravity. If one man could accomplish such feats, perhaps there were others who could as well. He did not know.

Ghazal nudged him twice to wake him from his inward drift. Then she pointed forward— two plates had been set out.

"When did this arrive?" he asked, surprised.

"When you were thinking," she replied.

His stomach gave a violent protest— he had eaten little since yesterday; even pomegranate and mulberries had only eased his hunger. He washed and ate like a man who has been starving. Ghazal ate slowly beside him. Food steadied him; energy returned; the fog in his head thinned.

When Ghazal cleared the bowls, he noticed a chain around her ankle.

"Strange," he said. "I've seen men left free and women bound with chains— odd world."

She sat beside him.

"Perhaps you are also magician," he said.

She kept silent.

"Try to think of a way to escape— since you found me last night and provided food, my brain feels less muddled. I will sleep a little."

She watched him strangely and he lay down, placing his head in her lap. He tried to think, but soon sleep took him.

He did not wake on his own next time. He was roused.

The light that had warmed the room had gone out; darkness swallowed the cell. The lantern's glow seemed to shiver and die against the shaking walls, and a thick, absolute darkness took over.

●●

The night was drifting toward its fevered peak... Rakh'aan's lights still shimmered across the valley, lively and restless. People moved about in slow waves— eating, drinking, laughing, celebrating and the air was thick with smoke rising from tandoors and bonfires. Everywhere, aromas from half a dozen cuisines mingled like old songs braided together.

At the very center of the settlement, the illuminated palace of Sultan Alesar Attali stood in full splendor— not with modern electric glare, but with the vibrant glow of ancient craft. Hundreds of glass lamps, oil-fed and jeweled like ornaments, flickered across the courtyards and balconies. Beneath the palace lay the administrative chambers and the royal prison. Above them, in the higher terraces, were gardens— yes, real gardens... complete with flowing channels, carved stone benches, and hidden alcoves where the royal family lived in lush comfort.

Tonight, the Sultan was in one of the grand halls, speaking with his officers. In a different wing, Princess Manaal presided over a small private mehfil, while dancers, musicians, acrobats, and jugglers performed with bowed heads, trying to earn her smile.

Elsewhere in the harem, Prince Abaan drowned himself in wine, music, and the whispers of courtesans. And far beyond the northern range, Prince Aariz led a small mounted troop toward the palace gates.

Down in the lowest chamber, practically the palace basement— Aryan sat chained in one of the prison barracks. Against the opposite wall lay another prisoner— the man who had entered Rakh'aan alongside Aryan, the man whose companions had murdered the minister Alesar Saidow. The other six had escaped, but this one had been caught, and Aryan's presence with them had marked him guilty by association.

Now, both of them were to be executed at dawn.

Just then… above the palace, a huge pink cloth glided across the sky, floating like a living wave— before slipping through a terrace opening.

And inside that cloth… a woman was forming.

Aryan finally broke the silence.

"You know I can kill you, right?"

The man, Nabeev— turned his head, smirked, then returned to staring at the ceiling, utterly unbothered.

"You think this is a joke?" Aryan said sharply.

Nabeev smiled again. "Then do it. Go on."

Aryan hissed, "I'll wait. If by some miracle we survive the execution, I'll finish you myself. But why waste my hands on your blood when you're dying tomorrow anyway?"

Nabeev shrugged, amused.

Aryan continued, "Tell me one thing— why drag me into this? If your only goal was to kill Minister Saidow, you could have entered as simple traders. Why rest your gun on my shoulder?"

"Because traders get questioned," Nabeev replied lazily, "They check your hands. Your load. Your contact. Too risky. We needed free entry."

"Why kill Saidow?" Aryan asked— "You're from Aramin's royal force… right?"

Nabeev's eyes narrowed— "Believe what you want."

"I know you work for Elman, one of Aramin's military chiefs. You people live for his orders. You killed Saidow for him— why?"

Nabeev remained silent for a long moment.

Then he only said— "My name is Nabeev. And you… I'll feel sorry when you die tomorrow."

Meanwhile, the pink cloth that had floated into the palace spiraled downward in an empty hallway… and from it emerged a woman.

A breathtaking one.

Her body formed out of the drifting silk as though sculpted by a sorcerer's fingers. Golden hair, ocean-blue eyes, impossible curves, a dangerous beauty wrapped in a half-fallen garment of rose silk.

Then—

Footsteps.

Instantly her flesh hardened into marble. The woman became a stone statue— flawless, decorative, indistinguishable from the other statues along the corridor.

The Sultan and his officers passed by.

None noticed.

None paused.

When silence returned, the statue softened again— turned human… and sniffed the air like a hunting panther.

Then she moved gracefully, regally— toward the lower levels.

At the stairway, a guard's hand shot out, unnaturally long, grabbing her arm.

"Stop! Who are you?"

She was no longer in his grip.

In a blink, she was behind him— limbs contorting into the shape of a spider. Her elongated fingers wrapped his throat, tightening like steel. The guard staggered, suffocated, and collapsed.

She stepped over him, her fingers shrinking back to human form.

Down another flight, two more guards appeared. She lifted her arms— which turned into two serpents and the snakes flew forward, eight or ten feet long, coiling around both guards' necks. They slammed into walls, choking, until their bodies fell limp.

She descended to the deepest floor.

Seven guards.

Seven victims.

Her hair fanned out— turning into writhing serpents that launched toward them. Within moments, every guard in the hall was down, unconscious.

She inhaled again.

Her steps led her to the barred gate.

Her tongue forked like a serpent's and slid into the lock.

A few soft ticks… and the lock snapped open.

She pushed the gate.

Inside, prisoners were pressed against their bars, watching with terror and awe.

"Aryan!" she said.

"Samara!" Aryan gasped— "I knew you would come for me!"

She smirked softly— "And I knew you would land yourself in trouble the moment I blinked."

"That's what you taught me— a man grows by taking risks."

"Not when they cost you your life."

"Fair enough. Just get me out."

She opened his lock the same way. Aryan threw himself around her in a tight embrace.

"Oh, you can't imagine how—"

"Move." she snapped— "You can hug me after you stop getting arrested."

She knelt, placed her hand on the metal cuff around his leg— the flesh of her palm melted, slipping through the ring, expanding just enough to stretch the metal until Aryan's ankle slid free.

"Open mine too?" Nabeev asked hopefully.

Aryan's arm stretched four feet and slapped him sideways.

Samara grabbed Aryan— "Forget him. He dies tomorrow anyway."

They hurried back into the hall.

The snakes that had crawled over the bodies slithered quickly back up Samara's limbs, turning into strands of her hair again.

They reached the wide foyer— the one with statues of beasts.

Samara moved toward a marble peacock statue.

"Come," she said.

Samara flicked her wrist at a precise angle, and life surged into the marble peacock. Its stone wings shivered as if waking from centuries of sleep, then spread with a low tremor. The creature was large enough for both of them to sit astride.

Samara slid forward against its neck, gripping its feathers, and with her signal Aryan climbed on behind her, holding on.

The peacock let out a sharp, ringing call, beat its wings hard, and lifted itself through the open section of the corridor. The sudden ascent threw them off balance, but they steadied themselves quickly.

By then, several guards had arrived. Seeing them escape, some began shouting, and others sprinted down the lower levels.

The palace sprawled across a vast area in multiple wings, and the animated bird could not simply fly straight out. Instead, Samara steered it in wide arcs, skirting along the periphery. In one such sweep, Aryan's gaze snagged on a courtyard balcony— and there, he saw Manaal.

His eyes froze. So did his breath.

"My God… when will I ever get to breathe in a vision like that again?" He pressed a hand dramatically to his chest.

"What do you mean— is that why you came here?" Samara snapped, glaring at him.

"Why else? To sell donkeys?" Aryan shot back— "I'd heard so much about Manaal's beauty… I just wanted a glimpse. One look, and she's stolen my soul."

"You're insulting me." Samara's anger crackled.

"Why? I'm not allowed to fall in love with Manaal? Tell the peacock to circle once— just once. let me fill my eyes with that tyrant of beauty."

"In her eyes, your worth is no more than a slave's," Samara hissed— "Better not forget your place."

"My place? Even her father's place used to be beneath our slaves. Time changes, that's all. And why would I mind serving her? Let her enslave me."

"You're not even worthy of pity," Samara spat.

And the moment she said it, her flesh dissolved— vanished… leaving behind only the drifting pink cloth swirling in the air.

The peacock's motion ceased instantly. Its wings folded; its glow died. It stiffened into stone again— heavy, lifeless and began to plummet.

Aryan panicked, grabbing at nothing.

But Samara was gone.

And he was falling with the stone bird.

He crashed onto the gravel path— right in front of Prince Aariz's approaching cavalry. The peacock shattered into dozens of pieces. Aryan lay flat on his back, stunned, staring up at the sky. The soldiers halted at once.

Before anything more could happen, two guards rushed out from inside the gate.

"Who is this?" Prince Aariz thundered.

"Minister Alesar Saidow has been murdered, Shahzade," one of the guards answered swiftly, "He's one of the assassins. The others escaped— only he and one more were caught. This one just tried to flee with outside help. But fortune has betrayed him."

Aryan sighed heavily.

Half an hour later, he stood inside a chamber, head lowered like a condemned man. Prince Aariz paced in front of him. Two guards stood alert at the door, and a court minister waited silently in the corner.

A soft knock. The guards stepped aside.

A young man entered with a soldier— bowed deeply before the prince.

"Stand beside him," Aariz ordered.

The youth obeyed, coming to stand next to Aryan.

Aryan stared at him in confusion.

The young man was nearly his exact age, his build similar, even his features bore a trace of resemblance— though Aryan was clearly the more handsome of the two.

Aariz studied both faces for a while, then clapped his hands once.

"Good. You may leave."

The youth, unsure, bowed again and left.

Once he was gone, the prince turned to Aryan.

"Now tell me— who was that girl? And how did she breathe life into a dead marble bird?"

"That only she can explain, Shahzade," Aryan replied smoothly— "If I knew such magic, would I be standing in your custody?"

"The prisoners say she came for you. That she risked everything to save you. You must know her."

Aryan looked at him nervously.

"Listen carefully," Aariz said, stepping forward— "Whether you were part of Elman's men or not, you're being counted among Saidow's killers. Tomorrow at sunset, Nabeev dies… and so do you. If you want mercy, you need to give me answers— and you need to do something for me in return."

"Whatever you command, Shahzade," Aryan murmured with practiced obedience, "If you spare my life, I will fulfill whatever task you ask."

"Then start by telling me about the girl."

"Yes, Shahzade. I don't know her real name— I only call her Samara. I'm from Shahanabad in the West of Rakh'aan. She fell in love with me there. She spends most nights with me… takes me wherever she wishes. She can bring life into anything lifeless— make it run, swim, fly. She says she likes me. I don't know what she really is."

Aariz's eyes narrowed.

"Such power belongs only to Queen Abira. Could it be her?"

Aryan shook his head quickly.

"Shahzade, I'm a mere shepherd. Why would a queen fall in love with me? I think... she might be some human sorceress."

"And if she loves you so much, why did she abandon you mid-flight?"

"Jealousy, Shahzade... forgive my boldness. While flying, my eyes accidentally drifted toward the Princess— and I admired her beauty. Samara... didn't take it well."

"You saw Manaal?"

"I've already received punishment for that crime, Shahzade."

Aariz exhaled sharply.

"Fine. Then listen. You will perform one task for us— a killing. Do it, and you may live. Refuse, and you die tomorrow with Nabeev."

Aryan felt the earth tilt.

A killing?

"Tell me," he whispered, "what do you want me to do?"

"Tomorrow morning, Princess Manaal departs for Almaat for a pilgrimage. Her guard commander is Darab— the young man who stood beside you. You will take Darab's place and travel with the caravan. Around the same time, Princess Kazima of Qazaar will also reach Almaat for the same pilgrimage. Almaat is sacred place— no weapons, no guards, no violence. That is why any royal caravan travels lightly."

Aryan's heartbeat climbed.

"You want... me to kill Princess Kazima in Almaat?"

"No," Aariz said coldly— "I want you to abduct her. Take her somewhere into the desert. Keep her for a few days — however you wish. Then kill her and bury the body. No trace. No witness. After that, flee anywhere in the world."

Aryan felt faint.

"This is madness, Shahzade. She's a princess. Even without guards, reaching her will be difficult. Taking her outside Almaat alive… impossible. They'll cut me down before I take ten steps."

"If you want to live," Aariz said, meeting Aryan's eyes, "you will find a way. Once inside Almaat, our people will guide you step by step. Just remember— before reaching Princess Kazima, you must shed Darab's identity. You will abduct and kill her under your own name."

Aryan understood.

This was not mercy. This was just a way to use him before killing him later. Still… death tomorrow or a slim chance at life? A doomed mission or immediate execution?

He had no choice.

When Aariz asked— "Death or life?"

Aryan dropped his shoulders, exhaled heavily, and chose life.

●●

CHAPTER 5

With Elma carried on his back, the climb to the patch of greenery drained almost every ounce of strength Safir had left. By the time he finally reached it, he exhaled a long breath of relief and let her slide gently down to her feet.

"Now you can walk, right? Your battery must've recharged a little by now."

"Hmm." Elma murmured, still. breathless.

Safir scanned the place around them. The green stretch was fading into slopes that had been washed clean by last night's rain. The earth was damp, puddles glimmered here and there, telling tales of the downpour. It was a comforting sight, but also a worrying one. They might find fruit— enough to quiet Elma's hunger, but he saw no signs of any real shelter. Surviving a night without fire in this cold was another battle altogether… and with everything soaked, where would they even find dry wood?

"What're you thinking?" Elma asked. "My guess is— we should climb higher. From up there we can at least see which direction we're supposed to take."

"Hmm… let's go."

There was no trail— only rough earth and scattered stones. So, they carved their own path, step by thoughtful step, making their way toward the top of the small ridge.

"You know," Safir said, panting slightly, "a good knife would've been perfect right now."

"Why?" Elma glanced at him, puzzled.

"I was remembering those 'Man vs. Wild' survival shows. They teach you how to live in extreme conditions.

Even here, in the middle of nowhere, we could manage and a knife just makes everything easier."

"We have a rifle," Elma reminded him— "Isn't that more dangerous than a knife?"

"That's the point. A rifle can only kill. A knife can peel, slice, cut meat, cut wood… and yes, it can kill too if needed. It's a tool you can use a hundred ways. Even if we hunt something, how will we skin it? How will we prepare anything? How do we make a shelter? With bare hands?"

"So those shows don't teach you how to survive without a knife?"

"They do… but it's painfully hard and takes forever. Those methods are for people planning to stay long-term. We just need to get out of here as fast as possible."

Elma sighed— "Food we might find, but if we fail to find shelter tonight, we're dead."

"Exactly. You can survive a day or two without food, but if you can't get through the cold night, then nothing else matters. If we at least spot a human settlement— anything… there'd be some hope."

"I wish we had our phones…"

"Oh, we'd still have no network here. Useless either way."

"I wonder what our families must be going through… they must be losing their minds. My mother— she must've cried herself half blind by now."

"Maybe they've made peace with the possibility we're okay."

The conversation drifted to home. A quiet, heavy silence settled on their shoulders. Safir knew the army units targeted by the TTP would've already figured he and Elma were taken by mistake— because the kidnappers meant to grab Rimsha. He also knew search teams must be looking for them… but unless they knew which faction of TTP had taken them, there was no chance of rescue. And even he didn't know which faction it had been.

Elma suddenly broke the silence— "Tell me about your life, Safir. You must've fallen in love before Rimsha— right? Before Islamabad, before all this?"

"Our lives aren't exactly romance-friendly," Safir replied— "We grow up with studies, fights, stupid adventures… and by the time college teaches you maturity, families are already talking about marriage. Honestly, love found me through Rimsha— otherwise I'd probably be a father by twenty-two."

"So, no girl before her? No one who caught your eye? I mean, you're handsome— someone must've liked you."

"Maybe… but if they did, I never knew."

"You're on social media, right? Facebook, Instagram, TikTok, Twitter?"

"How did that come up?"

"Oh please! Half the love stories today start on social media. Post to chat, chat to inbox, inbox to WhatsApp, WhatsApp to life… I've met so many Majnu-types this way. My inbox is full of morning roses and goodnight hearts."

Safir snorted— "There was one. But madam wanted the romance without revealing her identity. Her profile name was 'Cute Girl.' That's all she'd ever say. Wouldn't give me her name, her city, her number— nothing. Just messages, poems, songs… good mornings, good nights."

"And? Didn't you feel anything for her?"

"At first, I did. But her secrecy became irritating. You can't stay in love with a ghost."

"Maybe she had a reason," Elma argued softly— "Maybe she was Indian and thought you'd stop talking if you knew. Or maybe she was poor and thought you'd look down on her.

There are a thousand fears… fears of losing the only connection they have."

"And what's the use if nothing real can come from it?"

"Maybe one day she'd have told you everything. Did you ever think of that?"

Safir shrugged— "Anyway, once Rimsha came into my life, I stopped checking Facebook altogether. And when I did, once every month or two, her messages were waiting. Sometimes I replied, sometimes I didn't."

"Poor girl…" Elma whispered.

"You don't know she was a girl. What if it was a 'meetha' guy? Those exist too. Half the profiles online are fake."

"Ugh, you're horrible." she snapped— "You think so cheaply. Not every girl is like that."

"Not every girl. But some are. She could've been one."

Elma pouted and fell silent. The rest of the climb they walked without a word.

When they reached the highest point, the world revealed itself below them— behind lay the barren expanse they'd crossed, ahead stretched rising hills dotted with green slopes. Thin water channels glimmered among them. But there was no sign of any human settlement in sight.

Though nothing there offered comfort, there was one hopeful sight— near the waterline stood trees heavy with fruit— plums, by the look of them. Enough to feed them both.

Their choice was obvious.

They descended towards the trees. The sun had sunk low behind the western ridge; an hour of daylight, at best, remained.

Half an hour later they reached the trees— and their joy burst out at once.

"These look untouched." Elma said, astonished.

"There's no rule that every place must have animals or humans," Safir replied, grinning as he plucked the first ripe plum.

The fruit was sweet, juicy— life itself. Hunger eased, thirst vanished, and when both were full, strength flowed back into their limbs. Even Elma looked alive again.

Now they headed toward the tall watch-tower-like structure they'd spotted earlier.

By the time they reached the base, darkness was slowly falling. The place was clearly abandoned— scattered gear lay rotting around it— a soldier's duffel, two torn jackets, and a ripped tent.

With no better choice, they cleaned everything as best they could. Even washed by rain and dried by sun, the gear still carried a stale smell— something unpleasant but tolerable. In their condition, it felt like a blessing.

The platform was built high, about twenty-two feet— with a fragile wooden ladder. Some rungs were missing, making the climb difficult, but survival demanded effort. In three careful trips they managed to haul everything up.

The platform was covered on all sides with nailed planks and topped by a roof. Roomy enough for two people to lie down if they squeezed close. They folded the torn tent into two layers for bedding and sat, back to the wall, staring out at the fading sky.

Darkness was settling fast. A streak of red glowed on the horizon, birds were flying home, and the wind whistled across the empty hills.

"Do you think this place is safe?" Elma asked, releasing a long, weary breath.

"Only on one condition," Safir said quietly, eyes fixed on the ground below— "That the Taliban or TTP men don't reach this spot while searching for us. If they do… then this tower becomes a mouse trap. Either we die here, or we land back in their captivity. But the problem is— there's no place safer than this right now."

Elma pulled her knees up, hugging them. "Who would even build a watch post in such wilderness?"

"Borders are like this," Safir replied— "You can't put fencing everywhere, nor can soldiers sit in every direction. Armies focus where movement is easier. Places like this are left as buffer zones— sometimes for stopping infiltration, sometimes for watching the other side. This stretch has been a battlefield for years. Maybe two-four years ago, some unit opened a front here. They used this tower to keep an eye on movement. And when activity shifted… they abandoned it. Whatever gear was useless, they dumped it here. Lucky for us, I guess."

"Will this be enough to survive the night?" she asked softly.

"Something is better than nothing. Imagine if we hadn't found even this… we would've spent the night curled under a tree like terrified rabbits. Once the sun sets, the wind turns colder and the temperature keeps dropping."

Elma's voice trembled— "Never thought I'd live to see a day like this…"

"Oh come on," Safir teased, "think about how cool this story will sound when you're old and telling it to your grandkids."

"And what would I tell them? Who I was with then?"

"Who knows— maybe they'll be my grandkids too." He winked.

"Dhatt!" Elma flushed crimson and folded into herself.

"Who knows," Safir continued, smirking, "by the time we reach home, I might fall in love with you. Instead of dropping you at Mahepora, I might kidnap you straight to Shahelaar."

"Stop your nonsense— I'll shoot you."

"You're cute when you threaten."

Elma wrinkled her nose— "These clothes… they stink. You got drenched yesterday and dried in them. Everything here smells disgusting."

"Well, you were drenched too." Safir chuckled— "Maybe a little sweat got mixed in… that's probably why you smell so strong. Surprisingly— bad smell isn't bad right now. It's weirdly exciting."

"Maybe it's just youth," she laughed weakly— "Even I'm not finding the smell unbearable."

"And opposite sexes get affected differently. If we were same-gender, we'd be irritated, not… this."

"True…" she murmured.

Darkness thickened. The silence grew deeper— no footstep, no animal, no rustle. Only a thin sliver of moonlight stretched across the valley. The night was long. And dangerously cold.

They wrapped themselves in the two torn jackets and tried to doze sitting upright with their backs against the wooden planks. But cold mountain nights were unforgiving — each time they drifted off, the icy wind jerked them awake. Elma, in lighter clothes, shivered the most.

Seeing that, Safir gently wrapped the duffel-cloth around her shoulders— "Here. Sleep a little."

But by midnight, their bodies gave up.

Their fingers were numb. Their jaws trembled uncontrollably. Breath came out in sharp white clouds.

"At this rate, we'll be half-dead by morning," Safir whispered, teeth chattering.

"What do we do…? We can't light a fire."

Safir inhaled sharply— "There's only one way. We get inside the two layers of this tent... together. Whatever warmth we have left— we share it."

In any other situation, Elma would've snapped at him. But the cold had eaten her strength, and her voice was barely holding together. Refusing wasn't an option anymore.

They slid between the two fabric layers of the tent. Their bodies brushed— both flinched, but soon accepted it. Safir pulled her tightly against his chest and covered them both with the duffel cloth. Their faces were buried inside, breathing each other's warm breath.

It helped... but not enough.

Safir whispered, "Our bodies are too cold. We need to generate heat."

"How...?"

"Through sex."

"Pagal ho gaye ho, Safir... I'll just leave. I'd rather die." Elma snapped.

Safir didn't raise his voice— "And what about what they would've done? Choosing between death and survival is different. You didn't want to die when that man tried to force himself on you this morning. Those Hazara girls back there — they survive only because they give up resisting. If you had been caught with them, even you would've been alive... unwilling, but alive."

"There is something else about compulsion..." Elma murmured, voice weak.

Safir replied quietly— "I didn't mean full-on sex... just something to warm up both of our bodies. If you mind, let it be. Let's just chill like this." —and he fell silent.

Elma lay still in the dark, thinking. Survival had its own laws... brutal, unfair, yet real. And she too knew— they wouldn't make it till morning like this.

A few minutes later, Elma gave her answer with a movement of her hands.

Safir understood.

When Safir got a positive response, he also started moving his hands and lips. There was a lot of commotion in a limited space between the tent cloth. This exercise of about ten minutes heated up the bodies of both of them.

A strange kind of intoxication began to engulf both of their minds. It began to demand a destination, but they also stopped.

Once they'd built enough warmth, Safir tightened his arms around her and forced himself to stop. Elma struggled too— but finally managed to pull back from the edge. They lay there, breath steaming, bodies still trembling but no longer freezing.

They drifted into an uneasy sleep— jolting awake every now and then… but somehow, they survived the night.

At dawn, the cold tore Safir awake. He slipped out quietly, covering Elma as best he could with the duffel cloth. The eastern sky was turning pale, promising sunlight— and life.

Minutes passed. Light increased.

Then— Safir startled.

Far in the south, a thin column of smoke rose into the air.

Someone had lit a fire.

Which meant someone… was right there.

His heart pounded with hope and fear.

He shook Elma awake.

●●

The moment the lantern died, darkness spilled across the room like a living thing. Rayyaan couldn't see a single shape, yet he could feel the world outside convulsing as if Judgment Day itself had descended. It sounded like a battlefield in full fury— cannons thundering, blades clashing, elephants and horses trampling the earth, screams shredding the air, the ground beneath him trembling as if bearing the weight of a thousand deaths. The uproar hammered against the weakening walls as though they were made of paper.

A terrifying question rose in his mind— Were all those people sorcerers? Was all of this truly magic?

"Run... this wall is about to break." Ghazal whispered — her voice barely more than a breath.

"And you?" he asked in panic.

"Don't worry about me. I can protect myself. They know I'm weak because of you... they will focus on you. Save yourself. I'll find you later," she said quickly.

The next instant the entire wall beside them collapsed with a deafening crash.

"Go!" Ghazal shouted.

Rayyaan lunged to his feet and ran. He couldn't see what lay beyond the shattered wall— the night was ink-black, but Ghazal had said run, so he obeyed. He stumbled over the rubble, regained his balance and kept going.

He had thought he was still inside a building, but a few steps later he felt grass underfoot and saw the blurred outlines of clouds drifting across an open sky. The warlike chaos still raged somewhere behind him... but the darkness revealed nothing. Blind, breathless, he kept running in whichever direction his feet carried him. He crashed into trees, tore through bushes, fell and rose again, refusing to stop.

Minute by frantic minute the chaos faded behind him. The night sounds thinned to crickets and insects. His run softened into a staggering walk.

He realised he was deep inside a forest. A heavy hush pressed around him; the sky above filtered in faintly through the canopy. Darkness on the ground was so complete that his eyes were nearly useless, yet his legs kept moving.

Two hours passed like that— wandering, stumbling, half-awake, half-drowned in fear.

A pale whitening appeared along the edge of the sky. Birds that had been still and silent all night opened their wings and began to chirp. His eyelids burned with exhaustion. Then, between two clusters of trees, he saw a small Mazaar.

It was made of stone, whitewashed with lime, enclosed in a circular boundary whose three-foot walls were punctured with small openings. Four pillars held up a sloping roof like a humble shrine-house. A small grilled iron gate prevented animals from entering. No houses, no humans, no trails— only wilderness, grass, and trees on every side.

For him, it was a blessing.

He pushed open the tiny gate, slipped inside and collapsed in the narrow space beside the tomb. His body was burning with the heat of fear and exertion; his breath scraped in his throat. When it steadied, sleep claimed him instantly. As his body cooled, he began to shiver, so he pulled the thick sheet lying on the tomb and wrapped it around himself before curling into sleep.

He didn't know how long he slept.

A droning hum reached his ears— insects or voices and consciousness began to pull him back. He blinked awake. The sun was already up; yellow morning light quivered on the treetops. With enough rest, he felt surprisingly refreshed.

He sat up.

A group of people stood outside the Mazaar, staring at him. Middle-aged men, old men, young boys, older women — all tribal-looking, all tense, suspicious, silent.

He forced a polite smile. It softened none of their faces.

"Do any of you understand Pashto or Urdu?" he asked gently.

"Yes," someone said behind him.

He turned to find an elderly man with a white beard, wearing a long white kurta and tahmad.

"My name is Rayyaan Afridi— son of the jagirdar of Kaanwabeel," he said softly— "Two nights ago I lost my way in the rain, fell into the hands of people who robbed me and tried to kill me. I escaped last night and wandered until I found this place. Please… may I hope for your help?"

The tension on their faces eased slightly— perhaps because he was clearly an outsider who had unknowingly slept on a sacred resting place.

"I apologize if I offended anyone." Rayyaan added quickly— "I was exhausted and freezing… I took shelter here and covered myself with the sheet. I meant no disrespect."

The Older man signaled him to step out and said something in their dialect and the group dispersed. The old man beckoned Rayyaan to walk with him. When they left the grassy clearing, a narrow path appeared— invisible in the night.

"My name is Hikmatyar. You may call me Abba-ji," the elder said, "I am a servant of Gulzar Shah… and people come to me for help with their spirit-related afflictions. If you wish, you may tell me everything. Perhaps I can help."

Rayyaan did not wish to tell him everything— not the parts that sounded impossible even to his own ears. So, he told a half-truth— that a girl named Ghazal belonged to a robber clan, that they had drugged and robbed him, thrown him out, where other men caught him; and he escaped during a clash between two groups.

Within minutes a hidden village appeared— a poor settlement of huts made of reeds, wood, straw and stones, untouched by modern development. People were beginning their day— carrying loads, cutting fodder, tending livestock. Men, women, old people, children— all living the same simple life.

Everyone greeted Abba-ji with respect.

"What is this place called?" Rayyaan asked.

"Gulzar Shah ki Dyodhi," Abba-ji replied.

The names struck Rayyaan instantly— Gulzar, Dyodhi… exactly what Saarah had mentioned. His heartbeat spiked. Had he escaped from enemies only to arrive among their allies?

"You look troubled," Abba-ji said.

"No… just thinking. Is there a doctor nearby? I'm injured."

"No doctors here. Only our hakeem."

The local hakeem tended his wounds. Abba-ji offered a simple breakfast. Rayyaan tried to chat with some villagers but their dialect had too many unfamiliar words.

"Abba-ji… I know this region is in the Swat Valley— around Karagal, but I need to return to my land in Kaanwabeel. How can I get there?"

"For me to say exactly is difficult," Abba-ji replied— "Some men go to towns to sell wool and fruit… but none are here now. Head west and eventually you'll reach a larger settlement."

"One more thing," Rayyaan said cautiously— "While wandering the forest I met a girl named Saarah. She said she belonged to this place— but vanished suddenly. I worry for her. Did she return?"

"All the girls here grew up in my arms," Abba-ji said gravely— "None are named Saarah. No girl here has gone missing. Had it happened, I would know."

"Perhaps she gave me a false name."

Abba Ji studied his face closely for a few moments, then stepped outside. From beyond the doorway came the sound of him shouting something in the local rustic tongue. After finishing whatever he had to say, he returned inside.

"It is also possible that she gave the wrong directions to Gulzar Shah's dyodhi. People often misstate their own name or the name of a place when they are being cautious."

"Yes, that could be so."

"But the night before last, that girl made you her prey. Then last night, the people who caught you— what purpose could they possibly have had, when you had already been robbed? And how did you manage to escape their captivity?"

Rayyaan had to steady himself again. What had happened the previous night was not something he could tell. It would only be taken as a lie or dismissed as a disturbance of the mind. So he said that he himself had no clear idea what those people's motive might have been, but that sometime during the night a rival group had attacked them. Amid the chaos of their internal clash, an opportunity to flee had opened up for him, and he had taken advantage of it and run.

"In all these surroundings, I have never heard of anyone being robbed before— so who were these people you ran into?" He seemed about to say something more when a sound came from outside. He gestured toward it and said, "Come— step outside for a moment."

They stepped outside. Fifteen or sixteen girls and a few men gathered. They stared at Rayyaan with curiosity— but Saarah was not among them.

"These are all the girls here," Abba-ji said.

Rayyaan shook his head in refusal. Abba Ji motioned for everyone to go back, then patted him lightly and led him inside again.

"Then he must have given the directions wrong. Or it's possible he gave both the name and the address incorrectly," Abba Ji said, settling into a cane chair.

"Are there other tribes around here as well?" Rayyaan sat down on the low wooden stool placed opposite him.

"Yes— there must be ten or twelve tribes in all, small and large."

"Is there any settlement, tribe, or village here by the name of Dera Jamal Khan?" As he asked this, Rayyaan watched his reaction closely.

But Abba Ji was visibly shaken. A flush rose in his eyes, his face tightened, and he sprang to his feet at once.

"Tell me," he said in a low, almost growling voice, "who are you?"

"Rayyaan Afridi… the only heir of Jagirdar Waqar Afridi of Kaanwabeel."

"How did you learn that name?"

"Before you answer, I must know whether you are friend or foe to the people of Dera Jamal Khan."

"Neither friend nor foe— we keep our distance from them."

"Are those people so dangerous?"

"They are no concern of ours. Their world is separate from ours. We do not cross each other's paths."

"They robbed me."

"Impossible! Why would they trouble themselves with humans or human things?" Their eyes filled with an astonishment that belonged to an earlier age.

"Why— are they not human?" Now Rayyaan was the one bewildered.

"Tell me the truth, the whole truth." Abba-ji sat back down and took his hand— "What exactly happened to you? There must be something I need to know."

Rayyaan told the tale slowly, without hiding or softening a single detail. He described the wedding with Ghazal, the nightmarish village, the monstrous wolves, the floating stick, the snake that swallowed him— everything. Abba-ji listened without the flinch of surprise he would once have expected; only at the mention of Ghazal's marriage did his eyes light up, and he leaned forward as if to catch every word more tightly.

"When I first saw you, I felt there was something special about you," Abba-ji said when Rayyaan finished.

"Special how?" Rayyaan asked, startled.

"You, my son, have crossed beyond the ordinary human lot— you have become the son-in-law, in a sense, of Dera Jamal Khan's people, and thereby an opponent of a rival fellowship."

"So, you mean… are they ghosts and demons?" Rayyaan swayed.

"No— not exactly… but they are not human."

"Then what are they?" Rayyaan's confusion deepened.

"Have you ever heard of the jinnat?" Abba-ji asked.

"Some. Arabian Nights, tales at home… I never really believed such things."

"They are real, son. As real as you or I. Not fairy stories. They are mentioned in the Quran. Look at what you saw among them— was it not real to you?"

"Can you tell me about them?"

"No human being can truly claim to know everything about them… only God knows, or perhaps they themselves.

As far as I know, among all living beings in this realm there exist two kinds of species that are superior— one is the human being, who is called ashraful makhlooq, and the other are the jinnat, who are superior even to us. They are not made of clay like us humans, but of fire. Most of what they eat and drink is different from us— though they do take many things from us as well. If they do not wish to, we cannot see or hear them, but they can always see and hear us. They can overpower us, make us do whatever they want.

They can even take our lives. Our strengths are limited, but theirs are unlimited. They are immensely powerful and mayaavi. They can take any form, any shape. They can alter, mould— everything around them— houses, dwellings, trees, plants, water, everything, according to their will. We humans can never match them. If they wished, they could erase all trace of humankind from the world, but they do not— because they too are bound by certain laws and boundries, and God has created many restraints and methods to keep them in check."

Rayyaan listened in silence, his eyes widened, while Abba Ji continued speaking.

"People say they are extremely devout and spend most of their time in the worshiping God. Generally, they do not interfere in human society and keep away from human settlements. Their settlements are usually found in desolate areas, and we humans and they do not cross each other's paths.

Yes, sometimes such incidents do occur when a khabees jinn comes to engage with a human, but it is precisely to bring him back to the right path that people like us exist. Otherwise too, they do keep company with humans— but without coming into people's notice, in the very shape of a human. This is the first time I have heard of a marriage between one of their girls and a human. It is possible that such incidents have happened before as well, but I have never heard of anything like this."

"You said that people like you exist to keep the khabees jinnat under control— so does that mean you are more powerful than them?"

"No— no human can be stronger than the jinnat. But when a stray spirit misleads a human or causes trouble, there are methods of knowledge at my disposal— not brute force, but rites and remedies— which can rein them in. That knowledge came to me through Baba Gulzar Shah."

"And where did you acquire this knowledge from?"

"From Baba Gulzar Shah… He was blind by birth, but possessed an exceptionally sharp mind. At a very young age, he not only memorized the Qur'an but also completed his formal religious scholarship, and went on to learn many kinds of effective ritual practices. Then he left his home, family, and city behind, came into this jungle, and settled here permanently. This was sixty years ago— at that time, this was the only human settlement in all the surrounding areas, and I was a small child who lived right here.

From childhood itself, I was so deeply influenced by him that I became his disciple and began acquiring knowledge from him. When I grew older, because of our household work of selling wool, I too began travelling toward urban settlements, which gave me the opportunity to learn the urban language. Later, when Baba grew old, I withdrew from work altogether and devoted myself completely to serving him. In his final days, he shared many secrets with me."

Before continuing, he paused for a moment in thought, weighing whether he should reveal those secrets before Rayyaan or not—but in the end, the decision went in Rayyaan's favour.

"He was not only a Hafiz, but also an Aalim and Kaamil. He was skilled in sifli amal as well, and would often relieve people of their aseebi troubles. In those days, these wildernesses were home to many settlements of the jinnat, and they even had a proper darsgah, where Baba would go to teach their children.

Because of this, Baba did not merely command respect among them— he was granted the honour of sitting in their company and for the khabees among them, he was a figure of fear as well. It cannot be said that he was more powerful than them, but he possessed the methods and prescriptions to restrain them, intimidate them, and even keep them confined when needed. This is why he carried a presence and authority unlike any other.

I was his attendant. I was neither a Hafiz nor an Aalim, and as for becoming Kaamil— mastering those prescriptions and methods was beyond my capacity. Had I failed in my efforts, I could have become the target of their anger. For this reason, he could not pass the entire legacy on to me. Still, he taught me a great deal— bestowed upon me many abilities, because of which I stand today at a position where I am accorded this respect. I cannot confront them directly, but to a certain extent I can protect humans from them, keep them away from human beings— and that is precisely what I do."

"Who are the 'khabees'— the evil jinnat?" Rayyaan asked.

"Yes— just like us humans, they too have a social fabric. They have households and families, joy and sorrow, marriages, gatherings, celebrations, conflicts— everything exists among them. However, their actions, rituals, or occasions have no direct connection with us humans. This may be the first time that a human has been deliberately entangled in one of their internal conflicts. Just as among humans, there are both good and bad individuals among them as well… and those who are evil are called khabees."

"Then what do you think— what exactly has happened to me?"

"You were unquestionably made a pawn. That girl was probably the most special among them, and Shah Alam was her suitor... but the girl herself must not have agreed. Perhaps no one else dared to step forward to marry her out of fear of Shah Alam, so they turned you, unknowingly—into her husband. Naturally, had you known anything, you would have refused, but you were completely without knowledge from the very start."

"What should I do?" Rayyaan asked.

"My heart says this place is fatal for you. You are safer in sunlight than in darkness; in the dark their powers increase manifold. You must leave as soon as you can. Reach a settled village before nightfall; spend the night in a mosque if you can."

"I do not know the way."

"Come with me." Abba-ji rose, took Rayyaan's hand and led him out.

A little while later, in a manner reminiscent of Bear Grylls on Man vs. Wild, he was moving off to one side with his head lifted like a camel's— intent on getting away from that cursed region as quickly as possible. Abba Ji had helped guide him part of the way, and another man had assisted as well. The hope was that by continuing straight ahead, he would eventually reach a nearby settlement.

He moved along a line of thick trees on the left; to the right lay a slope of scrub and stones that fell to a river. The route seemed to track the river as if the landscape itself were guiding him home.

A sudden laugh stopped Rayyaan mid-step.

He looked around; nothing visible. The sound came again— a soft 'shsh-shsh' and this time he saw where it came from— a branch of the tree to his left. Something sat there.

By its strange form he might have called it a man; yet whatever recognition his mind supplied did not fit the circumstances. A chill ran down his spine— this was not a human being. At that thought his courage deserted him.

●●

Princess Manaal's caravan was flying toward the city of Almat.

The caravan itself was uncanny— mounts that were not simple horses but ghulaam-Mareed— a sort of jinn retainer in equine shape, with broad wings enabling them to fly. A dozen such mounts bore three riders each on their backs; only one steed carried the princess alone. Three of those winged horses carried nine female attendants; the remaining eight bore two dozen men who doubled as servants and, if need be, armed guards.

A compact pledge "Bahashi Qaul" had been taken from Aryan— he must fulfil the task assigned to him without fail. The pledge was binding in their society— a spoken oath from which there was no honourable retreat. Aariz had warned him too— among those sent with him were killers, swift and silent; if Aryan deviated from the order he was given, those men would end him with poisoned blades— so he must take no liberty beyond his assigned charge.

Rakh'aan— a settlement in the desert stretching between Iraq and Syria— was remote, a land where human habitations lay sparsely and far. The princess's target, Qazaar, stood near the wastes by Modar in present-day Turkmenistan; Almat lay in a mountain region inside Iran. If Princess Kazima was to travel from Qazaar to Almat, the caravans should arrive together.

Almat was the only sacred city in their world— founded by one of their prophets. Not only were all the relics associated with him preserved there as centres of pilgrimage, but the House of God built by his own hands was the most vital link in that entire tradition. There was also a pool of consecrated water there, about which it was said that every jinnat must drink at least one sip of it in their lifetime. Because of this, it was considered a duty upon every being of their world to visit Almat at least once. Ordinary people might come only once in their lives, but those who were influential and held rank could come more than once.

In Almat, only the local administrators managed the entire governance of the city. Everyone else was an outsider — among them a large number of pilgrims, and then those who sold goods and services to meet their needs. Some of these people came and went, while many settled there for long stretches of time, making the city their temporary home.

The winged Mareeds could fly swiftly, yet the journey consumed eight hours. They had set out at first light; now the sun, a red ball, burned over the dunes. They avoided human settlements on purpose, though ordinary human caravans passed beneath them unnoticed— humans could not see them, nor sense them. To human eyes Almat was hidden, a city perched on a high hill amid desert ridges.

Along the way Aryan kept his retinue placed so he could steal glances at Manaal from the ranks. She had noticed him lurking and looked back more than once, but had shown little reaction.

By dusk they reached the plain below Almat and pitched camp before the ascent of stone steps that led to the city. Tents spread everywhere and weary travellers rested, bathed, ate— the kind of bustle that follows a long journey. Manaal withdrew to the hammam to wash away fatigue. The rest busied themselves with other tasks, and Aryan, without a particular duty, lingered about to observe the Qazaar caravan and confirm who accompanied them. Distant fields of tents, flickering lamps, the smell of food and spices in the air— all marked the approach of evening.

They planted their tents and prepared. The princess bathed; the camp settled. Aryan, meanwhile, casually made his way among the guards to watch and wait.

After a bit of searching, they finally located the caravan from Qazaar— and Aryan kept a careful distance while studying the faces of the people around it. The princess herself wasn't visible yet; she was likely still inside her tent or on her way somewhere, but even seeing the rest of the entourage was hardly insignificant. There were nearly two dozen people in total— five handmaidens and eighteen male attendants. Aryan memorised every face, fixing each one in his mind. He was about to turn back when the princess finally stepped out of her tent— she seemed headed toward the bath. Five handmaidens walked with her, and the rest of the attendants formed a protective ring around her.

Aryan's gaze stayed locked on Princess Kazima. He was trying to see her through the eyes of a man who would have to kill her. She was young and beautiful— perhaps not as breathtaking as Manaal, but still striking in her own right, with a softness to her face that spoke of innocence. Aryan's heart trembled. The thought of killing her unsettled him deeply. But if the people of Rakh'aan had decided her fate, then refusing the task wouldn't save her— it would only ensure that both of them died. At least in the first scenario, he still had a chance to survive.

He hardened his heart as she passed before him and disappeared toward the bathing area.

Just then, a hand fell on his shoulder. Startled, he turned — and froze. Standing before him, draped in soft silk and sheer chiffon, her face veiled except for her eyes, was Samara.

Aryan exhaled sharply. Instinctively, he glanced around — his assigned watchers had already raised the thin blowpipes to their lips. One wrong move, and the venomous darts would be in his flesh.

Meaning clear—

Keep to the plan— or die.

"How did you recognise me?" he whispered, staring into her eyes— he was still in Darab's form.

"For me, what's difficult about that? You know I can smell your scent anywhere. I came here searching for someone else— then spotted you, so thought I'd stop and ask after you. How did you end up so far from Rakh'aan? And for pilgrimage of all things. With Rakh'aan's people no less. What happened— made peace after I left you?" Her tone dripped with taunt.

"Peace? What peace... I admitted my mistake and agreed to their terms. I told them I'd accept their service. Eventually they trusted me and made me commander of the princess's personal escort. She wished to visit this place, so I brought her," he said weakly, trying to weave a story.

"In someone else's face— how clever." She laughed, sharp and mocking.

"Just precaution... Prince Aariz didn't want people discovering this man was already dead— the one whose shape I'm wearing. Perhaps he was someone important, someone whose absence would raise suspicion."

"So now you belong to Princess Manaal," she said, a cold edge forming in her voice.

"Yes, now I'll stay with her. Good too... this way I'll get to see her up close all my life. Isn't that wonderful—"

Before he finished, Samara's foot slammed into his stomach. He doubled over, gasping. She cast him one contemptuous look and swept away. His watchers didn't move. Aryan straightened slowly, clutching his abdomen, watching her retreat until she vanished in the crowd.

Two hours later, they began ascending the long stairs of Almat.

At the very base, everyone's entry was recorded— their names, their descriptions, their purpose. Aryan was registered under Darab's identity, and he disliked it immediately— Darab wouldn't be returning with the caravan, so what explanation would they give? The climb took nearly half an hour, and at the top, a city carved into the mountain slopes sprawled ahead. Most structures were built from sandstone, ancient in style. There were only two stairways in and out— one for entry, one for departure. Every other side was either sheer cliff or brutally uneven rock impossible to traverse.

At Manaal's order, they slipped into the empty wing of an unused building. There, for the first time, Manaal addressed him directly. She ordered him to remove his disguise and handed him a vial.

He scrubbed his face thoroughly— and another man began doing the same. Slowly, the false colour, stitched brows, and pasted skin peeled away. Aryan's true face emerged.

And alongside him, the real Darab's.

Aryan gasped.

"You are no longer part of our caravan. From this point, you proceed alone and fulfill the task given to you. After today, you have no connection to us." Manaal said, her voice firm and cold, eyes fixed into his. Then she turned and walked away.

Everyone followed her— except seven men who stayed behind with Darab. The rest vanished around a corner.

"Now you will wander these streets alone, searching for Princess Kazima. We will remain around you. If you show even a flicker of cleverness— remember, we will not hesitate to take your life." Darab said, patting his shoulder before moving off.

Aryan drew a deep breath and walked into the holy city.

Though they had scattered, the watchers remained in his orbit, blending into the crowds like ordinary pilgrims. They didn't look at one another, didn't signal, didn't acknowledge each other at all— but Aryan knew they were everywhere.

It didn't take long to locate Princess Kazima near the Prophet's tomb— and he began hovering in her vicinity, making sure to be noticed. Her attendants formed a protective ring, but it wasn't impenetrable. Almat was a sacred place— no one expected danger here. That laxity was Aryan's advantage.

For two hours, he followed the royal group through the major sites. A few times their gazes crossed— and he smiled each time. Kazima didn't return the gesture.

Finally, at the Hauz-e-Abar, Aryan found his opening.

The place resembled a vast synagogue— an enormous central hall with a circular pool in the middle, fed by a spring erupting like a fountain eight to ten feet high. Pilgrims circled the outer arched corridors thrice, then approached the pool, drank a handful of water, circled twice in the opposite direction and left. Despite the constant drinking, the water never overflowed; hidden vents drained the excess.

The hall was packed. It was impossible for Kazima's guards to keep every stranger away.

Aryan slipped close.

At that moment, one of his own men collapsed dramatically— writhing as if in terrible pain. The crowd erupted. Panic surged through the hall. In that chaos, Darab and his men forced themselves between the guards— scattering them just enough.

Aryan stepped in.

He pressed his closed fist to Kazima's waist.

"My ring holds a venomous dart. If it pierces your skin, no healer will save you. Walk quietly with me, your highness — just need a word," he whispered.

She turned sharply, eyes blazing— but the pressure of his fist made her freeze. Her expression held rage— and helplessness.

He shoved her forward, guiding her toward the exit. Not easy— the hall was erupting into chaos. Her guards finally sensed danger. Darab's men alone weren't enough to keep them back. Their only move left was—

Panic.

They triggered a full stampede.

In the violent crush of bodies, Aryan scooped Kazima onto his shoulder and sprinted through the hall's exit. The moment they emerged, someone slammed into him so violently that he and the princess crashed to the ground.

He didn't need to look. He recognised her from behind.

Samara.

She didn't even glance his way.

He tried to get up— tried to lift Kazima… but she began convulsing violently. Her skin turned a spreading shade of blue.

Aryan's breath died.

The game was over.

The crowd scattered, and within moments the chaos of the hall spilled outside. Kazima's attendants surged forward. Darab and his men emerged too. A crushing circle formed around Aryan— tightening, growing, hardening. There was no gap wide enough for him to escape. People were staring from every direction— above, below, around… eyes filled with fury.

An elderly man knelt beside Kazima, examined her limp hand.

"A poison has been used on her," he said gravely.

"He's the one— he's the one who delivered the poison into the princess's body!" Darab lunged forward, screaming, "This man belongs to Elman, the chieftain of Aramin. He and his men murdered Rakh'aan's minister Alesar Saidov, but he escaped custody. He must have come here for Princess Manaal— he wanted to abduct Princess Kazima for some purpose but poisoned her by mistake. Look at his hand— look at the poisoned-dart ring!"

"Wait— no, no, I didn't do anything— listen to me, please, this was an accident!" Aryan stammered, trying to defend himself, but his words found no ears.

Two men from Kazima's security detail slammed into him, grabbing his arms and trying to wrench the ring off his hand. Meanwhile, the completely blue-tinged Kazima's body had gone still— lifelessly cold. Gasps escaped many throats; others let out shrieks of shock. Aryan's spirit collapsed. It felt like the sun of his life had set right there.

He tried to break free— but now half of Kazima's entourage was on him, clawing, gripping. And right then, a piercing roar cracked from the sky— like a dragon warning the world. Every head snapped upward.

A massive bird— dragon-sized— was diving straight toward them, flames bursting from its beak as it plunged. Its target was the very crowd trapping Aryan.

People scattered.

The creature struck with a furious swoop, its talons clamping around Aryan before he could react. He screamed, thrashed, tried to break free, but the grip was iron. The monstrous bird hurtled upward with him, the ground shrinking away beneath his dangling feet.

It carried him toward the roof of a nearby structure— an open terrace and released him. Aryan tumbled across the stone floor, rolling painfully.

The giant bird circled once and landed before him— and even before its body fully steadied, it had begun transforming. Wings folded into arms, talons into feet, feathers melting into skin.

Samara stood before him.

Aryan staggered to his feet, bruised and battered.

"Why did you do that?" he snapped, fury burning in his eyes.

"I saved you— exactly what you were going to do in the end anyway." Her smile was cold, poisonous.

"You think I was actually going to do it?" he said incredulously.

"You're forgetting— you swore a Bahashi Qaul. You had no choice. Without completing it, you would've been killed from both sides. Only by doing it could you hope to save your own life."

"How do you know all this?" His eyes widened again.

"I came here with my own purpose. But when I saw you, I had to ask— how suddenly had you become valuable enough for Rakh'aan to make you commander of Manaal's guard? And that too, in a stolen face? It was clear— they were using you. And you're not yet capable enough to save yourself. You needed help— because of the vow I made to your father."

"And this is what you call help?" Aryan scowled bitterly.

"Absolutely. I was watching everything. When you returned to your own form— and the real face of the man you were impersonating appeared, I understood that they wanted to keep his identity alive. They wanted him recorded as having returned, so that anything you did later wouldn't trace back to them. After that, I hunted one of Manaal's men, subdued him, and learned the rest. Their plan was simple— they'd aid you only as long as things were going well. If you ran off with Kazima— good. You would do exactly what they'd planned. But if things went wrong, they'd expose you as the killer of Alesar Saidov and Elman's accomplice— then eliminate you before you could speak a word."

"I could have escaped with her."

"No. You don't even know she has two security squads — one visible, one unseen. You fooled the visible one. The hidden squad was closing in— I knocked you down at the very moment one of them was about to stab you with poison."

"Then why knock me down— why poison her?"

"Because your freedom depended on it. Your vow ends only when Kazima's story ends. And she's not dead. Nor will she die. She is in a deep, unbreakable unconsciousness. Only one thing can end it— Aab-e-Noor poured down her throat."

"And what is that supposed to be now?"

"A rare extract from the Orycan flower... rare, but not impossible to obtain. Once they realise it's Zahr-e-Alshet, they'll know only Aab-e-Noor can cure it. They'll try to find it."

"And where am I supposed to get this Orycan? I'm the one who led her to this fate— don't I deserve to try?"

"In Panjshir. But for you, getting it would be far harder than for them. Forget it. What matters is— I've saved your life again. And now you're coming with me to Masrib."

"No, no— listen... listen. I've only just left the nest— only just spread my wings. I won't give up this early out of fear. I'll make mistakes— but I'll learn too. Does Manaal know what her people were going to do to me if I failed?"

"Why do you assume she's innocent? If her brother and father are devils, she is one step ahead of them. Aryan— this is my last warning. I won't save you again. Now you're the enemy of Kazima's guards, Manaal's guards and the keepers of Almat. Everyone here wants you dead. No one will help you. Come with me."

"No. Now it's a matter of proving myself. I will."

"Last time— drop this foolishness and come with me." Her voice hardened.

Aryan didn't answer, but his face said everything— he wasn't going with her.

Samara climbed onto the far wall. Guards and local soldiers began converging on that area from all sides.

"Burn in hell, then," she spat, leaping off the wall. Mid-air she transformed back into the enormous winged creature, and vanished into the sky.

Aryan shook his head at the bitter irony— and jumped after her, landing on the adjoining roof. He bolted away immediately.

And behind him, a calm holy city exploded into chaos.

Wherever he ran, someone appeared to catch or kill him. He darted across roofs, over walls, through balconies— evading one pursuer only to face another. Chaos everywhere. No refuge anywhere.

Finally, reaching the city's edge, he slipped into a dark ruin and lost his trackers. He hid there, gathering breath, then climbed toward the outer wall.

Getting down wasn't easy— steep rock faces everywhere, but not impossible. And the utter darkness, with no lamps or patrols, helped him. A thin crescent moon hung above; stars shimmered, but not enough to expose him.

Reaching the ground safely, he circled wide and returned to the open desert plain where the tents of pilgrims stood. He wrapped part of his turban cloth over his face— unlikely anyone would recognise him now.

He slipped to the rear of Rakh'aan's tents. The Mareeds guarding them remained focused toward the front. Aryan entered from behind quietly— no one noticed. The tent was empty— meaning Manaal and Darab hadn't returned yet.

He waited.

Half an hour passed.

Footsteps approached.

Aryan gripped his dagger and pressed himself against the entrance flap.

Manaal walked in first.

Before she could even react, Aryan lunged— seizing her and pressing the dagger to her throat. Her handmaidens screamed. Manaal was completely stunned. Outside, Darab and the others would have sensed something instantly.

But now the game was his.

Dragging Manaal in front of him as a shield, he stepped out. Darab and the others had drawn their weapons.

"No, no, my dear brothers— you already played your move. Now it's my turn. The moment Princess Kazima fell, my vow ended. I owe your prince nothing. Tell him this— when I heard of Manaal's beauty, I decided she would be my bride. Now I'm taking what is mine. Either we both leave alive— or we both die."

Darab growled, teeth clenched, "You'll die the worst death imaginable."

"No problem. Death from others is always ugly. Now move aside."

"You're insane— listen, we can talk. We can save you," Manaal whispered, struggling.

"Worry about yourself, sweetheart. I'm shameless by nature."

They stood helplessly and watched as he reached the Mareed assigned as Manaal's mount. Aryan made her climb first, then sat behind her— pressing the dagger harder into her skin and ordering her to command the creature.

Manaal, furious and humiliated, still had no choice. She gave the order.

"Don't try following us— or I'll take her to my home, where she'll live as my captive, and all of you will die," Aryan barked at Darab.

The Mareed ran— its giant wings unfurling and with one powerful leap, it soared into the sky.

Below, Darab and his men stood like statues, eyes blazing as Aryan and Manaal vanished into the darkening horizon.

••

CHAPTER 6

The direction in which Safir had seen the smoke— reaching it required crossing the river, and to do that, they had to walk along the bank for quite a distance until finally they found a spot where the water only reached their knees. That alone felt like a stroke of luck, otherwise who knew how far they would have been forced to wander along its edge. The icy water troubled them, but since they had to keep moving, soon their feet warmed up again. Once on the other side, they resumed walking toward the direction from where the smoke had risen.

Daylight had fully broken. They couldn't yet see the sun from where they were, but the growing light around them made it clear that it had risen. A faint breeze drifted through — light, cold, and sharp.

The smoke gave them a sliver of hope— dangerous, yes, but hope nonetheless. It revived them. They climbed down from the machan, relieved themselves, washed their faces in the river, used a datun as a toothbrush, ate a few plums from a nearby tree to ease their stomachs, and set out again. Rifles hung from their shoulders; neither wanted to be careless from any direction. They walked with vigilant eyes, scanning everything around them. Their ears stayed alert, noting every sound that the wind carried. They had left behind the tent cloth and the holdall, but they had worn the torn, dirty jackets — making them look equally scruffy. But for now, warmth mattered more than appearance.

"Last night… we won't ever forget that helplessness," Elma said as she walked beside him.

"And what about the rest— do you think you'll forget any of it? Elma, ordinary people live their entire lives without a single moment of the kind that can change someone forever. It's rare… a matter of fate. I'm a man, living out in the world, so I expect that someday life might throw something unpredictable at me— something unforgettable. But someone like you, who's always lived a sheltered life… it's rare to experience something that sears itself into memory. Since the day before yesterday, nothing that has happened to us is ordinary. These are the kinds of moments where lives end… or change. They still can. You're focusing on only one part of it."

"That wasn't a small thing for me… no man had ever touched me before."

"If we're counting touches, then even when they dragged you out of Rimsha's vehicle, their hands weren't gloved. Or does that not count? Or are they not 'men' to you?"

"Don't twist it… when someone grabs you by force or tries something— you don't call that a touch. We girls notice the kind of touch where our own willingness is involved."

"Oh? So last night wasn't entirely helplessness— there was willingness too?" Safir nudged her with his elbow.

"Shut up." She blushed, her cheeks turning red.

"Just say it— that wherever I touched you, or wherever you touched me… all of that was your first time. New. And unforgettable."

"It wasn't your first time?"

Safir opened his mouth to say something, then closed it again.

"You must've done everything with Rimsha already… that's what came to mind. Girls can stay untouched till our age… but you boys can't."

"It's not like we earn medals for staying untouched."

"Still… we feel we shouldn't share our loyalty with just anyone. Only someone who reaches the depths of the heart, someone who promises to hold your hand for life, someone whose touch doesn't feel like sin… only he deserves that closeness."

"And when helplessness comes, anyone can do? Look— boys have helplessness too. That surge of youth doesn't always stay in control. The control girls have— we don't. And that's not something to boast about. It's just that for girls, society is harsher. One stain can destroy their whole future. They must guard their character. But boys don't have that restriction. In fact, they marry off wayward boys to 'fix' them."

"True… our 'purity' has less to do with willingness, more with society's rules and expectations. If I'd grown up in Europe or America, maybe I'd think differently."

"So really— no one's ever touched you willingly? Not even once? That doesn't necessarily mean marriage, you know."

"No. I never gave anyone that chance."

"Why… even at home, Owais, Rushan, Hanzala— good-looking boys."

"Aak— never. They were always like brothers to me. Nothing like that ever came to mind. You tell me— did you ever feel something like that for Zafeera, Namra, or Inaya? Your relation with them is the same as mine with Owais, Hanzala, Rushan."

"No. Honestly, I hate that kind of relation. Someone you've known since childhood as a sister, someone who calls you brother— falling in love with her or marrying her… I can't digest that. Even if religion permits it, not everyone's mind can accept it."

"You did everything with Rimsha, right?"

"What does it matter now— she's gone." His voice grew heavy at her memory.

"Was Rimsha your first? Or did you… before that too?" Elma insisted.

"I'd done it before, before going to Islamabad. I won't say more now… please, change the subject."

"The girl you first did it with— did you love her? Any desire to be with her?" Her voice trembled as she asked.

"No… no desire. She was married. Her husband was gay. Half the boys in Shahelaar had already been with her."

"Hmm." Relief flickered in Elma's expression.

They fell silent for a while— lost in their thoughts.

An hour after crossing the river, they finally reached the place. Sunlight had begun gilding the treetops. Before reaching it, they had seen sheep— and immediately guessed these might be nomadic Gujjars camped there.

Following the flock, they reached the group. The Gujjars looked stunned to see two people wandering in such a state. There were around fifty nomadic families— makeshift huts, but enough to sustain life. Safir's wallet was intact; he offered them money, and they agreed to help.

First, both bathed in hot water, changed into the traditional tribal clothes the Gujjars gave them, and washed their own clothes to dry. They were given tea, some bakery food, and assurance that they would be taken to the nearest settlement— an eight-hour journey.

Until their clothes dried, they stayed there. They couldn't tell which country they were in, nor whether Pak army, Taliban, or TTP were nearby— but it seemed unlikely for now. The group's leader was a strongly built man named Babar. Safir had paid him. Babar promised he'd leave with two men whenever they were ready.

Sunlight filled the valley; warmth returned— such a relief for both.

Now they sat away from the camp, near a rock. From afar, they looked like Gujjars themselves.

"You look good in these clothes. Keep dressing like this." Elma teased.

"Yeah— and you look good too. So, you should also dress like this. Tell your father to stitch only these from now on."

"If you want it, I'll do it."

"Why— because I want it?"

"No reason… I'll just think of it as repaying a favor."

"What favor? You saved my life— and you're talking about favor?"

"I'll never forget how you ran after me… risked your life. Isn't that a favor?"

"I thought you were Rimsha."

"If you had known it wasn't Rimsha but me— would you still have run?"

The sudden question left him speechless. His heart answered instantly— yes, he would have but the words didn't reach his tongue. His silence became her answer. Elma looked away, disappointment clouding her eyes. A sharp ache rose inside her.

"What am I thinking… stupid. Why would anyone risk his life like that for someone from an enemy estate? Anyway… we're out of danger now. Hopefully tomorrow we'll be home. Will you miss me?"

"I will… of course. Moments like these aren't forgotten easily. And why wouldn't I remember you when everything else will be remembered?"

"So, you won't remember me— you'll remember the incidents. And since I'm part of them, I'll get remembered by accident." She pouted.

"Why do you want me to remember just you?"

Elma couldn't answer; she looked away.

"Fallen in love with me?"

"Hunh… I'm not that unfortunate. I just meant— you'll remember this weird time we spent together, that's all. Anyway… don't try meeting me afterwards. My people might think you're one of those Shahelaar boys who tried to abduct a girl from Mahepora."

He laughed lightly.

They spent two hours talking about everything and nothing— until it was time to leave. Their clothes had dried; they changed back. Not knowing when they would next eat, they filled their stomachs with whatever was available. Babar chose two boys to accompany them, and to hide the rifles under their cloaks, both Safir and Elma were made to wear loose pherans so they looked like part of the group.

Their journey began again.

Babar led now; Safir didn't try guessing directions. Who could know these lands better than the people who roamed them daily?

The journey lasted nearly three hours.

And it ended in a place filled with dry, jagged rocks— perfect for ambush, cover, and conflict. The moment they entered the area, they sensed danger, but too late— Babar grabbed Safir from behind, and one of the boys seized Elma. From all around, armed men emerged— faces they recognised. The same men who had taken them from Nabiullah's house in Shazoom.

Their hopes froze to ice.

Babar and his man released them, stepping aside. Safir stared at Babar with betrayed eyes.

"Don't look at him, boy— these people roam only with our permission. They can't refuse us. When you two went missing, we spread the word among every local in these parts. Whoever found you had to bring you to us."

Safir clenched his jaw helplessly.

"Take them. We'll part ways here," the same elder ordered. He gestured— Elma was to be taken separately; Safir separately.

Their pherans were removed; the rifles were confiscated. Several men dragged Elma away. Safir could do nothing but watch her being pulled out of sight.

"Zama ta staargo khukal-a ye," she said softly as she left — then turned away.

It was a Pashto saying— you are the beauty of my eyes. But what could it mean here? Safir couldn't understand.

Elma disappeared from view. Eight men remained with Safir and led him in another direction.

And his mind kept circling that final sentence. Why that saying? Why there? Why now? She wouldn't say it without meaning. If she had fallen in love, she could've said something clear— not a proverb.

He strained his mind.

Then suddenly— like a flash— he remembered.

He understood exactly what she meant.

A sharp gasp escaped him.

●●

He looked like a little old man— barely four feet tall. As if age had stripped him— hair and brows thinned away, only two or three teeth left in his mouth, a body so frail it seemed a mere puff could blow it off. Skin clung to bone, but there were no deep wrinkles; the skin had a certain sheen. His complexion was clear, with a faint greenish tinge— the same dark green showed in the pupils of his eyes. Those eyes were unusually large, as if his face contained nothing but them.

He smiled through thin lips and watched Rayyaan. The moment their gazes met, he hopped like a monkey among the branches, dropped down, and came to a stop before Rayyaan using all four limbs like some small quadruped; then, in that odd, animal way, he began to inspect him.

"Where are you going, babu?" he asked in a feeble, elderly voice.

The question jolted Rayyaan— his throat prickled. He cleared that prickling with a huff, wetted his dry lips with his tongue, and tried to decide whose servant he might be. The people connected to Ghazal would not harm him, and Shah Alam would be more interested in torturing than killing. In such a tangle, surrendering weapons out of fear made no sense. Daylight lessened dread; otherwise, if this creature had met him in the dark, he wouldn't have had the leisure to think at all. Luckily, Abba ji's kindness had already given him some understanding of his plight, and that knowledge softened the fear.

"I was going to drive a peg into the sky, chacha— will you come?" Rayyaan asked in a teasing voice.

The little man smiled, and the absurdity of the answer eased him— "Yes—why not? Let's go," he said as if Rayyaan were an old, childish friend— "We'll drive the peg and tie our chickens to it."

Rayyaan walked on; the creature trotted beside him like a four-legged companion— walking four steps on all fours, then rising to two feet and leaping to hang from a nearby branch like a monkey, continuing onward by swinging from vines and boughs.

"Let's check the house first— see if the chicken's still there or some crow has run off with it." Rayyaan teased.

"No crow can take it— my chicken would roast that crow and eat it," the creature replied.

"Tell me one thing— how many megapixels are those eyes of yours? They must zoom a lot?" Rayyaan joked.

The remark flew over his head. He stopped, scratched his head, and looked at Rayyaan as if waiting for an explanation. When none came, he slapped his forehead and moved on.

"You're definitely praising my eyes. They're very beautiful— my sheep are fond of them. They won't give milk without meeting my gaze."

"Is it just a chicken and sheep in your life, chacha, or do you have a lady-friend too?"

"Yes, I do— why not? A whole dozen. But they're a nuisance, so I tie them up."

"All right, chacha— stop the nonsense. Tell me, how will you stop me? If I reach a settlement before sunset, I'm gone from you."

He slowed, matching Rayyaan's pace, and before Rayyaan finished the sentence, he shoved him toward the river. Rayyaan felt the impact like a bull's butt; his footing collapsed and he slid down a steep slope, tangled in thorns and scrub, tumbling and half-laughing as the creature watched, clutching its sides. Rayyaan slipped into the flowing river below.

He feared a broken bone, but the water was deep where he fell, so he only got drenched. He flipped the bird at the old man, who broke off laughing, and then Rayyaan dove and swam. He surfaced for breath, dove again; the water was cold, but he had no leisure to mind it— the current itself was a help, carrying him fast in the direction he needed. From time to time, he glanced back; the little creature hung in the trees, swaying and trying to keep up, but its path was clogged with obstructions while Rayyaan had a clear, fast-moving channel. Bit by bit it fell behind until it disappeared altogether.

Rayyaan did not want to stop, but the river looped where he needed to go straight, so he climbed out. The wind slapped at his soaked clothes and he shivered. He took shelter behind a rock, stripped, wrung the clothes until water ran from them, shook them out, and dressed again— hoping that sun and breeze would dry them in an hour or two.

A short way on he found a horse. It did not look tame exactly, yet the mane was long enough to be used as a rein. If he could manage it, the horse would be a great help. The animal grazed, and Rayyaan approached without startling it. The horse looked him over; after a cautious pause, it came closer at his call. He touched the beast gently; it showed no skittishness, so Rayyaan began patting and soothing it.

When he trusted the animal enough, he clutched the mane, vaulted up, and swung onto its back. The horse reared, trying to unseat him, but Rayyaan wrapped an arm around its neck, gripped the mane, squeezed his thighs tight and held on. After three failed attempts, the horse accepted him and broke into a run.

That was exactly what he wanted— horse and rider tore across the wild ground. Thick wilderness fell away, giving way to scattered trees and thorny scrub; the slopes were rough. Then, before long, his luck soured.

As he crossed a field, he spotted a rider under the cover of a tree— revealed only when he was almost upon him. The rider sat on a glossy black horse; both horse and rider were draped in black. The rider's face was not a face— there was only a hollow darkness where features should be.

Rayyaan's heart hammered; sweat slicked his skin. The figure stood up like some statue that came to life and began to follow him.

Rayyaan's tether could not make the horse run any faster; the animal, of course, was not empty of endurance. He raced as best he could, but the black rider was not alone. Figures that had been statues among the trees now animated and joined the chase. Men came out of cover until the tiny, solitary hunt became a pack. The scene felt like a herd of lions circling a single struggling deer; Rayyaan found himself the quarry.

Direction slipped from his mind. He no longer cared where he headed— only that the horse kept going. The sun surrendered; a deep gray dusk pooled and thickened, swallowing the ground. By the time the last rays died, mist had already gobbled the earth beneath the horse's hooves. When he looked back, the black riders were disappearing into the mist and, as if watched, the dark swallowed them.

Ahead, there stood a wood of strange trees whose dangling things were not leaves or fruit but long black locks, drapes of silk. No mist clung there; the air was unnaturally still, yet the black tresses seemed to sway as if wind would topple them. No sound disturbed the place, but the sight alone tightened Rayyaan's chest until it felt as if his ribs might close over his heart.

Rayyaan pulled the horse's mane to slow it— but the animal didn't even feel the command and charged straight into that strange grove. The black strands of hair wrapped around its legs, and the trees themselves seemed to bend, trying to trap them in their embrace.

The farther the horse went, the thicker those silky masses became, and the trees overhead knitted into a ceiling that shut out the last traces of light, plunging everything into a darkness like the heart of an amavas night.

When the horse stumbled and slowed, Rayyaan leapt off — but found no ground beneath him. He fell onto something soft, velvety, and rolled again and again. As his body rolled, the silken threads on the ground clung to him, wrapping him tighter, until by the time he stopped moving, he was bound fast— as if a spider had cocooned its prey.

The more he struggled, the deeper he sank. It was as though every tree around had poured its silk upon him. Slowly the moment came when he could neither move nor breathe— and that was when his mind said goodbye to the world and plunged into darkness.

Then, into that black grove, a white horseman entered— and it seemed the darkness began to melt away. The silken clumps recoiled in fear, the frenzied trees stilled. The great bundles of silk began to reshape themselves— into human forms.

And what forms they were— each one a shrunken old man, like the creature he had met earlier on the road. Bare bodies covered only by a scrap of skin-like cloth. They growled like cornered cats, retreating from the white horseman, clutching at the trees as if they were leaves or fruit hanging from branches. The trees, meanwhile, no longer seemed trees at all— but women standing silently, holding to their chests the many impish children born of them, those devilish little things glaring with wide, fierce eyes.

The white rider— cloaked from head to toe in white, astride a snow-pale horse— reined in beside Rayyaan.

The rider bent down, and behind the veil, Rayyaan saw the face— it was Ghazal.

Tears welled in his eyes. He tried to speak her name, but she raised a finger, forbidding him, and extended her hand.

He caught it and rose. Understanding her gesture, he mounted behind her.

The horse leapt forward.

The enchanted grove fell behind; mist loomed ahead, and within that mist emerged the black-robed riders who had vanished earlier. The chase resumed as before. Rayyaan clung to Ghazal's waist like a child, his body pressed to her back, as the horse flew at impossible speed toward some unknown horizon.

When they reached the grassy plains where the trees ended, the horse's wings unfurled— vast, glistening and it left the ground. Soon scattered trees below were racing backward under its hooves, its wings beating hard, lifting them higher.

Rayyaan's senses dulled; wonder, fear, even the surge of excitement all abandoned him. He felt nothing, as though his power to react had been numbed.

He turned his head— behind them, the other riders had also taken to the sky. Their horses too had grown wings. They followed like black hawks chasing a single white dove. There was no sun, no moon— only stars, faint but enough to see clearly. Below stretched forests, rivers, valleys, cliffs, and here and there human settlements— houses glowing like fireflies in the dark.

After a long pursuit, he realized the number of dark riders had dwindled; only three remained. Ghazal turned her horse toward them. At that, they scattered; she singled out one and gave chase.

Now the hunter had become the hunted.

Half an hour passed in a furious aerial dance, but the quarry eluded capture. When they reached a dense black forest, the fleeing rider dived down and vanished among the trees. Ghazal descended too; darkness and the chirring of unseen insects surrounded them. The horse folded its wings and began to walk.

At one spot, it stopped. Four narrow rocks rose around them, and one broad slab stood above like a roof, shading a hollow in the middle. Ghazal dismounted and lay down there; Rayyaan dropped beside her, panting, trying to steady his breath.

She suddenly laughed.

"So scared! For such a tall man… I thought you'd have some courage, but you—"

"Believe me, sweetheart, even Rambo would've been like this. In the human world, I could handle any danger. But when the whole world is strange— when nothing makes sense— then even Rambo would've been trembling like me."

"That's true… Are you hungry."

"Of course! Haven't eaten since before noon."

She pulled a small pouch from within her cloak— some sealed tins and a bottle of water.

"Here— eat. It's for you."

Whatever the food was, it was unfamiliar to him, but delicious. Within minutes he'd finished everything. His belly full, a deep drowsiness came over him. After so much running, exhaustion was only natural. Leaning back against the ground, he closed his eyes. Ghazal lay beside him, watching— but he slept as if he'd sold all his horses and was free of every worry.

After some time— he didn't know how long— someone shook him hard. He blinked awake to find Ghazal calling his name.

But even as he focused on her, everything changed— the whiteness turned to a human glow. Her voice deepened. The delicate brows grew white, a beard and moustache sprouted, wrinkles creased her skin. The pointed white hood became a green cleric's cap, and her flowing cloak turned into a kurta and lungi.

She— was now Abba ji.

Rayyaan jerked upright.

"A-Abba ji— you!"

"Yes, me." He patted Rayyaan's shoulder.

Rayyaan looked around. There was no darkness, no horse, no Ghazal, no stony shelter— only the shrine of Gulzar Shah. Morning light seeped through, and Abba ji squatted beside him, watching.

"You were supposed to be in Mahepora— how did you end up here?" he asked in astonishment.

Rayyaan held his head in both hands, trying to gather his scattered thoughts. Everything that had happened felt like a nightmare— too unreal. If it were true, how could he have returned here? He should've been anywhere but this place. His mind tangled in confusion.

"What's wrong?" Abba ji asked, stroking his head.

Rayyaan told him everything— every detail.

"I can't understand how much of it was real, and how much imagination, or dream, or if all of it was just my mind's creation," he said, anxious and bewildered.

"When you left here, you were in full control. At what point did your consciousness break?"

"In that forest— in that mass of silk. Before that, I never lost my senses for even a moment."

"Then up to that point it must all have been real. Beyond that, perhaps dream— or vision from your subconscious."

"But even so, that forest was far from here. I couldn't possibly have walked back in my state. How am I here then? And another thing— yesterday around eleven or twelve, I ate at your place. By that logic I should be starving by now— but I'm not. My stomach feels full."

"Perhaps someone brought you here half-conscious, fed you, tended you. Some things you truly saw, some your half-sleeping mind imagined. Those who stopped you or tried to capture you were Shah Alam's men. Those who helped and brought you here— they were Safdar Hayat's."

"Or… maybe it was Ghazal herself."

"Could be. Look, son— whatever it was, one thing is clear. Even if you didn't enter this by choice, you're trapped now. And they won't let you go. You can return only if you free yourself— and there are only two ways to do that."

"And what are they?"

"Either leave this world by giving up your life— or face whatever lies ahead, fight, and emerge victorious."

"But how can a man fight them?"

"Yes— perhaps not an ordinary man. But you are under their protection too— you're their son-in-law. They themselves will help you. Yet before that, you'll need my help."

"What kind of help?"

"Come," he said, rising to his feet.

●●

The sun's heat had begun to needle his skin, forcing Aryan to open his eyes. The very first thought that flashed through his mind was whether he was safe. Seeing no immediate danger around, he exhaled in relief. And then— his thoughts shot straight to Manaal.

She wasn't there.

He jolted upright, heart thundering. After escaping Almat, he had steered toward Panjshir, but even after flying through the remainder of the night, the Mareed had managed to carry them only as far as southern Afghanistan. Before sunrise, over a stretch of barren, endless wilderness, the Mareed had finally exhausted himself and ended the journey.

Keeping the Mareed with them had posed its own risk — because he was bound to Manaal. The very moment Aryan fell asleep, she could command him to shield her, flee with her, or turn against Aryan entirely. So the moment they landed, he had forced Manaal to order the Mareed to fly straight to Rakh'aan and, if anyone asked, to claim he had left both of them in Aramin.

Once the Mareed vanished into the distance, Aryan had tied Manaal's hands and feet, left her on the sand, and allowed himself to collapse into sleep— hoping fatigue would eventually pull her under as well. Once both woke, he would decide what came next.

But she was gone. Simply… gone.

Had she gotten away on her own? Or had someone taken her?

He sprang to his feet and began scanning the landscape — rolling dunes of brown desert soil, uneven stretches of cracked earth, dips where one could easily hide. No sign of Manaal, no movement anywhere. Had she somehow freed herself and fled? In such a case, there was no telling which direction she might have taken.

For the next half hour he searched the surroundings, combing the ground carefully for footprints or any scrap she might have left behind. Nothing. Not even one hopeful trace.

In the end he sank onto a rock, frustrated and uncertain what to do next.

By now, Kazima had likely reached Qazaar. They would have understood she had been poisoned by zahar-e-al-shet and would be searching for Orycane already. For Aryan, finding Orycane before they did was crucial. Only then could he save Kazima and prove his innocence.

Manaal had served two purposes for him— first, a shield during their escape from Almat; second, a lesson he fully intended to teach her.

The first goal was accomplished. The second had vanished with her.

Should he stay here and search? Or set out toward Panjshir before he ran out of time?

Staying felt like a waste.

So, he rose and began walking— alone, without weapon, vehicle, or companion. Only his feet to rely on, and the destination so far that it seemed almost laughable. If he miscalculated, Qazaar's men could reach Orycane long before he did.

He regretted sending the Mareed away. He knew it was a mistake now, but it had been necessary at the time.

"Samara was right," he muttered bitterly to himself, "Aryan, you're still not capable of navigating anything on your own. A true leader decides quickly and correctly— not like you, blundering about and regretting every choice afterward. Manaal was your hostage, dear boy— if you'd used your head, you could've threatened her, scared her into silence, and forced that Mareed into obeying you for six or seven hours. He could've flown far enough that she couldn't influence him, and then returned when you needed him. You'd have had him for travel and she'd have no way to reclaim him. But no… you sent him right back. Didn't think for even one second about how you'd cross this blistering desert at noon. Idiot. Absolute idiot. You're not worthy of restoring Altunia's honor." He kicked at the sand, furious with himself.

The sun climbed higher, blazing overhead. Sweat drenched him as hot winds scraped across his face. Still he walked.

Two hours later, a faint patch of green appeared among the dunes— a settlement. Fifty or sixty old-style houses, perched on a greenish island of land. Even without looking closely, Aryan could sense it wasn't human. The aura was unmistakable— this was a jinn settlement. And like most such places by day, it lay in a lifeless stillness, as if abandoned… though he knew very well it wasn't.

Was Manaal here? Had she taken refuge in this place?

The thought quickened his steps.

Before the settlement, he passed a strange graveyard— disturbed graves everywhere, dug open after burial and left exposed. In the middle lay a freshly dug grave, opened perhaps a day or two earlier. Aryan bent to look inside. No corpse.

Two possibilities— either a corpse-eating creature roamed here, or a Ghoul lived nearby.

Neither was comforting.

He moved on.

Half an hour later he reached the settlement. To human eyes, every home would look ruined and deserted. But Aryan could see clearly— doors that seemed shut were ajar for any jinn, and inside every house, jinn lay in deep daytime slumber.

He checked seven houses. Not a single being was awake.

So, he washed himself with the water he found, ate whatever food was left out in the jinn households, and lay down under a shaded corner. He intended to sleep two or three hours, then begin the journey to Panjshir. By then, Manaal had slipped entirely from his mind.

But someone's presence tugged him back to consciousness.

His eyes opened.

Three figures sat around him— two men and a woman. Aryan sat up abruptly. They stepped back.

The sun was now tilting westward, the heat finally easing. He could travel again— provided these three didn't bring fresh trouble.

"Who are you, and what are you doing here?" one man asked.

"My name is Aryan. I'm a traveler. I came from Rakh'aan and I'm headed to Panjshir. My wife was with me, but when I woke, she had disappeared. I've been searching for her… saw this settlement… everyone was resting, so I lay down as well. Have I done something wrong?" A careful mix of truth and fabrication.

"Hmm… nothing wrong. We just saw a stranger lying here," the man said, "You say your companion vanished? Where?"

"Back there— behind that tall ridge."

"Maybe someone took her. Or maybe she wandered off and lost her way. You should have searched that area."

"I did. Couldn't find her anywhere. Anyway… are there more settlements nearby?"

"Yes— three or four of our kind. And several human villages farther east. Was she human?"

"No… no. Is there any large settlement around?"

"Northwest lies Kandahar, a big one. But why would you need that?"

"I passed a graveyard coming here. Almost all graves were torn open— including one freshly dug. Why?"

"All our graveyards and the humans' as well— share that fate. A Ghoul lives somewhere nearby. It devours the dead. We've tried everything to get rid of it, but nothing works." A heavy sadness fell upon all three faces.

"And we're just grateful it doesn't attack the living," the second man added.

"But my companion has disappeared," Aryan said— "Isn't it possible she fell into its hands?"

"We've never had any living person vanish. So we can't say." The man shrugged.

Aryan had a feeling Manaal had escaped on her own. She would reveal her identity anywhere she reached, receive help instantly, and find her way back to Rakh'aan without difficulty. But another thought crept in— what if she had fallen prey to the Ghoul? Wouldn't that make him responsible?

Should he not at least make one attempt to find her?

"Does this Ghoul have a lair? Or does it roam anywhere?"

"There's a place we've seen it go to many times. It may be its den. But it's too dangerous for any of us to enter."

"You've never checked?"

"We are ordinary jinn, boy— not Hikmatyar Ghazavi. We can't fight it alone. And that place only allows one person in at a time. If one of us goes in, he'd be trapped. And we don't want to provoke it. At least it only eats the dead. If it starts hunting the living, we're finished. But… if your wife is so important, you may take the risk. Your matter is different from ours. If anything goes wrong, the consequences fall on you, not us."

Aryan fell silent, torn.

Why should he risk his life for Manaal? She hadn't valued Kazima's life. Why should he value hers?

But his heart pulled in her direction. He remembered the stories he had heard— stories that had brought him to Rakh'aan in the first place. Even when they fled Almat, a part of him had imagined keeping her close… making her part of his life.

In the end, his heart won.

"All right. Tell me where it might be. I'll look."

The two men nodded and signaled the woman to return home. Then they motioned Aryan to follow them toward the east.

That side was desert too, but with patches of green near the settlement. The sun dipped lower, the air turning easier to breathe. Aryan sensed plainly— these two were using him. They couldn't face the Ghoul themselves, so they were sending him in first, using him like a rifle rested on another's shoulder.

But he had to see. He had to be sure Manaal wasn't trapped there.

After half an hour they reached an isolated patch of land — uneven ground, scattered craters. One crater in particular lay ahead; the men pointed.

"You'll have to go down there. We've seen it enter this one several times."

"Only one person can fit inside. We don't dare go," the second added.

"All right. If it's not there?"

"He should be home at this hour. They rarely wander once dusk begins."

Aryan nodded and walked toward the crater while they hid behind a rise of earth.

The entrance looked like the burrow of some colossal beast. To enter, he would have to lie flat and slide in. He lowered himself, listening. Silence. Darkness.

Finally, he gathered courage and crawled inside. At the beginning the tunnel was tight, but as he advanced it widened and spiraled downward. Eventually he could sit, then stand. Cool air soothed his overheated body. A faint glow appeared ahead.

The tunnel emptied into a large hall— stone everywhere, and strange torch-like flames burning in niches. Smoke drifted upward into vents carved into the ceiling. The smell of charred something hung in the air.

Aryan scanned the shadows— someone had to be maintaining these fires. But the place was full of jagged rocks and blind corners.

Then something slammed into his back.

A kick— so powerful it hurled him nearly twenty feet. Aryan smashed into a boulder, pain shooting through his bones.

Groaning, he turned— and his mind jolted.

A towering figure nearly ten feet tall stood before him. A massive, deformed creature— no clothes, bulging eyes, monstrous claws glinting in the firelight… and a low wolf-like growl rumbling from its chest.

Staring at it, Aryan understood instantly— compared to this thing, he was nothing.

He spoke with honeyed urgency. "Look— look, brother… listen to me— can't we talk this out? Has fighting ever done anyone any good? Think a moment… what will you gain by killing me? Yes— there'll be meat, but my meat is poisoned, brother, believe me. Eat me and you may not see tomorrow's sun. Have patience, I beg you." He instantly turned on the charm, buttering him up for the moment.

The creature paid no heed. It lunged with a roar at Aryan, and before he could blink it had reached him, scooped him up with both hands, and flung him so hard that he smashed into a rock and crumpled. Pain rippled through his limbs; anger flared in the monster's chest for a second, but seeing his own size, it controlled itself.

"Listen, brother— my beloved has gone missing. I was only looking for her. I thought she might be here, but now it seems I was mistaken. There's no point in making matters worse. I'll go back. Forgive the error of my coming here, brother." Aryan tried to hobble back, speaking like a supplicant.

But the Ghoul— because that's what it was, reappeared as if by sorcery, struck his waist with a brutal shove, and Aryan tumbled forward with a sharp cry. He writhed and begged, yet nothing moved the creature; it savaged him with merciless blows. Aryan did try to fight, but each attempt failed— every time the thing seemed to vanish from its place and appear behind him like a phantom. In a short while his strength ebbed— he lay limp and lifeless, the will to move gone, death a thin silver arch at the horizon of his vision. Numbness spread; he surrendered as if to a slow, inevitable blade.

Then, as if some temper had cooled, the creature's fury ebbed. Its expression softened a shade. It settled beside him, regarding him with intent curiosity. Then, to Aryan's dismay, it leaned in, wrinkled its nose, and sniffed his neck, hair, and face.

"If you mean to eat me, just eat. Why savor the scent and whet your appetite?" Aryan croaked weakly.

The creature spoke then— its voice deep and surprisingly measured, "Who are you?" it asked for the first time.

"Hello— asking who I am only after all this," Aryan mumbled— "What does it matter who I am? Kill me and eat me— what difference will it make?"

"Are you connected to Hikmatyar Ghazavi?" the question he was asked left Aryan in shock

"How do you know my link to him?" Aryan shot back.

"By your smell. I would recognize it even after years. You are surely the son of him— Aryan Ghazavi."

"Oh—so what? Even if I am, what of it? Kill me if you must. Any other torments you plan before that?" Aryan managed a bitter laugh.

The Ghoul laughed too— low and almost gleeful. Aryan found himself staring, bewildered at the creature's sudden mirth; it rolled like a child, mocking him.

"The son of Hikmatyar Ghazavi— so weak, so faint-hearted. The true heir of Altunia reduced to this— if anyone saw you now, what would they think?" the Ghoul taunted, pointing at him as if ridiculing a spectacle. Aryan winced.

"There is no Altunia now, and no father left anywhere. So, who I belong to means nothing. Today my story ends here." He shook his head in despair and said.

"What do you think I'm going to do to you?" the Ghoul said, getting up and sitting down in front of Aryan.

"What else can you do but kill me, big brother... And once I'm dead, what difference does it make whether you bury me or eat me?"

"No... that was certainly your fate before, but not any more," he said, his tone completely serious, and the moment he heard this, a surge of life returned to Aryan's body.

"Then what are you going to do to me?" he asked, sounding a little more alert.

"Your father caused me great suffering. I will pay him back. I will keep you as my slave. For Hikmatyar Ghazavi, that is no small punishment— to see his heir living as a Ghoul's thrall."

"If you want revenge, you could kill me," Aryan said— "Keeping me a slave is fraught with risk. I could escape, or take your life— killing is simpler."

"Because your father is not dead," the Ghoul replied— "No one knows where he is or when he will return. He will accept your enslavement; he will not accept your death without finding a way to repay. I do not fear your people, but Ghazavi is different— he is a force beyond anyone. There is but one beginning that subdues him… and an ancient secret — someone is searching for Ghazavi across Altunia. If you fall into that one's hands, you will be kept until your father is found— centuries if need be."

"Who is this?" Aryan asked, curiosity pricked sharp.

"There is one," the Ghoul said— "One so much your father's enemy that he has come long before to hunt him. If you fall to that hunter, expect to be held until your father is found."

"May I know Your name big brother?" Aryan asked.

"You can call me Omar," the creature said.

"Tell me— why take revenge on my father? What did he steal from your field— turnips, perhaps?"

"For a while I was a notable figure in Panjshir— there was a reign to my command, a glory to my name. But I refused the tyranny of your father's patronage. I resisted his servitude. For that he humiliated me, struck me down in front of my people, forced me from my land, and left me in these wastes to become a devourer of corpses. That is why I am a Ghoul. It is true that I am stronger now, but I cannot return to my old dignity with that stain on my name. Now you have come into my hands— an opportunity to return to my people in triumph. I will take you as my slave and parade you before them— Ghazavi once disgraced me— now his son returns as my thrall." He laughed, intoxicated by the thought.

"Fine, brother— fulfill your desire. But tell me— have you eaten my beloved?" The one favor he still hoped for— that Manaal might be alive.

"No… I saw them take her," Omar said, eyes brightening, "She's a pretty girl—your beloved."

"So—she's alive?" Aryan's voice caught.

"I cannot say for sure whether they killed her or kept her. I only saw them take her."

"Who took her?"

"Qasra people… as far as I could understand them, they belonged to the Qasra tribe itself. They are feral tribal folk living toward Amir Mohammad Kalay, who abduct women from regions stretching from Afghanistan to Syria and Oman and sell them in cities. Now, if your beloved hasn't created any commotion, they will sell her, and if she tries to make any trouble, they will not hesitate to kill her. I get plenty of corpses from the Qasra people— for me, they are nothing less than angels."

The news made Aryan's brain tilt. It was naïve to think Manaal would submit quietly to such men. As a princess she would possess the pride of birth; anger would double her resistance. She would not stay silent unless she hid her identity— and if she revealed who she was, the Qasra might hesitate before killing her outright.

"If you want to restore your lost dignity, you must help me," Aryan said, springing up, all the creature's wounds forgotten.

"What help?" Omar eyed him with sharp intent.

"The Qasra may be angels to you, but to restore your dignity, you must come with me and rescue her. Imagine— you will return to your people with Hikmatyar Ghazavi's son and daughter held as my slave."

"What concern is it of mine to save her— it will be enough for me if I return after turning you into my slave."

"No… you don't understand. I must save her. If she is not saved, I will take my own life; then your dream of restoring your dignity will remain a dream. Either come with me to save her, or forget your return. For me it makes no difference whether you kill me or I destroy myself."

"You cannot do that," Omar said, squirming.

"If you wish to test me, go ahead… Time is slipping away very fast. Think carefully— lest it be too late."

Omar stared at him for a moment with eyes that seemed ready to devour him— then, the helplessness showing on his face, he let his shoulders drop… a gesture that made it clear he was ready to accept Aryan's terms.

They retraced the way Aryan had come. Omar's bulk seemed to be dragged along, and on the narrow stretches of the path the monster diminished in size; by the time they reached open air he had shrunk until he looked thinner than

Aryan. As soon as they breathed the open wind, he swelled again into his vast frame.

Aryan glanced back toward the place where those who had brought him had been; in the distance the two figures slipped away, and humor rose bitterly in his chest.

"What is it?" Omar barked.

"Nothing— just laughing at the state of things. Tell me — when did you see her? When did they take her?"

"In the morning, when I returned from the hunt. They were carrying her away."

He realized then that Manaal must have freed herself while he slept and run on— if the Qasra people had taken her earlier, she would have raised an uproar and perhaps woken him. Since nothing disturbed his sleep, she must have escaped his side after he fell asleep and been seized later.

The sun sank lower, a dim, red globe; its heat faded into a cool, traveling dusk. Now they could travel without the brutal sun on their backs.

Omar walked ahead, and Aryan trod in his wake. He should have teased the creature, joked to break the tension— old habit, but his thoughts were consumed by Manaal's fate and the heavy responsibilities toward his people. The charge of sending a Qazaar princess into the jaws of death already rested upon him— and if anything happened to Manaal, the blame for a second princess would fall upon his head as well. And Omar would return him to his people as evidence of shame; Aryan had resolved before leaving Masarib never to reveal his identity to anyone.

Lost in these thoughts, they covered an hour and reached a settlement nestled in the hollow of a stony hill. In the dimming light, he could just make out earthen houses. The village was awake; men had gathered in the center, carousing— drums, shouts, drunken revelry; women and children watching like an audience. Several bonfires and torches lit the square, scattering the encroaching night.

They crouched behind a mound and watched. Among the crowd someone was hauling a cart; on it stood a human-sized cage. Inside that cage, Aryan recognized Manaal even from a distance— her state made his blood boil. She was completely naked; not even a scrap of cloth covered her body. Men around the cart leered and made obscene gestures; the sight ignited a white-hot fury in Aryan's chest. His hands clenched until his knuckles whitened.

●●

CHAPTER 7

Safir lay on his bed, staring up at the roof while his mind kept drifting back to Elma. Physically he was in the house, but mentally he was elsewhere. The thought that gnawed at him again and again was this— he himself had reached home safe, but where and in what condition was Elma? Her touch, her scent, the way she had looked at him— all of it made him feel alive in a way that kept pulling him back to her. The memory of it would come and the cruel possibility would follow that she had been taken by those men and now, somewhere among those tribesmen, she might be suffering. The idea tormented him.

He had felt something like this once before, when Rimsha left him— for many nights after that he couldn't sleep; and even after she died, the remorse had not weighed on him like this. What he felt for Elma was different; it signaled a change in him. The bond that had begun to grow with Elma was of a different, present kind. The things she'd said as she left only hit him later, and then he could not reply because she had already gone. The same lines, he realized, were the sort of messages her "cute-girl" fake profile on Facebook used to send— the last message lying unread in his inbox. He finally understood why that profile had behaved the way it did— it was her. It was the mask she used to speak to him while hiding her identity. He thought he was either a gay guy or a flirtatious girl— and that was why, after showing some interest at first, he'd started ignoring her. Now he realised why she'd been reluctant to meet up or reveal her identity.

But then why, and how, did she fall in love with the son of an enemy fief? The only explanation that made sense to him was that a girl coming of age is like a mirror— whoever stands before it, that face settles into her heart. In her tender years, Safir teasing her and claiming he would carry her away must have lodged itself somewhere deep within her. And since such things were part of their tradition, it was not altogether impossible. He had said it casually and forgotten it, while Elma must have clutched those words to her heart and begun dreaming of that very future. It was true that meeting each other or even coming face to face in the outside world was almost impossible, but in the age of the internet, how difficult was it to find someone on a social site? If she lacked the courage to speak with her real identity, she would have taken the route of a fake profile. It was another matter that even then she failed to earn Safir's trust, and he moved ahead on a different path.

He had gone back to his laptop and read through the whole thread from the fake profile. Snatches of meaning that had escaped him earlier were now plain as day. But by now there was no one to answer.

That morning, when the two groups had delivered them to the TTP, one faction had taken Elma while another had taken him to a nearby village. From there they had procured a vehicle and, by evening, reached the Shahelar border where Safir's father and brothers were brought in to bargain. He had come back home in a hollow state, cleaned himself up, and sent Sohail to do one task. The terms the family had struck with that TTP faction were ugly— those men handled dried-fruit exports and regularly shipped cargo from Gwadar and Karachi. They wanted to smuggle an opium consignment out of the country and, in exchange for Safir's life, his father Anas Khasoor had been forced to accept their condition.

Words alone could arrange such deals, and so the arrangements had to be made. Safir had resolved to go after Elma himself, regardless of whether that pitted him against one wing of the TTP or the whole organization. He would deal with whatever came. If he died trying, so be it.

His thoughts were interrupted by louder noises outside; it sounded like people calling his name. He sprang up, slid into his slippers, and hurried out along the corridor to the wide balcony. From there he could see the lawn in front of the haveli lit by high-mast lamps. A whole kafila had entered — a vehicle, many horses, and men armed with rifles. His family stood their ground in front of them. At the head of that gathering stood his father Anas, shouting; his brother Farrukh was with him. Safir squinted and recognized faces— the men of Mahepora; on the vehicle were Elma's father Huzaifa and cousins Owais, Rushan, and Hanzla. Heated words flew between the two groups.

He ran down at once to prevent things from worsening. As he approached, all eyes turned toward him and the quarrel abruptly stilled.

"What's this? What's happened?" he asked as he reached them.

"You went with Elma— where is my daughter? If you came back, why didn't she? Where has she been left?" Huzaifa roared.

"I don't mean to be rude, but please calm down and hear me out. If you know anything else, you must know that Elma wasn't taken by me— the TTP took her. They're not relatives of ours," Safir answered, trying for a controlled tone.

"Then why did they leave you and not her?" Owais asked.

"That question you should put to them. Didn't you know some of the Lakwal faction are in your jagir?" Farrukh said, barbed.

"Look Safir— instead of arguing, answer straight. You know how dangerous this is," Hanzla said, addressing him bluntly.

"So why did these armed men come and storm our haveli? There was no need for such an assault." Anas's anger had not cooled.

"They didn't come to attack; they came to secure us. If you're offended, we apologize. But tell us plainly where Elma is and why they didn't leave her." Rushan pleaded.

Safir told them as much as he dared. He described how the Lakwal group had attacked the army convoy to seize Rimsha; tricked by that ruse, they had taken Elma. He had thought she was Rimsha and had rushed to save who he could, then got caught himself. When the men realized their mistake, they kept him alive to extract a profit; they had led them all away at night, and in the morning, they realized the girl they'd taken was Elma, not Rimsha. She had concealed her identity then, and Safir had not known who she was. Later, they'd gotten an opportunity to escape, but tracking the route had been messy. The path of rescuing them had twisted— the herders they'd trusted to help them reach safety had, by the time of dawn, led them right back into the hands of other TTP men. Some took Elma; some took Safir this way. In exchange for his survival, his father had to cut a deal.

Silence followed. Huzaifa's temper flared again— "Why did they keep her?"

"They may not realize who she is. Maybe they plan to keep her captive; perhaps if things go badly, she will reveal herself and bargaining will begin." Safir stopped there— he could not tell them the whole truth that the men intended to sell her into laundi; telling that would have driven them to madness.

"Are you telling the truth?" Huzaifa asked, incredulous.

"What's the point of lying, Chaudhry Sahab? If I had taken Elma for myself, I would have said so outright and made preparations. We would have kept the haveli ready; you would not have had to go into Shahelaar." Safir's voice held a sting of wounded pride.

They let the thought sit. Then Huzaifa's face hardened — "We'll ask. If they refuse to return our girl, we'll line their bodies like corpses. Come."

Their mounted men awaited their signal. When the order came, they mounted, the jeep revved, and the kafila turned back. The gate slammed shut behind them.

Safir shot a quick look at his father and brother as the column left. A new thought kept gnawing at him— if the men didn't know Elma's true station, would learning it change their decision? They would understand the price of keeping a Mahepora girl. But he couldn't sit waiting. He would go try to save her himself.

Half an hour later Sohail returned. Seeing him, Safir straightened.

"What happened?" he asked.

Sohail's breath wheezy from running— "I've been at it for three hours. During the attack on convoy, one attacker's identity was traced to Musa, so the army searched everywhere for him. He couldn't stay and probably slipped across the border. The last hope was Ameer Khrotai— when we stormed Bagraat, someone from Rushdabad I know was there. I tricked him with a lie that we needed Ameer; he gave us Ameer's location and even spoke to him on the phone. So now we have a place to go."

Safir rose to prepare at once.

"What do you plan to do? You told me to find Ameer, so I did— but these are militants. We can't afford a permanent feud with them. We bargained for your return; remember that this is a fragile arrangement. Think before you act." Sohail warned.

"I'll manage. Where is he?" Safir asked.

Sohail gave the location— about ten kilometres from the haveli.

"It's only ten now— why go at ten o'clock? We can leave in the morning, take men with us, keep things under control." Sohail insisted.

"No. I'm leaving now. You rest. If I need you, I'll call." Safir patted Sohail's shoulder to reassure him and, as a precaution, took a Mauser.

Sohail knew his stubborn streak and could not stop him. But he could not grasp why Safir, who'd just been spared, would rush back into the lion's den. He had fetched Ameer's location at Safir's request— why Safir needed him now remained a mystery.

He left Sohail in a state of indecision and went down to the kitchen where Namra and a servant were. He asked for something to eat and both of them hesitated. He had to tell them, then, that he was leaving on an emergency errand which might keep him out until late, so it would be best to eat first. They fed him in the kitchen. Had he added a stay in Peshawar to that, he might not have had a proper home-meal for another week— today was only the third day he'd had a decent meal.

After food he mounted a bike and rode off.

The road was so poor that what should have been a ten-minute ten-kilometre stretch took him half an hour. It was night and there were no streetlights there; darkness ruled everywhere, so he could not press on fast.

The location Sohail had given for Ameer was a little cluster of eight or nine houses, almost hidden on the slope of a densely wooded hill— no electricity, and from outside it looked as if every home lay buried in darkness. The silence was such that it felt like no one lived there; in any case it was past eleven by the clock and that hour in those parts was deep night.

He steeled himself for what might come and knocked on the door of the house where Ameer Kharotai was supposed to be.

The door opened quickly. The man who answered held a lantern; in that light Safir could see that this was not Ameer, and that the man had a gun in the other hand.

"Came from Shahelar?" the man asked, eyebrows raised.

Safir nodded once.

"You could have come in the morning," the man said.

"There's no time," Safir replied.

"Hmm. Come in." The man stepped aside.

Safir entered, and the door was shut behind him. The man led him through courtyard, veranda and a narrow passage into a room where another man already sat whom Safir could now tell was Ameer Kharotai. He was a solid-built Pathan in his early thirties, his heavy eyelids and the chilam in his hand showed that he was high. Another lantern burned in the room; the man who had brought Safir set his lantern down near Ameer and sat beside him. As was the custom there, the bedding lay on the floor, so Safir too knelt and sat before him.

"What's wrong? What trouble has sent you here so late?" Ameer asked, glaring.

"I want Elma," Safir said, peering into his eyes.

"Who is she?" Ameer asked.

"The daughter of Chaudhry Huzaifa of Mahepora."

"That'll cost. Two lakhs," Ameer said flatly.

"I'll give four lakhs… but first you need to know where she is."

"Why— is she not in Mahepora?" Ameer's expression showed surprise.

“No. She’s with Nabiullah— maybe in Shāzoom,” Safir said it as if he had weighed the words already, for he expected the reaction.

Both men were startled. The one who had brought Safir went for his gun in a flash; Safir kicked the weapon from his hand and the man stumbled backward. Ameer rose, but Safir smashed the chilam into his face— hot coals inside spat and struck the man. He screamed and fell back.

Safir drew his Mauser… his plan was to disable them with the pistol before they could recover and extract the information by force. But plans do not always go by the book. As he drew his Mauser, Ameer lunged and shoved him hard; Safir lost his balance and stumbled. The other man made a move for his weapon and Safir leapt onto him, and they both wrestled to the floor. Both of them had weapons in their hands, which made the situation dangerous. They were locked with each other, each struggling to force the other’s weapon away. Seeing them grapple, Ameer started moving toward a wall, where Safir could now see a rifle kept inside a cupboard. If the rifle came into Ameer’s hands, Safir’s chances would be finished for good.

Seeing no other option, he turned his wrist in that direction and fired— the bullet struck Ameer in the back, and with a sharp grunt, he collapsed right there.

The sudden shot stunned everyone; for a moment the men loosened their grip and Safir used that instant to wrench the Mauser toward his chest and press the trigger. The man’s eyes widened; pain carved deep lines across his face. His body slackened and he fell helpless. Safir planted his foot on his pistol hand and held his Mauser leveled at Ameer. At the sound of the second shot Ameer looked at his companion, and the man, shaken, collapsed where he was.

The man whose arm Safir had pinned thrashed a while then went limp; his resistance drained away and he lost consciousness. Safir looked at that man closer and saw the bullet had pierced toward the heart. The chest was soaked with blood. He was not yet dead but the odds of survival looked grim. Fear rose in Safir's mind— if the shots had alerted other accomplices nearby, they might come looking — a peril Safir could not afford. He had come to gather information by force, if need be, not to wage a pitched battle.

He crept close and crouched beside Ameer. The wound had left the man helpless; he lay bent and mute, teeth clenched against a pain that quivered through him.

"I didn't come to take anyone's life— I came to ask," Safir said, regret in his voice— "But danger forced my hand."

"Do you think you'll make it out alive?" Ameer panted.

"No one can promise that. But you can live if you help me. Help me and you survive— and you can take revenge later." Safir tried to sound practical.

"How?" Ameer groaned.

"You and your men attacked the army thinking you were grabbing Rimsha, but you took Chaudhry Huzaifa's daughter Elma by mistake. I ran to save her… and they captured me and turned the idea of shipping opium into a deal. They decided to keep me alive in exchange for using my family's export contacts. They plan to keep Elma as a laundi and hand her to a Zargam as part of a bargain. Do you understand what that means?" Safir asked.

Ameer answered, voice thin— "Zargam is a Taliban commander fighting the Northern Alliance toward Panjshir, and Shahzeb Barqzai has direct access to him… earlier, when they were fighting against the government, they used to take support from us… now that the government has come into their hands, they are driving the TTP men out from that side… the border is a safe haven for us… if that support is taken away, the Pakistan Rangers will become a torment for us." He explained in a choked voice.

"Yes, but what does all this have to do with Elma and Zargam?"

"We will have to please Zargam through that girl, so that he arranges to deal leniently with our faction… the men he has toward Nuristan… he has enough influence over them that they will not create trouble for us." His voice was trembling now.

"Hmm… so with the change of government, they are pushing the TTP away from their border, and to escape that, your group wants to bribe him with a beautiful girl. Fine… now tell me this— how can I bring Elma back? Would it be right to go to Shazoom… as far as I understand, if they have already left with her, then they won't be found there.

"Go toward Panjshir— try to find the Zargam. She may end up with him or be moved through his territory," his voice kept growing fainter, and his eyelids began to droop.

"All right… thank you! Let me see where the bullet has hit… and what I can do for now."

Ameer said nothing and closed his eyes— when Safir tried to lift him, a deeply agonized groan escaped him. Safir slipped his hand inside Ameer's shirt and felt around, then understood that the bullet had struck the spine just above the waist and shattered it. Everything below was soaked in blood… when he pulled his blood-smeared hand out, he wiped it on Ameer's own shirt. Ameer was clenching his teeth, trying to swallow the pain— his eyes had shut again. Safir laid him flat on his back.

"The bullet has hit the wrong place… saving you without taking you to a hospital will be difficult, and the hospital is very far from here. Tell me— if there is someone close to you, I can inform them so they can take you to the hospital. As for me, arranging anything like that here is not possible," he said this as he rose to his feet.

Ameer gave no reply— he lay there just as he was. Safir waited for a while, expecting him to say something, but Ameer's condition made it clear that in his attempt to endure the pain, he had lost consciousness. Safir did feel a measure of regret for him, and there was remorse too over his own haste… but what could be done now. He knew that once he left this place, Ameer too would die, just like his companion. Shaking his head in quiet regret, he stepped out of the room, wrestling with the apprehension of what effect those two gunshots might have had outside. Were there other companions of Ameer nearby who might now be lying in wait for him?

Yet by the time he reached the courtyard, he noticed no such movement, and standing there, he began to consider whether he should slip away quietly or make some other arrangement. If no one had seen him arrive, how would anyone know who it was that had finished the two of them off inside? After a moment's thought, he arrived at the conclusion that leaving silently was the wiser course— that alone was right.

He opened the front door, peered out— silence again and slipped into the dark. He mounted his bike, shoved the Mauser back into its holster and prepared to ride.

But as he revved the engine a shadow lunged from the right and fell upon him. The shadow's arm extended; another Mauser aimed for Safir's skull. Despite the thin starlight, he recognized the figure.

It was Owais— Yasir Hamaar's son, the elder Chaudhry of Mahepora and Elma's cousin.

••

Rayyaan fell in step quietly behind Abba Ji. Everyone in the settlement who saw him looked surprised— by their count he should already have been gone. He followed Abba Ji into the hut. The old man closed the door carefully and motioned him to a low, nailed stool.

"Baba gave me many amulets and practices at the end of his life that help against wayward jinn and fanatics," Abba Ji said, "but since I was not exactly Hafiz or a fully trained Alim or Kamil, he could not pass every method to me. Many of those methods would be useless to you, because you do not know how to use their workings, but there is one talisman that might help you."

"And what is that?" Rayyaan asked, watching him with searching eyes.

Abba Ji took the rudrāksha mala from his neck and put it over Rayyaan's head.

"Never take this rosary off," he said— "This tasbih reached Baba Gulzar Shah through the very people you fear; Baba gave it to me. Its property is this— once a person wears it, those people cannot use any charm against him that works from afar."

"What do you mean?"

"I mean— you know how immeasurably strong they can be; after you wear this, if they come to fight you, they will be able to use only as much power as you yourself possess. Remember how, when you were captive of Shah Alam, his voice became unbearable for you— that voice was stronger than human endurance by many measures. Now he cannot wield that beyond a human scale against you. If they come, they will have to fight you at your standard. Their magic, their deceptions, their guile will not affect you more than they would affect any other person. They can still change shape, increase their size, but they will have to face you on equal terms."

He was explaining and Rayyaan listened, stunned.

"That is the only help I can give you."

"But you are entrusting me with something so precious — won't you need it?"

"No. We are both human and our strength is human; could I stand against you? No. Think of it this way— you among humans still have the time and the capacity to fight, to defeat someone, to stand up and act. An old man has none of that. With this, you can face any one of them— I cannot."

"Will I really be able to face them?"

"Yes— and do not forget that they too may have many tactics that can be tried against one another. After all, when they see you standing up to Shah Alam and his companions, they will themselves step forward to help you. That girl will stand by your side, the one whose husband you are. They may grant you many more such stratagems— you only need to muster the courage to fight."

He fell into thought. Escape was impossible now; he had seen that. What else remained besides laying down his head in a mortar? Even if this had not started by his will, he could decide to end it on his own terms. He had never lived fearing his life— he had always welcomed danger. Adventure was the nourishment of his spirit; this, too, was another kind of adventure.

"Okay— I'm going to do it," he said at last.

"What?" Abba Ji blinked.

"I mean, Abba Ji, I'll do exactly that. Ghazal may well not be only human— she may be among the jinnat but she is still my sharīke-hayāt. If anyone, even Shah Alam, makes trouble for her, how can I not face him? I'll face him— whether I live or die."

"Good— I will pray to God for you."

"Now please let me go, and tell me which way Dera Jamal Khan lies."

Abba Ji explained, and a little while later Rayyaan was walking along a path.

It was strange that the very beings he had never cared to believe in now walked as reality before his eyes. The world's knowledge of jinn perhaps had always been filtered through Arabian Nights or through folktales among Muslims; to ordinary people they were only characters for wonder. No definite proof had dragged them into the light, and Western scientists, journalists and scholars had mostly either ignored them or read strange phenomena as either ghosts or aliens. Whichever way you looked, every paranormal event had a natural explanation to some— but in Pakistan, India, across Asia or among conservative Christian circles, such events only reinforced belief in ghosts, whereas those hunting other worlds found their own 'proofs' for extraterrestrial activity. The strange world he was caught in could be read either way.

He ate a dry breakfast, as on the previous day, and set out. His route led him toward Dera Jamal Khan, threading through difficult, wooded trails. He let his thoughts churn as his footsteps pressed on. If he ever chose to tell the world about all this, would anyone accept it? Or would they brand him mad? He had no proof to show— only words and such words from an ordinary man would always be met with scepticism; only saints and mystics find patient listeners.

"Where are you going, babu… ha ha ha ha." a voice broke his reverie.

Rayyaan turned toward the sound and saw, dangling from a branch, a wild mass of jute-like locks, big green eyes, a grin that split up to the ears and a few black teeth glinting between cracked lips. A cold shiver ran down his spine. The creature looked frail and skeletal, but the shove it had given him the previous day had felt like a bull's charge.

He had already resolved to face danger; why fear now? Besides, Abba Ji's tasbih rested at his throat. If it really worked, then this creature was no match.

"I'm going to uproot, chacha— will you come?" Rayyaan taunted.

"Yes, yes— why not? Come," the jute-haired thing said, dropping from the branch and landing before him like a monkey— "I love uprooting and I know many ways. Let me see how you pull."

"Tell me one method you use to uproot," Rayyaan said as he walked beside it.

"Use both hands— plant one foot, put all your weight in and pull."

"Like Sunny Deol in Gadar?"

"What district is that— Khan or Deol?" it scratched its head.

"Never mind. Tell me how you pull?" Rayyaan pressed.

Before the creature could answer, Rayyaan leapt, seized its neck from behind and lifted it off the ground.

It gasped, eyes wide, then raged. It bellowed like a wild thing, but Rayyaan held it firm. The creature struggled with all its strength— and then, to its surprise, found its efforts futile. Perhaps the tasbih did hold power; the being truly seemed frail, unable to escape the grip. It snapped into different fearful shapes— a drooling wolf, a great dragon breathing little fires, a roaring lion… yet no guise could break Rayyaan's hold. When the creature had exhausted its tricks, Rayyaan let his hands strike in quick, bone-jarring jerks until the thing lay whining and small.

"Say one more trick and I'll fling you so hard that the earth will not keep your bones together."

"I understand." it croaked, broken.

"Keep quiet," Rayyaan said, releasing it.

They moved on.

"You pushed me the other day, I'd have avenged it— but I'm not in a mood for violence now. I'm going to see Ghazal," Rayyaan said.

"That girl will have you killed," the creature muttered.

"Shut up— she's my wife."

"Shah Alam won't spare you. You thwarted his plans."

"Let Shah Alam try," Rayyaan said.

They walked on in silence.

And perhaps Dera Jamal Khan was close by, which was why that creature sprang off in a single leap— here one moment, gone the next. Ryyan had no reason to concern himself with it; he kept moving along his own path.

And when Dera Jamal finally drew near, he again noticed the large, stretchable cats lurking in the surrounding bushes — creatures he had seen before. This time, however, he paid them no heed. If one of them chose to attack him, that would be dealt with then— for now, it was not even clear whether they were friends or enemies.

Then Dera Jamal came into view.

It lay just as lifeless and dead as he had seen it the day before yesterday in broad daylight— as though no one had set foot there for centuries. Ryyan looked toward the spot where, two days earlier, a clash between two elephant-like wolves had turned everything to dust— yet today it appeared exactly as it had before the fight… as if that battle, and the devastation of that place, had not been a real event at all, but merely an illusion, or a figment of his sleeping mind.

He returned once more to Ghazal's house and again searched it thoroughly, with complete calm and patience— but nothing of significance turned up there.

From there he returned to the lanterned platform where Darain Chacha had once squatted like a haunted idol. It was afternoon and fatigue pulled at him; he lay down on the platform and the warm, thin sun lulled him toward sleep. He could not afford to be careless— sleep light and watchful… so when he sensed someone near, he snapped awake.

He raised his head and looked; Saarah was seated beside him. He sat up immediately.

"Where did you go, babu?" she smiled.

"Cut the drama, Mallika-e-Husn— come in your true form."

"Why— are you so restless to go see your begum?" she said it teasingly, and in that instant her face changed; the girl sitting beside him became Ghazal so completely that there was no pause between them.

"That'll do." He lay back again— this time he rested his head in Ghazal's lap.

"So, Abba Ji told you everything." She ran her fingers through Rayyaan's hair with complete calm— "This is exactly what we wanted— that's why we kept sending you to Baba Gulzar Shah's doorstep. What Abba Ji told you— had we told you ourselves it would have sounded like a trick. The tales of jinn and ghosts you have heard of— even if until now you didn't truly believe— had we counted ourselves among them and misunderstood, either we would have been destroyed or we would have died trying to save you."

"Maybe you're right— but from now on bring the real matters to my notice so I can understand them properly and make decisions accordingly."

"Ask… what do you want to know?"

"Why was I chosen for this whole affair?"

"Do you believe in peshangoi— prophecy?"

"No— I think nothing is written in our life-book beforehand. Whatever is written, we write ourselves."

"Perhaps not every little thing is written, but the main events, the big incidents, are. For instance, when I was a child I was told that I would marry a man and that I would meet him in my nineteenth year, in the month of Shawwal… and see, in my nineteenth year, on a stormy night of Shawwal, you met me there where there was no expectation of a human being anywhere."

"Oh— so I didn't end up in these wastes by coincidence or because circumstances misled me— I was meant to come here, so I wandered."

"Exactly."

"All right— the other day, those two wolves… who were they, fighting over me?"

"One was a khadim of Shah Alam and the other belonged to Abba Huzoor."

"And who struck my head with the stick?"

"One of our own khadims— because we did not want the situation there to affect your senses badly; you were already incapable of understanding. Then we ourselves brought you to that river and stayed with you. We had mentioned Baba Gulzar Shah's dyodhi, so that you would reach there and meet Abba Ji."

"It seems you hold Abba Ji in great respect."

"Yes, because he is Gulzar Shah's khadim, companion and heir… Gulzar Shah was a master whose disciples included our Abba Huzoor. We expected that Abba Ji would not only lift your confusions but also give you such talismans that would make you stronger."

"Tell me this— those stretchable cats, whose side are they on? Friends or foes?"

"They are our khadimas."

"So, what happened in the jungle the day before yesterday?"

"They were shadowing us— we wanted to take you to Gulzar Shah's dyodhi, but Shah Alam's people found us. They were greater in number, so we got caught in their clutch."

"And then a serpent swallowed me— like in that silk grove where those silken locks wrapped around me. Does that spell merely render one unconscious, or can it take life as well?"

"It can take life— if the intent is to kill. But Shah Alam is more interested in imprisoning you at the moment."

"Yes— because he has conceived a singular punishment for me— until I die, I should witness his company, live— a sort of live blue film, and that too with you. What on earth is this Shah Alam? Never mind, tell me about the little man we saw the other day— did you see him?"

"I wasn't there… but some khadims had eyes on you. They saw him but did not attempt to stop him because at that moment our aim had merged into one. We did not want you to leave until this matter was settled. When you were swimming in the river, arrangements for your mount were made by our people."

"And those men in black?"

"We call them Dozakhi— the covert troops of Shah Alam. Cruel killers— they keep themselves in concealment because their faces are so foul and shredded that anyone who sees them is filled with revulsion. While fleeing them you entered that silken grove where Shah Alam's khadims were encamped."

"I didn't— the horse burst in. I felt like I'd braked it but the brakes failed. Then… how did I get back to Gulzar Shah's dyodhi?"

"I brought you back— I was not negligent about you. I had already heard that you were in danger."

"So, what I saw was not merely a dream or a product of bereft imagination— it was all real."

"We cannot say for sure— you were not entirely conscious; how much of what you saw was real and how much was the mind's conjuring is hard to tell."

"Now tell me— who is Shah Alam and why is he angry with me?"

"You carried away his favourite girl and he was enraged. Be thankful that after your capture he could not take us to his fortress; where he had imprisoned you, he could not station a full garrison. Abba Huzoor attacked the place and managed to rescue us. Two of our khadims had gone after you to help, but when they saw you delivered safely to Baba Gulzar Shah they returned."

"And Shah Alam… was he not present?"

"He had left by then."

"So, Shah Alam has a fort?"

"Yes— he is the sultan of our realm."

"Ah!" Rayyaan whistled— "So that's the matter… I thought kingdoms had gone with the British. Here the kingdoms remain— and you people aren't even human… and yet this fellow is the state's sultan. The sultan fell in love with a chieftain's daughter; she refused him. She married another and so he was affronted, but because no one in the realm dared oppose the sultan, nobody came forward to marry her. In that state of things, they forced me into becoming her husband."

"There was prophecy— it was meant to be," Ghazal said.

"Okay— tell me about your people, your world. I want to know."

"We resemble humans in many ways and differ in many. We are not made of clay like humans; we are of fire— fire is our essence. Where our settlements are spread across the wastes, life runs for us much like the courts of old ran for humans. Our food, our dress, our animals differ from yours. We rest and worship through most of the day and wake at night. Our lifespans are many times longer than humans'. We have no televisions or mobiles for entertainment, yet we have our own pleasures."

"You live apart from humans yet you know the language and ways of their world— how so?"

"We are not entirely separate. Many of our people live among humans in human guise— for months, for years, sometimes for whole lives. They don't reveal themselves; they keep their secrets. I grew up among humans in Shahelaar— I even studied in an English medium there and later returned here."

"You said Shah Alam could not bring me to the fortress for some reason. What was reason?"

"That was because of you. He could not take a human into the fortress; that would have sparked rebellion. The courtiers might turn against him— so he could not station his full force there."

"So, Shah Alam is a strange character. How did he fall for you— and why, being sultan?"

"Because I alone was a child raised outside, educated and sharp; my reputation spread across the province. He desired to make me his— not only to show superiority, but to secure his rule through the chiefs. If he holds the allegiance of men like Chaudhary Safdar Hayat, his hold on governance strengthens."

"If he thinks that way then where's the harm? If you'd married him, you would have become queen; that position no one else could have offered."

"Three problems. Number one— he is cruel, and most of the realm's chiefs oppose him, including my father.

Number two— from childhood I was different and set apart; I am no one's commodity. And number three— his particular virility is famed across the state— he is infamous for a lust that has ruined many. Sixteen wives did not die for nothing. I didn't want my ruin."

"Ah— so he wanted to parade his companionship. Fine. But tell me— how will this saga end? Shah Alam intends to imprison me and parade me, or kill me and shrug— but what is your plan?"

"What do you mean?"

"How do you intend to finish Shah Alam's side of it? Will you let him be dethroned and the new sultan spare you? Will you keep him imprisoned in a bottle at the bottom of some trench like mariana? Will you use a talisman and finish him off, and then the whole province will celebrate his death?"

"Those are possibilities— any one of them would end the matter."

"What's the program for tonight?"

"Leave it— will you eat naga fruit?" She glanced toward the tree.

A naga tree stood some fifty paces away in a courtyard. He had thought at first it would be destructive magic, but when she reached out its fruit came easily into her hand and she plucked three with one motion.

Rayyaan thought it better to eat the fruit than be astonished.

He spent the remaining day and night at Dera Jamal— in their house.

She had come to him two nights ago, and Rayyaan, ever fond, hadn't let the small life go. When tired, he had sunk into sleep like drowning.

In the night Ghazal woke him.

He woke from a deep sleep— it took him a few seconds to gather himself. She was fully awake and dressed while he was in his natural state. Outside came the noise and clatter of conflict as if a battle had erupted. On Ghazal's face worry showed even in the dim light.

"Quickly dress— Shah Alam has attacked." she said sharply, looking him straight in the eyes.

●●

Manaal's condition made Aryan's blood roar; he wanted to surge forward, tear everyone apart, and bring her away— but he knew that such a try would cost him his life in a heartbeat. Manaal could be cruel, he had told himself; she deserved lessons sometimes, but never this indignity.

"She's alive." Omar watched him.

"You can see she's alive— what else can you see?" Aryan snapped, fury burning in his throat.

"For me those finer points don't matter any more. You figure out what to do," Omar spoke with a kind of numbness.

"I'll save her— do I even need to say that? I told you she's my love; these savages can't do this to her. Look— look, big brother… I can't fight them alone, not inside their den. You must do something— do something, please. What are you waiting for?"

"They are like angels of fortune for me… I find many corpses for them," Omar said, lips hard.

"They used to be useful to you; now that you don't want to stay here, why care? You want me taken to Panjshir so you can reclaim your lost honour— well, this is your chance."

Omar made a face and stared toward the center of the revel, where Manaal had been dragged and where the crowd's frenzy had swollen. There was no way to take her out without smashing through the men; danger swarmed in every direction. Still, if Aryan was to recover his standing, this had to be done. Omar drew a slow breath and moved toward the crowd.

Aryan launched after him.

As they advanced, Omar shrank in stature and his face shifted; soon he wore the face of one of the very tribesmen celebrating there. The disguise was perfect— which was why no one looked twice at him. Aryan kept to the outer press of people, where he could be seen and singled out.

They drew close because everyone's attention was fixed on the spectacle in the centre. Half an hour passed; the revel thickened into something near madness. Perhaps the reason was that in the guise of Manaal they now held a prize of rare worth and were eager to profit.

Then Omar began to stir trouble. Dancing, he landed slaps and shoved men; always, the man whose face Omar wore turned and struck back at that figure. Omar's legerdemain— changing his appearance among the crowd, sowed confusion— people started fighting one another. The brawling spread like a contagion.

When the mob tangled, spectators tried to intervene, and the celebration turned into chaotic commotion. Sensing the opening, Aryan slipped forward toward where Manaal was held.

At Omar's signal someone shoved the carriage carrying Manaal so violently that the whole cage toppled. Manaal fell out with a scream. Immediately a free-for-all broke out; most of the men were drunk and hardly responsible for their limbs. The women shrieked and tore at them to pull them back, but the men were already at each other's throats— punches, kicks, and now knives and short swords flashed. Omar bent the cage-bars wide and, seizing Manaal by the arm, hauled her out.

She struggled but the exposure of her naked body lit a fire in the crowd; bestial looks spread over faces as if every man wanted to possess her. In that surge someone slung her over a shoulder and ran toward the alley where Aryan had been waiting in some contrivance. Several men followed; Omar stayed back and began to fight those who tried to stop the escape. Aryan and the man carrying Manaal rushed into a house and slammed the door.

Inside, Aryan shoved the man; all three landed sprawled on the floor. Manaal lay stunned; Aryan latched on to the carrier. The fight went frantic, fists and feet in the dark. The carrier might have been a heavier man, but his drunkenness made him clumsy; Aryan hammered him until he lay senseless.

Manaal looked like a statue as the struggle unfolded. When Aryan finally floored the man and got to his feet, she recognised him. Then she felt the shame of her nudity. She screamed while raising one hand to cover his chest and kept the other hand down.

Understanding her condition, Aryan began tugging at the clothes of the exhausted tribal man and had just managed to yank them off and fling them toward Manaal when another tribesman burst inside. The moment he saw Manaal, he lunged at her, but Aryan collided with him head-on.

Manaal hurriedly wrapped the two pieces of cloth around herself, above and below, in such a way that she was properly covered. In any case, since the garments were not stitched, size was not an issue at all. A lantern was burning there, in whose light they could see one another. Manaal stretched out her hand, grabbed it, and wrenched it from its place, hurling it to the ground. It shattered— and along with it the oil spilled out, and with the oil, the fire spread as well. Aryan was trying to bring this opponent down too by taking advantage of his intoxication when yet another tribesman rushed in. Right behind him, Omar also entered and began beating him… and soon he caught the man fighting Aryan in his grip as well.

"Take him away," Omar ordered, voice sharp.

"Come with me." Aryan took Manaal's hand.

She might have jerked away, but the danger made her keep his grip and she went with him. They slipped toward the back— darkness there, but they could see well enough. At the far end a clay wall rose; Aryan slammed his shoulder into it.

"You think with your legs, or what, fool?" Manaal snapped.

Aryan stared. She hauled herself up and, like a creature with long limbs, reached the top of the wall and clung there. With a mocking look she swung over and dropped down the far side. Aryan cursed and did the same. The other side was emptier, with routes that used the cover of hedges and hollows to slip away.

Omar, meanwhile, had assumed Manaal's shape in the press. The men who had been attacking now groped at the figure they believed to be the captive; none guessed the substitution. Where they expected to grab Manaal, they found a fighting, shifting target. Ultimately Omar shrugged them off and ran out. A fresh man collided with him and tumbled through the doorway. The commotion outside was wild, but the watchers' attention still tracked Omar, and they chased him.

He ducked through alleys, dodging men who surged after him. Those who saw him bolt after him; the crowd behind him grew and ran with howls. Manaal ran too— headlong, breathless. When Aryan scaled the wall and reached the outer ground, she was already well ahead. It dawned on him that this was her plan— escape him so she could vanish. He swore and shot after her.

Her running was fierce; she put space between them despite his desperate speed. He could not let her go; he ran until his limbs burned.

For the next half hour, the two of them kept running back and forth as if dogs had been set loose behind them. The sandy terrain had been left behind— ahead now began solid ground, where fields could be seen stretching into the distance. Even so, at this hour of the night there was still no sign of any human presence.

Running for so long and over such a distance was astonishingly hard for a princess— one who had been raised with such delicacy that even the smallest exertions meant for her had been entrusted to attendants. When she felt she could no longer take even a single step, she collapsed at one spot and began to gasp violently. By then her body temperature had risen to a searing pitch— her breathing was breaking apart, and her entire body was drenched in sweat.

Aryan reached her a minute later and fell down beside her, panting like a work-beast.

"You were never taught how to say thank you, were you?" he said, voice thin with breath.

She said nothing at first; she only looked at him and breathed hard. Then, without warning, she flung herself at him. He yelped and tried to fend her off; they rolled and thrashed on the ground. For five minutes they tangled like children, exhausting themselves. No one saw them. Had any outsider come upon that sight they would have had stories to tell.

Finally, they stilled, spent. She collapsed, wide-eyed and breathing hard.

"Do you have seizures, Maalikah-e-Aaliya?" Aryan said, lying near her.

"You dog, you wretch, you filthy swine… if I don't have your hide stuffed with straw one day, my name isn't Manaal." she snapped through gritted teeth.

"But I just saved your life from those savages… don't you think I deserve at least a little gratitude?" Aryan said in an injured tone.

"And how did I end up in that mess? Which swine dragged me out of my safe sanctuary into these godforsaken wilds? And because of whom was a princess— who has lived all her life among dozens of guards and handmaidens— forced to wander alone until those barbarians laid their hands on her?" Manaal said as if chewing embers.

"Well… if you look at me like that, I have barbed arrows of my own. Why do you think I had to abduct a princess and run for my life? You knew exactly what your brother had planned for me— how he had prepared my death— and you were completely on board. You marched into Almat with your entire security brigade fully aware of what they intended for me. So, if the one who intended to kill me became my hostage, how was I in the wrong? And once I had taken you, your safety was my responsibility— sure. But you broke out of captivity and ran. The moment you fled, you took your protection out of my hands. Whatever happened afterward… how am I responsible for any of it?"

The argument was fair. Manaal found no retort and fell silent.

Both lay there for a long time, staring up at the white, scattered stars overhead.

"What do you even want? Your entire point in abducting me was to escape Almat alive… So, once you'd escaped, why didn't you just let me go back to my escort? Why stop me?" After a stretch of silence, she finally turned her face toward him, her tone noticeably softer.

"For two reasons… First, I wanted to teach you a lesson — because you were just as complicit in the plot that tried to kill me and Princess Kazima. Second… I'd heard tales of your beauty. They say from North to South and East to West, there are only two maidens in all of Altunia whose beauty has no equal. I had decided I would see both and choose the one who stole my breath. The other girl was far away in Panjshir, daughter of some commander favored by Sultan Shah Alam. Too far from where I was. So I chose Rakh'aan first— Princess Manaal was closer. And when I saw you… the sight of you drowned every other desire. After that, the second maiden didn't matter to me at all. Even if none of this had happened, I still would have settled in Rakh'aan. You were always going to be the one I came for."

"That other girl belongs to Shah Alam… even mentioning her name in Panjshir will get you butchered," she said in a mocking tone.

"No need to mention her anymore. After seeing you, I don't want any beauty but yours."

"In dreams, perhaps. In reality, I'm a princess and you're a common slave. You reaching for me is like reaching for the moon— pretty, pointless, and impossible."

"Let's see… but you could at least be my friend."

"Don't forget your place. Princesses don't befriend slaves— or fall in love with them. Slaves obey. Their eyes don't rise above our sandals." Pride shimmered plainly in her tone.

"Alright, Your Highness… but I am not a slave, nor am I anyone's servant. I reached Rakh'aan as a donkey-merchant and joined your security squad under an entirely different mission. Neither title applies to me."

"Even if you were a common jinn, the answer would be the same."

"Don't forget— you're my prisoner. And as a prisoner, I could just as easily make you my handmaiden. I could take you, or sell you like any other captive."

"I'd rather die first, you uncivilized brute." Manaal retorted, her voice rising.

"And you might not get the luxury of dying first. Those men wouldn't have given you that option. They would've simply taken what they wanted."

"We?" Her eyes widened with suspicion.

"There's a Ghoul named Omar. I needed his help to save you. What could I have done alone? And the price of his help… well, I pretty much had to pawn myself." Aryan made a face.

"Oh… so the one who told us to escape from the back — that was your Ghoul friend. And where is he now? If he owns you, how are you here freely?"

"He got left behind somewhere… I'm praying he never finds us. Maybe that's how I'll escape my debt. Tell me something— once I fell asleep in the morning, you somehow freed yourself and ran. Somewhere along the way these Qasra men caught you— fair enough, they kidnap and sell women, it's what they do. But why didn't you tell them who you were? Had they known you were a princess, they wouldn't have dared treat you like that… might've even returned you to Rakh'aan unharmed."

"Are you insane? This territory doesn't belong to Rakh'aan. It's under Panjshir's control. And yes, I did tell them who I was in a moment of desperation— hoping for mercy. Instead, they were delighted. They thought they'd stumbled upon treasure. They still wanted to sell me— just expected a higher bid. First bid to Shah Alam, of course. He's obsessed with women… he'd have paid a fortune. They were drunk on victory and even drunker on liquor. In that state they forgot all restraint and wanted a taste before selling me. Maniacs."

"Ah… so that's why they were completely feral. Anyway — rest a bit. Then we need to head toward Panjshir."

"I'm not going anywhere."

"I'll carry you if I must."

She opened her mouth to lash out again, then bit down on her lip and turned her face away toward the sky. Aryan fell silent too, thinking.

All the running had taken them far beyond Qasra; this terrain wasn't one he recognized. Would Omar even guess which direction they'd gone? If they moved quickly, maybe Omar wouldn't find them at all… and Aryan would be free of his debt. And Manaal— well, she was with him now. He could resume his original plan.

He kept glancing over his shoulder, half-expecting Omar's huge frame to appear… but a full half hour passed, and Omar didn't come.

"Looks like he's lost our trail. We should move. If we go now, we might escape him entirely— and I won't have to answer to him again," Aryan said, rising.

"You go. I'm not moving," she said, bored.

"Ah… so you want a ride."

And then she shrieked as Aryan hoisted her over his shoulder. She pounded his back with her fists but he didn't budge, carrying her like a sack.

"Try one stunt— just one— and I'll knock you out cold and carry on without pause," he warned.

"Swine," Manaal hissed— then let her body go slack.

Aryan kept walking northward…

He knew nothing about these lands— only that there were farms nearby, which meant both human settlements and Qasra-type tribes could exist anywhere. Silence was safer. If he spoke, she'd scream. And screaming carried far.

Three hours passed before they reached the Dori River. On its sandy bank, Aryan dropped Manaal unceremoniously and collapsed beside her, panting like an exhausted bull.

"Tell me something, Maalikah-e-Aaliya… your touch is driving my senses absolutely wild. Nothing stirring in you? I mean, I'm a man after all— surely you're feeling something after being carried like that." Aryan turned his face toward her.

"Riding donkeys has never aroused anything in me," she said with a mocking curl of her lip.

"Oh really? Want me to prove my manhood right here? Think carefully… don't complain later."

"And how exactly would you do it? Climbing on top of me? Have you ever even climbed on anyone?" she asked, genuinely amused.

"No, not yet— but that doesn't mean I can't." Aryan puffed out his chest, and she burst out laughing.

"What's so funny? Fine, I'm inexperienced— so what? You must be inexperienced too. It's not like you've conquered worlds in the art of intimacy."

"I'm a princess, you idiot. For us royals, every pleasure is permitted. I have an entire harem of slaves for that… What made you think I'm some untouched, delicate little princess who's never known a man's company?" she said, turning toward him with a sly, taunting gaze.

Her words hit Aryan like a blade.

His throat tightened, his eyes stung. For a moment, he couldn't believe what he'd heard. He felt naïve— painfully naïve. The world had changed, and he was still chasing old-world ideals.

Manaal looked at his stricken face and broke into peals of musical laughter. Her voice carried through the night like silver bells. To Aryan, that laughter felt like humiliation he had brought upon himself.

"Love is not something people like us chase, fool. Love belongs to common folk. You should've dreamed of some girl of your own status."

"Why? Royals aren't capable of loyalty?"

"No. My father has three wives— each wife has her own male slaves. My brothers will also marry many times and keep harems of concubines for their desires. In such a world, why should I remain untouched for one husband— who will himself have other wives and slaves? Why should I bind myself by fidelity when no man in our world ever does?"

"Not all men are like that."

"Oh really? Look at all four great thrones of the broken Altooniya— Rakh'aan, Aramin, Qazaar, Panjshir. Every ruler is a lecher. Their sons and daughters— every one of them keeps a harem. Give me one example of a royal who lived for only one love."

"Hikmatyar Ghazavi."

"Hah! One man in centuries. Find me another. One. He was a madman to give all his devotion to one woman."

"He wasn't mad— he was a lover. You wouldn't understand," Aryan muttered, wounded.

"Nor do I want to. We get one life. If we cannot live it fully, what's the point? Now tell me— what lesson were you planning to teach me? If you meant to use my body as punishment— go ahead. It would hardly be a punishment. If you expected me to fall in love with you— never. And if you imagined making me your wife— write it down somewhere, I will still sleep with other men, I will betray you, and the day I find the right chance I will stab you in the back."

Aryan went silent.

No fitting response came.

She was nothing like he expected— nothing like the dream he had crafted. His illusions crumbled like a sandcastle hit by a harsh wave.

"Yes… you're right. I set my hopes in the wrong place. One should dream within one's station," he said quietly, "Good thing I learned that early. Go— you're free. I'm not holding you, nor restraining you. Whatever trouble you brought into my life, I forgive you. And whatever suffering I caused you— I apologize."

"Well, that was quick," she scoffed.

"Yes. I'm going to sleep now. Do whatever you want. In the morning, I'll head toward Panjshir. You can choose your own path."

"And if I fall into trouble again— like last time?" she asked.

"That will be your fate. And this time, I won't be coming to save you." He turned his back to her.

Manaal stared at his back… then lay down and looked at the star-studded sky.

She was furious at this fool for dragging her here— and even more furious that he now expected her to wander alone in a hostile land. What if she fell into the hands of savages again? Not every time would she escape. She decided she would not leave Aryan's side— not until they reached a large settlement. Whether he liked it or not.

Aryan, meanwhile, tried to soothe his freshly wounded heart.

It hurt— of course it hurt… but he needed an anchor. And that anchor became the other fabled beauty of Panjshir.

He would find her.

He would challenge Shah Alam if needed.

He would carve out a new life for himself there.

Lost in their separate storms, both eventually fell asleep.

At dawn, Aryan was shaken awake violently—

He opened his bleary eyes and saw Omar looming over him, fisting his collar, rage blazing in his eyes.

Manaal was already awake, watching with pale fear.

Aryan jolted fully into consciousness.

●●

CHAPTER 8

"The crack of gunfire had made me think they'd finished you off— but since you're alive, it means the ones inside did their work... Were there only two of them inside? Or did you waste two bullets on a single man? You came in a friendly guise— so why did it turn into a firefight?" Owais said, his voice thick with mockery.

"What do you want?" Safir glared at him.

"I'll tell you— first, get out of here. There could be more of them inside who haven't figured things out yet; if they see two people coming out, they'll put the pieces together." Owais sat behind him, easing the muzzle of his Mauser close to Safir's waist.

Safir started the bike without a word. He kept the headlamp off, though the engine's rumble cut through the profound night like proof that a machine was moving.

They'd not gone far before they saw another vehicle approaching along the same road. It too had its lights killed; by chance it came into their line of sight as it rounded a bend.

"Stop— get down. That's surely one of theirs," Owais said, punching Safir lightly on the back.

Safir pulled off the road into a clump of scrub and shut the engine. They were hidden from the road, but Owais kept the Mauser tucked against Safir's hip.

An SUV sped past where they had been standing, swallowed the corner, and disappeared from view.

"Let's go— leave this place fast," Owais whispered when the car had vanished.

"What do you want, exactly?" Safir asked.

"What a chance has fallen into my lap— an heir of our enemies, wiped out so neatly that no one would ever know who did it. Isn't that splendid? But not today. For now, move quietly— otherwise it might happen before you realise it." He sounded amused and dangerous both.

Grim-faced, Safir kick-started and sped the bike away.

"Turn towards Shapora ahead— if they chase us, they won't take that road." Owais moved closer and murmured into his ear.

Safir said nothing. The plan nagged at him— where had Owais sprung from, and what did he want? About three kilometres ahead lay a crossroads— one road led to Shahelaar, the other to Mahepora, with Shapora along that latter route. When they reached the first hamlet, Owais made him turn the bike inland.

"There's a ruined house up ahead— park it there," Owais ordered.

They drew up before a crumbling homestead at the edge of the village. Darkness and silence presided.

"So— what do you reckon those people were? How did they get here so fast?" Owais asked, climbing off the bike.

"I don't know." Safir's face remained hard.

"Either someone inside sent a message— one of those you didn't see, or someone in the neighbourhood tipped them off— 'Bullets fired at Ameer's place'—and his men ran. I heard two shots earlier— what happened?"

"You tell me your intention first. What do you want?"

"I wanted to know if you'd hidden Elma somewhere. We suspected you people might have spirited her away and had help. However, according to the army, these people had abducted her under the mistaken belief that she was the daughter of a colonel… Still, we wanted clarity. We had men looking into these people. One of them, Parvez, reached Sohail earlier. From their talk we traced some possible plan and that you would come to Ameer Kharotai. I came here beforehand— but couldn't go inside. Then two shots rang out and you came out alive. I want to know what went on— were they your men? Who shot whom? Which girl are you trying to snatch?"

"We aren't snatching anyone. It was a bluff— just to get to Ameer and know who Zargam is and why Elma would be handed to him."

"Zargam? Elma? What is all this?" Owais demanded.

Safir told him everything. As the tale unfolded, fury lit Owais's face.

"Bastards— filthy dogs. I'll show them what happens for such insolence." He ground his teeth, "Who fired inside?"

"I fired," Safir said— "When they realised, I'd come to ask about Elma, their tune changed. I meant to frighten them into talking, but things got out of hand and I had to shoot. I saw Ameer and one companion— both hit. I don't think either will survive."

"Good— such scum deserve it." Owais's voice had an ugly satisfaction. For a minute they were silent. Owais re-holstered his Mauser and studied Safir as if measuring him.

"It doesn't make sense that Elma became your enemy's bounty. You had no business in her abduction, yet you ran off at night to pull information— took two lives in the process. What's your motive?"

"She risked her life to save me. It's my duty to do anything I can for her."

"Is that all? Or something else?"

"If you must know— then know it. I love her. That's why I'll do anything to save her."

"I thought something was off," said Owais, "Are you prepared to live by our traditions if need be?"

"I might be shot for it... but maybe," Safir said.

"Then I'll shoot you too— our customs are customs," Owais said, eyes narrow.

"We'll see." Safir shrugged.

"For now— what's the plan?"

"I'll go to the border. I'll slip into Panjshir alone. I'll see if I can reach Zargam. If I get there, perhaps I can do something."

"If we come with men—?"

"If you bring men, fights will start along the way. I'll go alone. See what can be done." Safir's voice had set, immovable.

"You're not going alone." Owais rose— "I'm coming." He grinned, "Hanzla and Rushan are wives' men— we won't involve them. I won't tell the family; they'll go mad and charge off. I'll say I'm searching for Elma. Do we need to make some preparations… I mean, are we really going to storm in just like this, in two pieces of cloth, carrying only this Mauser?"

"Why do you want to come with me… go and prepare yourself, however you wish."

"So, you want to leave immediately— what a lover you are. Fine then… let's go like this. I have enough clout to arrange things even along the way," Owais said with a smile.

"Do you have a phone?"

Owais handed a handset. Safir dialled Namra from memory. Her phone, showing an unknown number, might not be answered— but to his surprise she picked up.

"Namra— this is Safir. Listen to me. Tell Abbū that I left for Peshawar last night. Something's happened; two TTP men are dead by my hand. I'll lie low for a couple of days. I don't have a proper line— just tell them I left at night." Namra's voice came through, a startled "hello" in the distance. Safir cut the call and handed the phone to Owais.

Owais rang his own people and said that news of Elma had arrived; he was heading out now and would keep them informed. They set off.

Riding at night was dangerous— army patrols could stop them, or a TTP band might intercept— but Safir could not wait.

They rode until a fuel station glowed awake and topped the tank. The question they faced was which route to take across the border and, from there, how to find Zargam. Panjshir was no small place— a valley with seven districts and five hundred and twelve villages— a broad province where the Northern Alliance held sway and the Taliban sought influence; routes were many and shifting. Finding where a single commander fought was not simple. Safir had no plan; he wanted to slip into Nuristan province, but Owais had a scheme and persuaded Safir to follow it.

By four in the morning, they reached the last settlement before the Afghan border— Maskeni… where Owais had a man, Fakhar. They woke him. Fakhar could scarcely believe that princes from Shahelaar and Mahepora had come to him together, but when Safir explained, Fakhar arranged help. He packed two light backpacks, fresh clothes, magazines for the Mausers, and drove them to the border. Their bikes remained in the village.

Fakhar told them they would cross on foot; from the border to Asmar, no other settlements would be encountered. He gave them some Afghani notes for payment. The mountains and river gullies there left no eye to watch them, so slipping over the frontier was not hard— yet they had to avoid soldiers and local militias— any traveller could be a threat.

Fakhar warned that beyond the border to Asmar the route would be twelve kilometres in a straight line, but the terrain offered no straight roads. They followed a tributary of the Kunar and walked. By dusk they neared Asmar— but a new problem awaited— a front line had opened there. Villages were locked down while two parties shot from cover. Who they were— Taliban, Northern Alliance, or a TTP splinter— no one could tell. Bullets had already pierced the air long before the men approached, but the sinking sun worked in their favour; darkness could hide them.

Once they reached the outskirts, they were stuck. Which way into the settlement? Two directions were gunfire zones. Asmar was not a single cluster but many hamlets, and the shoot-out lay directly on the side they'd approached. They could not risk crossing the exposed ground.

"What now? They could fight all night— their whole life seems to be nothing but fighting." Owais said, looking to Safir for an answer.

Safir had none.

They sat under cover where they were— two hours passed like that, yet the fighting ahead produced no decisive outcome; the sporadic gunfire continued.

"This night will waste away like this," Owais muttered, irritated.

"Let's move on. Whoever we meet, tell them we are guests of Ishaq— coming from Asadabad. If we look like ordinary civilians for both our sakes, perhaps they'll let us pass," Safir said, thinking fast.

"And if they search us?"

"We only have Mausers— keeps for our safety."

"I think we should fall back— our destination lies the other way anyway. We came here only for that Salarzai fellow. Let's head to the main road— someone will give us a ride."

"Alright…there really is no other route."

They turned back.

They had taken every precaution so far to avoid being seen, but heading for the main road inevitably meant running into other people. And as if fate laughed at their plans, it happened almost instantly.

No more than a hundred metres had they gone when a band of fighters, moving quietly in the same direction, appeared before them. Neither party expected the other; both were startled. Their Mausers were in bags while the fighters held rifles in their hands— but fortune favoured them— neither side opened fire. Seeing each other so suddenly, both panicked, then performed a small act of prudence— both raised hands. The fighters read them as non-hostile, and so did not begin shooting.

"Who are you?" one of them asked.

"My name is Safir Khasoor and this is Owais Hamaar… we're from Asadabad. We came to meet a man called Ishaq Salarzai— there's shooting over there so we found no road forward and started back," Safir said, hesitating; he was unsure if they would be believed.

"You came on foot from Asadabad?" the man eyed them.

"No— someone gave us a lift. They were heading to Hajiabad," Owais answered quickly.

"Who to see?"

Owais told them about Ishaq Salarzai, as Fakhar had explained. The fighters listened closely; they did not immediately show recognition, but scrutinised the two for truthfulness. There were five of them, and standing before them the travellers could face a fight— yet the fighters had no desire for that. The newcomers appeared urbane rather than local tribal men, and so the five were inclined to trust them. They motioned for them to follow.

Reluctant but unable to refuse, the two fell in behind. The route toward the fighting required them to stay shielded, to move from one cover to another with bursts of running. Bullets whistled past them from the front, but none struck. At last they reached the place where some overturned stalls lay and two men were fighting behind them.

The five halted, looked, and recognising the story, one of them vouched for Safir and Owais. He signalled two companions to lead them toward a house and they moved swiftly, keeping low. Reaching the door, they knocked; there was a frightened reply from inside. When they explained who they were and asked about Ishaq Salarzai, the answer came— his home was nearby.

"See that two-storey house? Right behind it— go. That side has no fighting. Move," one of them said.

They thanked him and slipped off in the direction given. There were many hiding-lines to use, so it was not as dangerous as it sounded; the men across the valley were Taliban, and at that hour they did not suspect them.

The two-storey house stood with a lane descending at its side; halfway down that lane, pressed to the wall of the two-storey house, was the building they sought. They knocked. For a moment silence, then a voice asked— "Who's there?"

"Owais— Fakhar Wahab from Maskeni sent me," Owais answered in a low voice.

The door opened quickly. They stepped inside and it closed behind them. Darkness lay thick, and the man who opened the door was little more than a shadow.

"Follow me," he whispered, moving aside.

They followed the shadow and crossed a threshold, descending a flight of dimly lit stairs. At the bottom lay a proper room, furnished for habitation; battery-powered lamps glowed and everything was visible. A mattress lay on the floor, laptop and satellite phone sat on a low table, and rifles and books were stacked. The man who had brought them in was a tall, burly Pathan, dressed in modern clothes. A young woman in the room grew visibly nervous when she saw them.

"Sit…Fakhar told me you might come, but I didn't expect you so soon," the man— this Ishaq— said as he sat down.

"We were heading back when Taliban crossed us. We told them we were from Asadabad, coming to meet you, and they kindly showed us the way. You live down here?" Safir asked.

"Upstairs is risky— one shell or projectile and you're done. Down here we have a chance," Ishaq said.

"Who's the other party?"

"Northern Alliance— fighting will drag on through the night. They'll keep pushing slowly."

"Who is she? Your wife?" Owais pointed toward the girl.

"No…not married. She just came this evening. Usually I let her leave— today she got stuck. She lives in Sankai. She'll leave tomorrow morning. Tell me— what help do you want?"

"Can we speak here with her present?" Safir wondered; the woman still seemed uneasy.

"Naima, go make food— keep an ear out. If a stray bullet comes, drop to the floor." Ishaq addressed the girl; she breathed relief and went up.

"When she's gone— tell me what you need," Ishaq said, eyes on them.

"It's a TTP faction." Safir began instead of Owais, "They kidnapped a girl and plan to present her as a gift to a commander named Zargam to secure leniency. We must get her back— whether they've reached him or not, we need to intercept."

"Is the girl so important?" Ishaq asked.

"If she weren't, we wouldn't risk our lives," Owais answered.

"I don't know Zargam; there are hundreds of commanders. Finding him by name across this country is near-impossible."

"At present he's somewhere in Panjshir, fighting with the Northern Alliance," Safir said.

"Then you must reach Panjshir. Most places are Taliban-controlled; only a few pockets remain where battles continue. I can't promise I know Zargam. Searching blindly is tough. And you two expect to extract a girl from their hands alone?"

"We won't go in with an army. There are many ways to get one girl out."

"Honestly, this task likely borders on impossible. But if you're confident, I can help. I'll make you fake IDs proving you're from Asmar— so you can move more easily. Also, one of my men takes a truck to Jalalabad to pick up goods; I can send you with him to Jalalabad. From there you can get to Dingak, and you'll find the frontlines' movements. If you need weapons, I can arrange them too— for a price."

"That's enough— do that," Safir said.

"All right. But there's a cost." Ishaq named an amount — five thousand, and more for two local facilitators and costs in Dingak. They agreed and handed over the money.

Ishaq quickly prepared ID papers that would show them as men from Asmar. He had all the necessary gear— lights, a small petrol-powered generator for the lamps. While the documents were being made, Naima brought food. Bullets and occasional blasts still rose outside, but for now those dangers were beyond their small room. After they ate, Ishaq spoke about the shifting Afghan situation; the two listened perfunctorily, passing time.

That night all four slept in the room. Naima's presence made both men slightly uncomfortable, but they had no choice. Ishaq even offered pleasures if they desired— an offer they flatly refused. They were there to free Elma, not for pleasure; soon they slept.

Ishaq woke early. He roused Naima, sent her to cook a sparse breakfast, then woke the two and urged haste. Outside the fighting had ended— two Taliban and five Alliance fighters were dead, others had escaped; Taliban forces had amassed in the area. They packed quickly. Ishaq led them, careful, through alleys to the main road where a contact's vehicle for Jalalabad was about to leave. They boarded.

The journey to Jalalabad took until afternoon. The man they were to meet awaited them and fed them lunch. He loaded them aboard a DCM truck bound for Dingak, which carried supplies that way. By the time they rode, dusk approached; they were to reach Dingak and meet Ishaq's man there by nightfall.

But an accident struck just as they neared.

The settlement they aimed for did not sit on the main road; you reached it by crossing the Pamaher River. The road ran along the valley, and most villages lay off the main track. As they approached the route descending to Dingak, a Taliban convoy crossing behind them came dangerously close. The driver prudently stopped.

The sun had vanished below the horizon— a blood-red glow hung in the west while darkness deepened at their feet.

Half the convoy had passed when the opposite slope erupted— RPG rounds and mortars shell slammed into the road and the valley. The area became a roar of explosions. Vehicles took the worst— windscreens shattered, flattened metal buckled, some trucks launched into the air. The convoys twisted and crashed— some rammed each other, some rolled down slopes. The attackers on the ridge struck with mortars and RPG, and the defenders returned fire from the vehicles and the cover they had.

Seconds later the volley of bullets and the detonations made ears ring. Smoke and fire belched upward; the air filled with choking plumes. Bodies lay— and whether on that side men were killed or not, here certainly many were.

They were trapped in the hubbub; stray rounds tore into the DCM and the front screen screamed under impact. All three hunched down, and in that moment, none could say how long they might survive. The Taliban vehicles near them lay at odd angles, and fighters using their cover were firing— so the whole flank was a maelstrom of incoming fire and the DCM in its path was ripped by a RPG projectile which struck it, sending its mass into the air in a fiery explosion.

••

Ghazal's words made one thing painfully clear— they had to run again. Rayyaan finally accepted that perhaps this land would never allow him the luxury of a peaceful night's sleep. He stood, slipping into his clothes with a reluctant sigh, thinking that perhaps he too should start sleeping during the day like these people— and spend his nights fleeing like Count Dracula.

"That old dwarf told Shah Alam about you." she said quickly while he dressed— "He's even more furious now. He's issued an announcement declaring Abba Huzoor a rebel of the realm. This attack is the consequence of that decree. He wants to weaken us so thoroughly that no one can protect you or me. I don't know how big this attack is, but if he's brought a full legion, then tonight every last one of our people might be captured. And if we fall into his hands, that would be no different than dying. We have no one to count on now— no reinforcements, no allies. We have to survive on our own."

She finished just as he tugged on the last piece of clothing— and just then, two shadowy figures slipped in through the window. Before either of them could react, they had seized Ghazal.

She struggled violently.

It was time to test the true power of the prayer-beads. If the tasbih truly worked, then these attackers would have to fight Rayyaan on his own terms— and Rayyaan was more than capable of taking on ten men at once.

The two were occupied subduing Ghazal, and Rayyaan lunged at one of them, grabbing him by the collar. The man turned, his expression twisted with murderous intent, releasing Ghazal and focusing entirely on Rayyaan.

But before he could act, Rayyaan drove a brutal kick into his most vulnerable spot. Color drained from the man's face as pain hollowed his features. In the next instant, Rayyaan swung him by the collar and smashed him full-force into the wall. A sharp cry broke from him as he collapsed.

Seeing this, the second man shoved Ghazal aside and charged toward Rayyaan. But Rayyaan met him with a clean, crushing punch to the nose. The man fell back, clutching his face. Meanwhile, the first attacker staggered up and lunged again, but how could ancient warriors anticipate a modern spinning heel-kick? His confusion lasted only until Rayyaan's leg whipped through the air and struck him with full velocity. The impact hurled him backward, arms flung wide— and the man toppled out through the window he had come from.

The one with the broken nose had recovered by then. He stretched his arm— eight feet long— toward a vase in the corner, intending to smash it over Rayyaan's skull. Ghazal reacted instantly, stretching her own arm to stop him, but

Rayyaan shook his head, stopping her. As the attacker swung the vase toward him, Rayyaan intercepted his elongated arm with lightning-fast reflexes, twisted hard, and sent the vase flying. The man extended his leg, trying to strike Rayyaan with an elongated kick— but Rayyaan grabbed his leg instead, lifted him effortlessly, and slammed him against the walls again and again until the room filled with his screams.

"Leave him— come on." Ghazal warned sharply.

Rayyaan flung the limp attacker out of the window like a discarded rag.

"Let's go," she said, grabbing his hand.

They rushed out of the room.

Ghazal's chamber was on the upper floor. They ran downstairs, passed through several corridors, and emerged into the backyard of the mansion. A white horse stood waiting. Ghazal leapt onto it, and with her signal, Rayyaan mounted behind her, pressing against her back.

She nudged the horse and it bolted forward.

In a single bound, the horse leapt over the eight-foot boundary wall and sped into the night.

This was the desolate, unlit land behind Chaudhry Safdar Hayat's estate— but it wasn't as empty as it seemed. Shah Alam's secret death-squad, the Dozakhi— their infamous black-clad executioners— were waiting in the darkness, anticipating that Ghazal or her father might flee through this rear exit.

They gave chase.

It was past midnight. Darkness reigned everywhere, yet Ghazal's horse ran as if it could see in broad daylight. The Dozakhi closed in from the right and left. Rayyaan later realized that they carried long black whips— fifteen to twenty feet in length. They cracked through the night like snapping serpents, slicing the air with a harsh "sadak—sadak" as they swung dangerously close. Rayyaan couldn't truly see them; he only sensed them— dark shapes merging into the darkness, invisible yet deadly.

"How many are there— these Dozakhi?" he shouted.

"Seven behind us— why?" she replied, as if she could see them clearly. Which meant she could see in absolute darkness.

"I can take them." Rayyaan yelled.

"Don't talk like a child— you can't fight them blind. If they catch us, we're finished."

He had to fall silent in irritation.

Then something changed.

The horse's wings… unfurled— massive, powerful— stretching nearly eight feet on each side in a few strokes. It beat them once, twice, three times, and the ground fell away beneath them. Wind roared past their ears. Below, the trees became a blurred shadow.

Up in the starlight, Rayyaan could see the Dozakhi more clearly. Their black horses now had wings too, soaring after them. Their long whips curled and snapped through the air like airborne serpents, seeking flesh to tear. But Ghazal swerved, dipped, rose, and banked through the air with uncanny precision, avoiding every strike. She could see them; he could not.

So, the vision he'd had last night wasn't the product of a half-drugged mind— this was real.

Only last night, the Dozakhi had been behind them and they was ahead. Tonight, Dozakhi bracketed them— left, right, and behind. And now, armed with those whips, they were far more dangerous.

But Ghazal was one of them too.

She maneuvered the horse sharply, breaking their formation. One by one, the Dozakhi fell back until roles reversed— they lagged behind and Rayyaan and Ghazal shot ahead. Their whips retracted. Below them, the land turned rugged— forests, streams, scattered lights like distant fireflies. The ground blurred beneath them as they soared in one direction.

Soon the flatland ended and mountains rose ahead.

Ghazal brought the horse down in a narrow gap where two massive boulders leaned together, forming a natural fissure. They dismounted.

"Come," she said, taking his hand.

There was no time to question. He followed her into the pitch-black passage.

She moved fast— almost running but this was no smooth path. The uneven surface made it nearly impossible for an ordinary human to keep pace in utter darkness.

"Ghazal— I can't run. I'm human. I can't see like you, and the ground is uneven," Rayyaan said helplessly.

She understood. She wrapped an arm around his waist, lifted his left arm over her shoulder, and gripped it firmly— like supporting an injured man.

"Listen— trust me. Just jump with me. Match your force with mine. Believe me— I won't let your foot stumble on a pit or stone."

"Alright."

He followed her lead, pushing off whenever she did— and together they leapt through the darkness, covering ground rapidly.

After some distance, they reached the edge of a ravine. Beyond it, Rayyaan could sense, not see— a waterfall pouring down like a shimmering curtain. Before he could protest, she leapt.

Rayyaan's heart lurched.

He braced for shattered bones— but first they passed through a hollow of air, then through the icy sheet of falling water— soaking from outside but remaining steady and then, after a brief drop, their feet hit solid ground. They staggered, but managed to stay upright. Seconds later, they steadied themselves against a rocky wall and sank down.

Cold rushed over Rayyaan's skin. Ghazal's body felt much warmer than his— He moved even closer to Ghazal… finding some relief.

"We're safe here. They can't track our scent," she whispered.

"You people can smell too?" he said in astonishment.

"Quiet— they can hear as well."

He fell silent.

For half an hour, they sat in absolute blackness, the thunder of the waterfall echoing around them.

"They'll think we followed the water downstream. They must have headed that way. We're safe now," Ghazal finally said, stretching and moving slightly away from him.

"And what if someone still finds us?"

"Then what are you here for?"

"Hmm…" He paused for a moment, thinking— "Did your people never consider, at the time of our marriage, that such possibilities existed? That he is the Sultan of the realm — and that your step would be declared outright rebellion, after which he might take direct action against you?"

"The people present at the wedding were the chieftains of all the nearby territories. They had assured Abba-Huzoor that they stood with us, and that such a situation would never arise. But it seems they either succumbed to some pressure… or Shah Alam bought them with promises. Still, all of this was set into motion by that old dwarf— the one who must've carried news to Shah Alam that you were capable of facing his men… and had openly, fearlessly joined hands with us.

That must have infuriated him— set him ablaze. And that is why he made his move tonight."

"Meaning if I had never reached Dera Jamal, none of this would have happened?"

"Yes— not tonight. But if those chieftains had already switched sides, then sooner or later this was destined. There's no point regretting it now."

"So, what next?" Rayyaan asked, frustration tightening his jaw— "Your people aren't strong enough to help us. Your father is most likely in Shah Alam's custody by now. What options do we really have?"

"One option is to leave these wastelands behind— go somewhere far away. Shah Alam isn't powerful enough to hunt us across the world. Let him spend his life searching."

"Fine— then let's leave at dawn."

"Leave Abba-Huzoor behind?" She snapped, fire rising in her voice— "In our society, women don't even have the right to express their own will. We are raised to bow to the decisions of men. Yet even in such a world, Abba-Huzoor raised me according to my own will. He gave me education… allowed me to see the world… gave me the right to choose. When Shah Alam sent a marriage proposal, even then, by our custom— Abba could have agreed without question. But he refused. He asked me first. And when I refused, he rejected Shah Alam… knowing the consequences. This calamity fell upon him because of me— because of my choices. And you think I will abandon him to his fate?"

Rayyaan felt cornered— "So what will we do?"

"We stay— and fight. Either we die fighting… or we triumph."

"Just the two of us!" he exclaimed in disbelief.

"No. Shah Alam is a tyrant. Countless people suffer under him. There are many who resent their chieftains… who hate Shah Alam. We must gather such people— organize them, form a force… and see this battle to its conclusion." Her voice trembled with determination.

"Ho gai phir to Eid," Rayyaan said reluctantly— "Well said, Razia Sultan. But this is a long process. It could take years. You jinn have long lifespans— you can afford to spend decades. We humans barely get a short life."

"So, didn't humans fight wars?"

"Against other humans, yes— not against jinn. Look… in face-to-face combat I can take on Shah Alam too, if I have to. But you forget— I have limits. You thrive in darkness; you can see in darkness. I'm human— I'm nearly blind in the dark. Your world operates at night. And your… long-limbed acrobatics—" He shook his head— "Against that, even two opponents become a problem. You can vanish from my sight — I can't vanish from yours. What sort of fair fight is that?"

"Yes… your limitations are real. You will face difficulties. But you can still stand with your wife. And if you don't want to, you may leave. I will fight alone— and if I lose, I'll die alone."

"You're asking whether I would abandon my wife in danger?"

"From your arguments, that does seem to be the implication."

"It's not that. I'm not scared of fighting. It's against my honour to abandon someone helpless— let alone my own wife. But I cannot deny the reality— this is a battle among jinn. My abilities won't ever match theirs."

"Listen…" she said softly, "For this world to function in peace, a balance must exist. God created everything with that balance— predators and prey, oceans, winds, skies… to prevent any species from overwhelming another. Pharaohs rose— but Moses rose against them. Humans were given power— but never so much that they could become gods.

Every tyrant in history has fallen— never has any era been ruled endlessly by one unchecked monster. That is balance."

"Okay, but what's your point?"

"Shah Alam is powerful— but also monstrously unjust. Everyone knows he cannot reign forever. For balance to be restored, God must have set something against him. That something is you. I'm convinced now that you've been sent to us for his downfall."

"Me?" Rayyaan blinked rapidly— "How?"

"Recognize the signs. God never speaks directly— He shows indications. Shah Alam has a boon— no jinn can kill him. That belief makes him reckless. No human can kill him — or so they think. Therefore, people fear him. Now see the signs— there was a prophecy that I, a jinn princess, would marry a human— in the month of Shawwal. It could have happened anywhere… in Shahelaar, in the human world… anywhere. Yet look how destiny twisted paths— Shah Alam saw me somewhere, became obsessed, moved mountains to acquire me. You, meanwhile, stumbled into our world through chaos… and the prophecy came true. How extraordinary that a human— capable of matching jinn in combat— ends up my husband. It can't be coincidence."

"You're saying— Shah Alam cannot be killed by his own kind; so destiny arranged for a human fighter— me… to be thrown into this mess through a chain of events linked to you. And your prophecy existed only to make sure that this clash would happen."

"Exactly. And when we tell this to those who hate Shah Alam, they will believe— truly believe… that his end is possible."

"But still… my limitations—" He hesitated again.

"Where there is imbalance, God creates a way. There must be a path for you too."

She paused… then her eyes lit up.

"Listen— one path exists. We need to go to Baba Abdali."

"Who is that now?"

"A great Sufi— so powerful that even God is said not to deny his words. Shah Alam's boon came from him. No one knows whether he is human or jinn. No one knows his true age. They say he existed in the time of the Prophet… meaning at least fourteen hundred years old, if not more. In our era, no jinn has ever met him— except Shah Alam. All we have are stories— that he lives far from the eyes of the world, immersed in divine worship, still present somewhere in these lands. When history has fallen out of balance, both jinn and humans have sought his help. "Although Abba Huzoor is two hundred years old, and even in his generation no one ever had the ziyarat of Baba Abdali, that does not settle whether he is still alive or not. All we have are the stories, which assure us that he will live for thousands of years, and that when we are in need of his help, we will find him."

Rayyaan shook his head— "In our world, people have ten children by the age of seventy. Your father is two hundred and only managed one daughter— who's barely nineteen!"

"Don't get distracted. If jinn reproduced like humans, there'd be no space left to stand. Focus on the real concern — how do we find Baba Abdali?"

"I don't know— I just learned today that there exists a being older than a millennium."

"He lives somewhere far from the world, hidden in darkness, devoted to God."

"And how do we find that?"

"Let me think."

She pressed a finger to her forehead, muttering aloud.

"No one alive today has seen him— except Shah Alam. Anyone who would know how to reach him must be at least three hundred years old… perhaps three hundred fifteen. Who among us is that old? Who… who… who?"

Rayyaan watched her tap her temple in deep thought.

"The oldest among us today is only about two hundred and fifty."

"Only two-fifty! Madam, four generations of humans die in that time. In our world we'd put such a person in a museum."

"Don't mock— he's respected."

"Alright, don't be upset. We'll hold on to his ankles if we have to. Even if he cannot take us to Abdali Baba, he might show us the path. We'll think about this tomorrow. At night we humans only think of sex— daytime is when important ideas settle in. Let me sleep… otherwise I'll be useless tomorrow."

She opened her mouth, then closed it, realizing he meant no disrespect— only exhaustion.

Rayyaan's clothes were still damp. To warm himself, he pulled Ghazal close. Her body's comforting heat washed over him, and with that relief, he abandoned every worry, every battle, every prophecy…

…and slept like a dead man.

●●

"You really thought… you could ditch me?" Omar snarled, shaking Aryan by the collar with both hands— "You thought you could escape me?"

"A— are bhai… it's not like that at all," Aryan stammered, terrified— "I waited for you for a long time… when you didn't show up, only then I moved ahead… trust me, brother, I swear."

But it made no difference. Omar must have been searching for them the entire night, and rage had settled on his head like fire. He attacked Aryan viciously— and Aryan tried to defend himself, even fight back, but in front of Omar he was a child. Within moments Omar had beaten him to a pulp.

He stopped only when Aryan stopped moving, collapsed on the sand like a limp sack. Omar dropped beside him, breathing hard. Manaal watched them from a distance— frightened, shaken. She had never even thought about this possibility. And now a new trouble loomed— if Aryan remained under this Ghoul's shadow until they reached civilisation, she would have to suffer the Ghoul too— a creature whose behaviour she did not yet understand.

When Omar finally came back to his senses, he turned to Manaal.

"What did you even see in this coward?" he asked curiously— "that made you fall in love with him?"

"Love?" Manaal's eyes widened.

"Why are you so shocked?" Omar frowned, trying to read her expression.

Manaal met Aryan's gaze— and his eyes pleaded silently. She understood immediately— Aryan must have told the Ghoul something like that to win his help. If she denied it now, Omar would certainly question why she mattered so much to Aryan— why he risked his life to free her. And if he discovered who she truly was… he could lose his mind just as the Qasra people had. She decided she would reveal nothing, and she would keep the façade alive.

"His innocence," she finally said, siding with Aryan, "The innocence you're calling cowardice."

"He is a coward," Omar muttered with disgust.

"Maybe for you… by the way, do you even know me?"

"No. Are you some princess of a kingdom that I should know who you are? You look like one— your face and your body both— that's why I'm asking. How did a cowardly, penniless, kingdom-less excuse of a prince like him trap you? He can't even guarantee you two meals a day."

"Then I'll leave him— and find someone else. I'm not short of options."

Omar grunted and fell silent.

For the next half hour, all three remained where they were. By now the sun had risen fully, flooding everything with light. A few humans from the surrounding lands also appeared and began working in nearby fields. The good thing was— unless they wanted to be seen, humans couldn't see or sense them.

"Let's go," Omar finally said, rising to his feet.

Aryan stood up quietly— unsure what to feel. The very woman for whom he had been willing to live as Omar's slave… he no longer felt anything for her. And now he couldn't even say it, because last night he had practically begged to keep her with him. Torn and confused, he looked at Manaal— and she silently begged him with her eyes— Please. Say nothing. Let me stay with you for now.

Omar stretched his body— and before their eyes transformed into a colossal horse with a horn-like protrusion on its forehead. It wasn't a real horse— no saddle, no reins. They would have to ride bareback, gripping his thick mane for support.

He tossed his head, signalling them to mount. Aryan climbed up first, then helped Manaal up behind him. Aryan grabbed handfuls of the beast's mane; Manaal, unwilling yet helpless, held Aryan's waist.

Her touch sent a warm, electric shiver through Aryan— but he restrained himself and signalled Omar to move.

Omar began running along the riverbank. When the river became shallow enough to cross, he plunged straight into it, spraying water as he thundered through. Then he turned Northeast— toward the land they believed was Panjshir… a long, unforgiving journey.

The day grew hotter. Omar ran. They crossed plains, stony plateaus, and sun-scorched hills. For Aryan, the harsh sunlight was tolerable— but for Manaal it was torment. Within two hours she looked exhausted and faint. Seeing this, Aryan pleaded with Omar to stop. After nearly three hours of running, Omar halted in a patch of greenery.

They lit a fire, roasted a few things over the embers, and ate. A small pool nearby provided them water to drink. Omar, having fed well the previous night, needed nothing.

After half an hour's rest, they set out again.

Manaal had no desire to move— but no one cared about her wishes. Aryan too remained silent; it was pointless to create trouble before reaching Panjshir. Best to make use of Omar's speed while they could.

The afternoon heat was vicious, but the wind from Omar's gallop made it bearable.

Hours passed quickly beneath them.

Three and a half hours later, they stopped again near a river. Human settlements existed here too— but since humans couldn't see or sense them, it made no difference.

After another short break, they continued— by now the sun had begun its descent.

As daylight faded, the heat softened, wind turned cool. Compared to the earlier journey, this stretch was merciful. Still, for Manaal the constant motion was torture— but she endured in silence.

Darkness settled, stars brightened, and Omar kept running without pause. They had noticed throughout the journey that Omar avoided every settlement belonging to his own kind— deliberately choosing routes that stayed clear of them. He clearly wanted no encounters before reaching his destination.

Four more hours later, Omar slowed. Distant lights shimmered ahead— not human lights, but those of their people. Relief washed over them— the journey would end soon.

Before entering the settlement, Omar stopped and signalled them to dismount. As they stepped off, he returned to his true form.

"Is this your place?" Aryan asked.

"No. That's still two hours away." Omar's tone was flat.

"Then why stop here?"

"Because I have unfinished business with someone here," he said with a strange smile, "Someone who humiliated me, standing with your father. I was weak back then— not anymore. Today I will settle every score."

"Who?"

"You'll see when we meet him. Girl— cover your face. No point tempting people unnecessarily."

Manaal had nothing suitable to cover her face. The clothes she wore barely covered the essentials. She looked helplessly at Aryan, who handed her his handkerchief. She covered half her face with it.

At Omar's gesture, they walked toward the settlement.

As they drew closer, they saw activity— men, women, children. People noticed them. Aryan and Manaal, appearing like ordinary jinn, didn't attract much attention… but Omar's gigantic build did. People watched with wary curiosity.

No one approached— they only observed from a distance.

Omar didn't wait. He grabbed one man by the shoulder. A few nearby raised their weapons instinctively— but did not attack.

"Where is your chieftain? I must speak to him," Omar demanded.

"He doesn't meet strangers," the man replied calmly.

"I'm no stranger to him."

"That's his residence." The man pointed toward a hill.

All three looked. Atop a small hill stood a grand, old-styled mansion. Dimly lit lamps glimmered through its windows.

Omar strode toward it. Aryan and Manaal followed.

People continued to watch but made no move to interfere. Manaal briefly considered slipping away— maybe seeking help to return to Rakh'aan. In a place full of jinn, she could easily find someone sympathetic. But this was Panjshir territory— home of Rakh'aan's enemies. Revealing her identity to the wrong person would mean death. And with Omar nearby… escape wasn't an option.

Still, she slowed her steps, letting distance grow between them. Aryan moved with her.

"Listen," she whispered.

"What?" Aryan asked quietly.

"Where is he taking us? Why should we care about some tribal chief of his? Tell me… if I separate from you here, can I get help to reach Rakh'aan?"

"Don't even think about it. You should have escaped earlier. This land belongs to the enemies of Rakh'aan. You can't reveal your truth to anyone. You'll need someone trustworthy… and that risk might kill you."

"Meaning I'm in danger here too?"

"In Panjshir territory you're in danger everywhere."

"Then why did you bring me here?"

"Because whatever danger came, I intended to face it for you… but now that we have no reason to remain together, you can face your dangers yourself. Why should I carry that burden?"

"Khinjeer," she hissed, teeth clenched.

The rest of the walk passed in tense silence.

When they reached the mansion's main doors, two guards appeared like phantoms— tall, broad, intimidating.

"What do you want?" one asked sharply.

"I want to meet your chieftain," Omar said— "Tell him Omar is here… to settle an old debt."

Once again, the two of them examined him carefully from head to toe— then they watched him take a few steps toward the main entrance of the inner building, and in the next moment he had reached it and gone inside. Behind him, they kept surveying the structure… it was built in the style of an imambada, with several domes rising above it and countless doors and windows visible. Most of them were wrapped in darkness, with light coming through only a few.

After a while, the doorkeeper who had gone in returned exactly as he had left.

"Come on." He signaled with his eyes.

He moved ahead, and the three of them followed behind him… the one who remained behind vanished again, ghost-like, to some unknown place. By now this was no longer something to puzzle over, so they kept moving forward, focusing only on the man ahead.

He led them through the main door, into a grand hall. Lavish seating lined the space. On the raised seat sat a regal man, drinking wine poured by two female attendants. Below, on cushions, sat several imposing figures.

The moment Omar saw the man on the throne, he froze.

The chieftain paused too, confused by Omar's reaction.

"Who are you?" Omar barked.

"Arshaan Haqqam," the man replied— "Chieftain of this land. Who are you, and how did you enter?"

"But… the chieftain here was Nazaar." Omar said in disbelief.

The moment the name Nazaar was spoken, Aryan jerked violently— staring at Omar in shock.

"Yes— there once was… but twenty, twenty-two years ago my father Altamsh Haqqam deposed him from the throne, and since then the chieftainship of this land has been in our hands." the man seated opposite retorted, staring at him.

"And where is your father now— could he tell me where Nazaar is, or can you?" Omar asked.

"Respect must be observed— I am not given to idle conversation." The man's brows rose.

"I must meet Nazaar at any cost— if he is alive."

"He is in our custody, and he will remain so forever… are you here to rescue him?"

"No— he is my enemy. I have come only to humiliate him."

"Oh… when age crept upon my father, he renounced rule and, ten years ago, handed his inheritance to me and withdrew into the wilderness for worship. I transferred Nazaar to Kohe Balesh. He is there now— if you truly are his enemy, I can arrange for you to meet him."

"That would be merciful— humiliating him will grant my soul a peace I cannot describe."

After a moment's thought he signalled to the wine-pouring female attendants. They extended long arms, producing a slip of paper and a pen, and passed them to him. He wrote a few words, stretched his hand so that Omar could take it, and Omar bowed and backed away.

Aryan and Manaal had also taken a step back at the sight of him; they, too, fell silent. They walked out of the building together. Once outside, Aryan could no longer contain himself.

"Why this obsession with Nazaar?" he burst out— "You were going to your own domain, your own tribe— so why suddenly pursue Nazaar?"

"He is as great an enemy to me as your father is," Omar said, voice filled with hate, "He was the most loyal of your father's retinue— the man who first came to me, offering me servitude. He humiliated me before my people, and after my defeat it was he, who consigned me to a damned life in those wastes. I cannot take another bite of life without facing him."

"Alright, but you say he's in Kohe Balesh— what exactly is Kohe Balesh?" Manaal asked.

"A mountain that houses Panjshir's central prison for political captives. Its administration is under Panjshir's government, though all the chiefs of the realm share its upkeep— each lord contributes. There they keep their political foes."

"And where is it?"

"Far from here— it will take another hour of travel."

Both Aryan and Manaal felt it was a waste of time— but for Omar, scorched by the fire of revenge, this solace was necessary. They slipped silently back out of the settlement. Omar shifted form and became that same horse again; both mounted and he galloped off.

For the next hour they rode on— valleys and climbs and scattered human habitations sliding past beneath them. Then they arrived at a greener stretch— a valley ringed by verdant slopes with a small central hill and several watercourses. Omar dismounted them and shifted back to his true form.

"This is the prison," he said, pointing toward the hill in the valley's middle.

"That may be, but there are no visible fortifications or entrance… how will we get in?" Aryan asked, perplexed.

"I know the way— I've been here before. Once, I too placed a prisoner in this place," Omar said, and on the move his form altered into that of a retainer who had sat in Arshaan Haqqam's assembly.

They followed him without question.

They descended the slope, waded a knee-deep watercourse, crossed some level ground and reached the base of the central hill. After a short climb they came upon what looked like a possible entrance— except a huge stone was lodged across it, sealing the way.

"What will you do now, brother? The path seems blocked." Aryan observed.

"It is always kept this way," Omar replied. He glanced at the stone and murmured a few archaic words as if requesting permission to enter.

Astonishingly, the stone moved away.

But the opening revealed not freedom but guards— armed men who had been waiting inside and trained their weapons on them at once. Aryan and Manaal raised their hands in alarm, but Omar was unfazed. He produced the paper that Arshaan Haqqam had written and held it out.

The guards' demeanour shifted as they read; they lowered their weapons. One of them then motioned for Omar, turning and walking away. The trio followed obediently.

They were led into a hollowed network cut into the hill — long corridors, stairwells up and down, barracks carved out of rock with iron doors. Lamps and channels of light made navigation easy; drafts showed the place breathed. Passing through the galleries they saw some barracks empty, others filled with prisoners— hollowed men who told their story through their faces. The place looked built to make escape an impossibility; those who came here would live out a captive's death.

The prisoner they sought was held in a lower, darker barrack where the light was thin and the air cramped. The retainer who had led them indicated the cell and stepped back.

Aryan studied the man more closely than Omar did— a frail figure with white hair and an unkempt beard, eyes hollow with weariness. He sat like a statue on a slab, and upon noticing them he slowly raised his head.

"Nazaar— how are you?" Omar asked, a venomous laugh curling his lips.

"Who?" Nazaar looked him squarely in the face.

"You won't recognise me in this guise… I am Omar— the same Omar who once came offering servitude on behalf of Hikmatyar Ghazavi. The same Omar whom you humiliated before my people. The same Omar you exiled to a blasted life. Remember? Or have you forgotten? You people took hundreds of domains; perhaps you drove out many Omars."

"Which domain do you mean?" Nazaar rose from his slab and came toward the bars to inspect him more closely.

"Shaluman— after you cast me out you enthroned your puppet Arba Ghaznavi."

"Oh— Omar Darvish. So, you have returned?" Nazaar tried to recall.

"Yes, Nazaar— and many times stronger… so that I may slap your face and teach you and that Hikmatyar Ghazavi a lesson in how I have avenged myself." Omar declared, word by word.

"How?" Nazaar's voice held interest.

"See this." Omar pushed Aryan forward— "Look at him, Nazaar, and recognise him. This is the son of your master Hikmatyar Ghazavi— Aryan Ghazavi— whom you abandoned thirty years ago under the guardianship of Sila's keep, asking Queen Abira to shelter him until Hikmatyar's return. But look— today he is a humble slave of mine; his life's bread I granted on the condition that he be my servant forever." Omar laughed derisively.

The revelation stunned not only Nazaar but also the soldier who had brought them here— and Manaal. Omar's earlier hints had sown suspicion in Manaal's mind that Aryan was the son of Hikmatyar's retainer, but now no doubt remained. Aryan's name spread in those faces; shock widened their eyes as they stared at him.

Nazaar reached out and touched Aryan's cheek as if to confirm the reality. Aryan felt a tremor under the old man's hand.

"Oh Aryan… why did you leave the masrib?" Nazaar's voice trembled.

"I thought I had grown enough to look after myself," Aryan answered, averting his eyes in shame.

"No… you are only thirty, my child. How could Abira allow you to leave the keep?"

"By my stubbornness— I demanded a chance to test myself. You released me until the arrival of Baba, and Baba never came. Who knows if he lives or if he is dead… how long should I have waited among those women?"

"Perhaps you were right… I don't know where the chieftain disappeared to— he never returned," Nazaar muttered.

At that moment the soldier who had escorted them tried to step away; his movement caught the attention of others.

"Omar— you should not have revealed Aryan's identity here… he is Shah Alam's man. Why would he want the son of Hikmatyar Ghazavi to escape from their hands? Seize him — before he exposes this secret," Nazaar said urgently.

On hearing this, the soldier retreated quickly. But Manaal — who stood at the rear and closest, sprang— she stretched out her leg and tripped him, sending him sprawling face-first onto the ground. Before he could recover, Omar leapt upon him, grabbed him like a small animal and slammed him so heavily against the wall that a piteous scream burst out. His skull split; perhaps his fate was sealed even before his fall.

But the scream did its work.

"Oh— what have you done? Now everyone will be alert. I will be cut off; without a fight we cannot leave this place," Nazaar said, grinding the bars with anxiety.

"Why should we release you— if a fight comes, I can fight," Omar replied.

"You cannot face them alone— and Aryan is not capable of fighting."

Footsteps were already coming rapidly in that direction. Aryan and Manaal both panicked, terrified by the turn of events— while Omar stood dumbstruck, bewildered beyond belief. He had not imagined such a scenario; his mind felt paralysed.

"What are you thinking— they are about to arrive." Nazaar's voice struck him like a blow.

●●

CHAPTER 9

When the DCM was struck by a RPG projectile and tossed up, Safir and Owais as well as the driver were violently flung inside the cabin— the vehicle vaulted and then flipped down the slope. Fortunately, when it rolled the damaged front screen faced the incline, so they escaped becoming prime targets for the bullets coming from ahead.

Thrown with the wreck, half to entirely out of the front portion, they fell clear. Owais was thrown fully out, Safir half-out, while the driver remained trapped behind the steering wheel— his head struck somewhere and split, blood running down his face.

The blast had stunned the three of them; it took a few seconds for their senses to return. In that interval the fuel tank, struck by a stray bullet, ruptured and detonated. The spilled diesel caught and the whole vehicle was swallowed by a spreading fire. The second blast shoved the DCM further and it tumbled down the slope. Owais had already been thrown clear— Safir managed to wrench himself out before the blast but the driver stayed trapped and went rolling down with the burning vehicle. Both men somehow steadied themselves and made their way down the slope to avoid falling into the line of fire; they peered below.

"We have to save him— he'll burn if we leave him," Safir said to Owais.

"Let's go."

They hurried down. A small mercy— seeing bullets whiz past, they'd already taken their backpacks and were holding them in front as makeshift shields— even if the packs were lost to the flames, they'd at least saved their gear. The DCM lay on a protruding rock, roaring in flames. The cargo inside was feeding the blaze, making it worse.

They reached the wreck. In the driving cabin the driver hung trapped, senseless, the fire creeping closer. The two of them moved quickly, hauled him free with care and dragged him away from the burning vehicle. All the while they kept an eye on the road, fearful another stray RPG projectile might roll down. Noise, smoke and gunfire echoed from there. They pulled the driver to safety before the flames reached him. Then they headed toward the Pamaher River. Above, the fighting continued— explosions and gunfire resounded, but they were lucky to reach the river without further risk. Safir laid the driver down on the sand; Owais checked the head wound.

"He's not mortally wounded." After a few seconds, he nodded at Safir.

Safir scooped water in his hands from the river and splashed it on the driver's face. The man stirred, blinked, and sat upright.

"Easy, easy… you're safe. Nothing wrong except a head wound." Owais soothed as he supported him.

The driver looked toward the road dully and then at the burning shell of the DCM on the slope; an involuntary, shocked sound escaped him.

"You should be thankful we got you out in time— otherwise you would have burned with it. Go and clean the blood." Safir offered a hand and the driver accepted it, standing up shakily.

He shuffled to the water and washed his face. Afterward he found a handkerchief in his shirt, wiped himself and bandaged the wound— the blood still flowed. Darkness gathered quickly across the sky and shapes began to merge into the night. Light from the roadside fighting still flashed in the distance.

"What now?" Owais asked the driver.

"You go— there's a road to a settlement that way. You'll get a lift or you can set out on foot. I'll see if anything's left." He answered in deep dejection and, without waiting for a reply, walked toward the burning wreck.

"Leave him," Safir said— "We must move. The night will only increase the danger."

Owais nodded and followed.

They followed the riverbank and crossed where a ford offered the shortest way. The river divided into many branches here; there were bridges, but using them would have required a long detour. So, they took the direct route. After some effort they left the wild tract behind and began seeing a few scattered houses, then fields, and finally the faint glow of a settlement in the distance.

They picked up the road that led to that cluster and walked on. When they reached the first habitation, two policemen appeared as if from nowhere; the nearby gunfight had driven most people to hide indoors.

"Who are you and how did you get here?" one of the policemen demanded.

Owais spoke. He explained the ambush and how they had escaped with their lives. He mentioned Burhan Shabai, who lived nearby. The cops checked the forged IDs Ishaq had prepared and then let them go. They did not know exactly where Burhan lived, but an elderly man on the way pointed them in the right direction. Burhan's house stood at the edge of a field and by the time they reached it the night had fully set in.

They pressed the bell— none… so they knocked loudly. Footsteps approached from inside and the door opened. A young man of Ishaq's generation stood there, dressed in traditional clothes with a sparse beard.

"Sent by Ishaq?" he asked sharply.

Both men nodded.

"Come in." He moved aside and closed the door behind them.

The place had electricity and they could see clearly. A small courtyard led to a kitchen on one side, a bathroom on the other, and a long veranda with rooms beyond. A couple of rooms were lit and a few faces peered through the windows. Burhan guided them into the innermost small room where chairs and a table were set; a computer glowed on the desk. He himself sat at the machine.

"Sit." He gestured; they dropped their packs and sat.

"Was there action on the highway just now? Were you caught in it or had you passed already?"

"We were in it— barely escaped. The driver's vehicle got destroyed and he was hurt. Barely survived," Owais replied.

"All right. Tell me what help you need. Ishaq didn't tell me anything."

"We're looking for Zargam— I don't have his full name. He's a Taliban commander and fighting somewhere with the Northern Alliance," Safir spoke without a preamble.

"Why? What's your business with him?" Burhan asked, surprised.

"There's a girl connected to us— TTP has abducted her. Border areas are their safe havens now; the group that took her intends to present her as a gift to Zargam to gain favour. We have to get her back," Safir said plainly.

"First tell me your relation to the girl," Burhan said, studying them.

"She is my cousin, and she is valuable to him because, at a difficult moment, she saved his life— and he has now come to love her," Owais replied frankly.

"Hmm… is she that beautiful? I never heard Zargam being placated with girls; he's not the 'give-a-girl-and-get-eased' type. Still, maybe presenting a girl and money could sway him."

"You could put it that way… beautiful, and a virgin as well," Safir said, somewhat hesitantly, avoiding Owais's eyes.

"Oh… then it's possible he might be pleased enough to grant some favor, but even that won't be sufficient. They will certainly pay some amount along with the girl. Do you have any idea when she was taken, and when they might deliver her to Zargam?"

"She was taken three days ago. They left Kaga two days before yesterday. I can't say about the ransom, but they might have a big consignment of opium they plan to send to Gwadar via our transport routes," Safir said.

"Look," Burhan began— "if they left with her two days ago, she is almost certainly in Zargam's hands by now. I know that man— not a Russian-type; ruthless and pretty deranged. If the girl's already in his stronghold it will be impossible to extract her. When American forces were here, there were slim chances, but now… it's nearly impossible. You might lose your lives trying."

"We don't care— we won't back down," Safir replied.

"I warn you— since this concerns a Talib commander, no one will assist you directly. I can, at best, tell you his likely location and point you to a man who'll sell weapons for a price. Beyond that, the risk is yours."

"Just tell us where he is."

"Okay— most fighting with the Northern Alliance is over and Panjshir is largely under Taliban control. Those Alliance elements who didn't collapse have either melted away, fled, or are scattered. The sector Zargam was fighting in has been captured for over a week and he's entrenched at Aroki. He's set a cantonment with nearly five hundred mujahideen. Extracting a girl from there would mean confronting them all— think coolly."

"We don't want to start a war. We just want to get the girl out by any means. Maybe there won't even be a shot fired."

"All right. Will you go tonight or in the morning? It's roughly a ten-kilometre trip. I can drop you off by vehicle but I'll leave you before the populated area."

"Fine. Feed us first. We don't know if we'll get another chance to eat; after that leave us where you can. If needed we'll take shelter near Aroki and plan."

Burhan nodded, stepped out and arranged food. While he was gone, Owais checked the internet connection on the computer and by coincidence— found his cousin Shireen online. He messaged her, asked about conditions in Mahepora. Shireen told him Mahepora's people had declared war on the TTP faction, mobilising fighters; she feared open clashes might break out that night. She also said the Bagraat group had accused the three neighbouring estates of killing their Chaudhry Abuzar and were preparing forces— Kaanwabeel was restless because Rayyaan's whereabouts remained unknown and suspicion was running wild; perhaps someone among them had snatched the chance to eliminate him. The situation was tense; anything could happen. For that reason, Shireen insisted he stay in Mahepora. Owais did not tell her the exact danger he faced; he only said he would try to reach Mahepora soon.

"Lots of unrest behind us— people are ready to kill," he said to Safir.

"Why? What happened?" Safir asked, alarmed.

Owais recounted everything and Safir's face hardened with thought.

"Kaanwabeel's anger is understandable— Rayyaan is like an only lamp to them. But how could he vanish? He wasn't seen during the attack nor afterwards. He didn't fall into Shahelaar's hands either— that's certain. You didn't capture him, so perhaps the Bagraat did— but who could have killed their Bade Chaudhry? Our families have no reason. We can't make heads or tails of this. Waqar Saheb dislikes such feuds — he has only one child and can't afford to lose him, and Rayyaan didn't live there anyway. He was returning the day the BadeChaudhry was murdered."

"I don't know... the situation is getting out of hand. Let's hope we can extract Elma without firefight and then sort things out there," Owais said.

By then Burhan returned with the food and they ate in silence. Afterwards, as Burhan had requested, Safir handed him money. Burhan left, returned shortly with an old Toyota Corolla— battered but serviceable.

They set off. Darkness reigned; there was no street lighting. The road was broken, and sporadic gunfire echoed in the distance. Around the Pamaher River wide tracts stretch for kilometres, with scattered settlements up to Mahmood Raqi. The highway runs along high ground; below it, a damaged track winds between inhabited patches into the valley. Beyond Aroki's fertile banks, a dry, brown hilly region supports settlements and several tribal enclaves.

Burhan stopped the car and pointed toward a hamlet in the distance.

"That's Shane Mir Wadi... Zargam will be there."

They shouldered their packs and got out. Seeing that settlement sent Safir's pulse racing.

"Listen, Burhan— I used your internet and logged into my Insta. I chatted with my cousin and forgot to log out. Please log me out now, and tell Shireen what I couldn't tell her— that the TTP took Elma to Panjshir and I've come to retrieve her. Tell her Safir is with me. If we succeed, we'll be back in two, three days; if not, assume we've died in God's way. Inform Safir's family too— they don't know anything about our movement," Owais said, reclining in the passenger seat.

"Of course… Allah Hafiz, brother."

"Allah Hafiz." Burhan reversed the car and drove away. They watched his taillights fade. Around them there was no habitation immediately; but three or four settlements lay three to four hundred metres apart ahead on the heights. Their target was the settlement on the rise where a few lights and building silhouettes marked the hamlet.

"Let's go— into the mouth of death." Owais patted Safir.

Safir said nothing; he walked on in silence.

As each step took them further across the ground, the tension in them tightened. There was no guarantee the people of Shane Mir Wadi would greet them kindly or even allow them to speak. They could always claim they were bound for Dingak with Burhan— but for this place there was no excuse. If they were seized by Zargam's men, there would be nothing to explain what they had come for. They could not possibly mention Elma.

Safir felt double the worry— alongside the fear of meeting Zargam's men, Elma's face kept rising in his mind and dancing behind his eyes. Who knew in what condition she might be? There was no certainty the TTP even managed to bring her this far; perhaps she had fallen victim on the way, or plans had changed. They were walking straight into the jaws of death without any guarantee— was that a sensible step?

"Wait," Safir put his hand out— "This place has been a battlefield for months. They won't be careless. It's true the moon is hidden and the dark favours us, but they will have binoculars with infrared lenses to keep watch. This location is ideal for surveillance. If they see us and catch us, they'll shoot from a distance. We have no excuse to say what we came for."

"Then what if we circle and approach from the main road and get in through that?" Owais suggested.

"They will surely have a checkpoint at the entrance and catch us there. Burhan said he'd seen this place used as a cantonment— a cantonment means they've arranged security in every way."

"Then what do we do?"

"My sense is walking straight at them that way would be stupid. They'll assume we're enemies and open fire from afar."

"So, the only way is to go to those fifteen or twenty houses we can see— stay put for an hour or two, then sneak into one and bluff our way. We can force someone to show how to get in, or use them as a pawn to enter. They'll travel in and out of those houses; their people will have reasons for movement that we can exploit."

"Then?"

Safir checked his wristwatch, thinking. "It's half past nine. Wait a bit, then make a move."

"Good idea. Let's do that." Owais snapped his fingers.

They changed course toward the cluster Safir had pointed out. A few houses showed tiny lights, though the wider settlement had no mains electricity. This hamlet lay lower than Shane Mir Wadi.

It took them five minutes to reach the edge. Rather than head into the village, they sat on a low mound outside. On the surface no movement was visible, but they refused to rush.

"Think someone could be watching us?" Owais asked, turning to Safir.

"How can we tell? We don't have thermal gear to spot someone in the dark. If someone's watching us, they'll move on us in a little while."

"But keep in mind— this place could be full of people in the same desperate state as us. Anyone wandering about like thieves will be taken for an enemy. Their interest won't be in asking if we're safe or detaining us politely— they'll shoot. We must act the same— no overthinking, no mercy."

"Hmm… have you ever killed someone?"

"Not deliberately. But when we went to take Iram in Kaanwabeel, Shameel died by my hand. The weight of that death still sits on my soul. I never go before Iram— no matter how much Rushan or Mahepora changed, I won't accept the man who killed my brother. He can never be forgiven."

"You like the tradition in which we score honour by taking each other's women, even if that means killing fathers and brothers whose daughters we intend to be with for a lifetime."

"If you press me, I won't speak soberly; Pashtun blood is hot. Rage takes over fast, we lose reason and then we don't know what we've done. If you're uncomfortable, why did you go to take Raika in the first place?"

"Because they started it— not us. They tried to take Inaya and in the struggle Rahil died. We went mad and attacked them; it's unclear whose bullet took Umair, but at least Farrukh and I still avoid meeting Raika. I don't like such methods personally."

"So, if we manage to rescue Elma from here— will you try to win her for yourself?"

"To be honest, I haven't thought that far. I don't think I'd try. If she wants to go with me she will; but her choice will not be bought with anyone's corpse."

"All four domains of Karagal are enemies to each other. It's hard to imagine love and marriage existing among us—

we win girls to lower rivals, not thinking of what those girls endure when they must live with the killers of their fathers and brothers."

"Have you ever wanted to do something like that?"

"You'll hate me, but once at an army function I lost my head seeing your Bade Papa's daughter Zafira— wanted to rush her, but then the Rushan mess happened and Shameel's death made me lose courage. Two of my family were ruined in that show, and among the remaining grandchildren of Khudabaksh Hamaar we have three lads; I'm the only bachelor left. I haven't resolved anything yet, but Pashtun blood is unpredictable— it can boil over."

"Ever told Zafira or tried to show her you liked her?"

"I never had the nerve... I do drop a 'love' react on her Insta photos occasionally; maybe she notices but never replies."

They passed an hour conversing like this. Nothing approached; that meant, to them, they had remained unseen.

At about eleven they rose. On the open ground, starlight let them see a little— and allowed them to be seen like shadows. If anyone found their behaviour suspicious, they could be shot from a distance. So, they walked toward the houses behaving as if they belonged there.

They stopped in front of a house that seemed the right one to infiltrate. A courtyard stood behind a high wall and the house itself faced it. The wall was tall enough to block direct sight. Following Owais' instructions, Safir took a Mauser from his bag, then, with Owais' help, planted his feet on Owais' shoulders and vaulted to the parapet. The courtyard beyond was dim— like a backyard with a tree and patches of vegetables.

He hung there for a moment, waiting for any reaction. When nothing happened, he dropped down to the other side. His feet hit raw earth without giving a sound. He stood, waited for any stir, and when none came, he moved toward a door which was padlocked from inside. He unlatched it and slipped inside; once in, Owais closed the door and locked it again.

They crossed the courtyard and reached the main house. The two doors they found were shut. They paused and listened— one door likely opened to a passage, the other to a room. The heavy breathing behind one door told them someone slept there; if no one had been inside, their effort would have been wasted because they would not dare break a locked door in such a place.

Owais knocked softly on that door— no response. He knocked harder. The silence tightened. Then a deep female voice from within asked— "Who is it?"

"Aunty— it's me, Rafia. I'm in trouble," Owais lowered his voice so it sounded like a frightened girl.

A person roused from sleep may not grasp the words right away, but a pleading woman's voice didn't seem to indicate direct danger. After a moment the door creaked open. In the dark they could not see the face clearly, but the person on the threshold glimpsed the light, moved to shut the door— and it was too late. The two forced the way inside; Safir seized the shadow and pushed the Mauser away from the man's head while Owais pulled a torch from his bag.

By switching on the torch, they saw an ordinary Afghan woman of about forty-five standing there, terror on her face. On the bed a man of the same age lay— perhaps asleep, but now awake and watching them with alarm.

"Sit down quietly and don't move in a way that forces us to shoot. We're not enemies of yours— we need help," Safir removed the Mauser calmly and spoke in a softer tone.

"What help?" the woman asked, bewildered.

"Turn on the light," Owais said.

She lit a battery lamp, and the room filled with a pale glow.

"Forgive us for barging in. Tell me, who else is in the house?" Safir asked.

"My two daughters are in the room ahead," she answered.

"Sit still. Are you supporters of the Taliban?" Owais asked; the couple looked nervous— perhaps gauging what stance to take.

"Listen— we are not with the Taliban, nor with the Alliance, nor with your side. We are Pashtuns, but we have no stake in their fight. We came for a girl from your neighbourhood who was taken and held near Zargam in Shane Mir Wadi. Can you tell us what you know about this?" Safir explained cautiously. On hearing this, relief washed over their faces.

"We are Tajiks— not supporters of theirs. My son fought with the Alliance and was killed; as punishment my husband's legs were cut by them. They gave us mercy for the sake of my daughters' bodies." The woman's eyes filled with tears and her voice choked.

They looked at the man on the bed and realized he indeed could not walk.

"Actually, we come from Swat valley. A faction took my sister and were to hand her over as a gift to Zargam. They passed Kaga two days ago, so they should be in the route by now. But we don't know for sure. Can you tell if they've arrived?"

"If he's there, we must go there too. Can you advise how to get in without confronting them?" Safir finished.

"Did anyone see you coming this way?" the man asked in a shaking voice.

"No— we came with full caution."

"We cannot help you directly… but perhaps our daughters can." The woman rose and went out.

They glanced at one another— wary that she might be playing them false, but her manner didn't suggest deceit, so they nodded. She returned in about five minutes with two girls. Both were tall and of ordinary beauty, appearing between twenty and twenty-five, roused from sleep and plainly bewildered; at the sight of Safir and Owais a thread of fear showed on their faces.

"This is elder Maria and this is younger Tamanna," the woman introduced them.

"Look, sister— you needn't be afraid of us. We're neither your enemies nor here to drag you into trouble. In truth, some people have taken a dear girl of ours and she may already have been taken to Zargam. We must bring her back at any cost." Safir spoke gently.

"That's impossible." The one called Maria answered with the first, involuntary disbelief.

"Maria— it's impossible for us too to leave her to her fate," Owais said.

"There are at least five hundred mujahids there at any time, and if trouble starts, they swell from five hundred to five thousand in no time." Tamanna added.

"That's all right… we'll see. Tell us if you can spare a little help?" Safir asked.

"What help?" Maria's voice trembled.

"Don't be afraid— we won't force you to do anything that endangers you or your family. Two days ago, they left Kaga with the girl, so naturally they should have reached Zargam by now, but since these people themselves are targets for Taliban, we can't be sure they arrived safely; maybe they were intercepted en route, maybe plans were changed. How can we confirm whether Elma has indeed reached there?"

"A girl did come through this morning… looked like a model, very thin but quite beautiful." Maria spoke, warmed by the courage of memory— "Mustaqim said she was Pakistani. I didn't understand why she'd been brought here, but there was a girl."

Blood thundered in their veins; their hearts raced. Owais switched on his phone and showed them a photo of Elma.

"Yes— that's her. But the people who brought her might still be nearby. They were supposed to meet Zargam, but he wasn't there; he was to return by night. Now we don't know whether he reached or not."

"How were you there, and who is Mustaqim?" Owais asked, puzzled.

She fell silent and looked toward her parents. They understood she was about to explain how she learned the truth of why those people were spared.

"Look, son— these aren't ordinary families with homes and children. For a long time, they lived fighting in hiding from American forces and the Afghan army. A whole generation grew up in that life. Fighting was their only purpose; they never settled into households. Yet bodily needs exist, and to meet those needs they adopted a practice for a long time— in their own strongholds they forced girls and women into service, and many women were taken for that purpose. Now that they have some control, they might try to settle and value family and affection. Because of our son, they were intent on killing us all, but they needed to stay here for a long time and required the girls, so they forced us to agree that whenever they called, the girls would have to go to them. Last night they called, so Maria went." Her father hesitated, then spoke.

"And who is Mustaqim and what did you see there?" asked Owais.

"There are ordinary mujahid, yes— but there is also a fort-like, huge compound with several houses inside— that is Zargam's base. About fifty men there are his close men. Mustaqim is in charge of coordination— people contact him to reach Zargam. We wouldn't necessarily know which commander someone reports to in the wadi, but last night I was at Mustaqim's place when some men brought the girl; he went to speak with them and told they wanted to meet Zargam, but Zargam had gone to Kabul and was supposed to return by night." Maria told them.

"You were told?" Safir asked surprised.

"Not told directly to me— I overheard Mustaqim speaking to a comrade, then he sent me away. On leaving I'd glimpsed the girl but had no talk with her. If she was brought for Zargam, she'll still be there for sure."

Safir and Owais exchanged looks. One thing was now clear— Elma had likely been brought this far. The question remained— how could they get to a place bristling with so many fighters? How could they enter the house that, Maria said, stood like a fortress under the watch of fifty men?

"Now tell us how we can get in without facing them. Assume we must go and try to rescue Elma even if it costs our lives," Safir asked the two sisters; they looked at one another.

"You can't go around the wadi— they keep constant vigil and will pick you off from a distance. The main route into the wadi is guarded; you cannot reach inside without confronting them."

"Aren't there ordinary people living there? Are they all his men?"

"There are maybe three to four hundred households in the wadi, but he dominates them all and knows everyone. Mostly Pashtuns who keep a 'soft corner' for him. That's why

Zargam made this place his base— no threat is expected from the residents."

"So, an outsider like us can't just go there."

"You can, but you need a reason and identity to enter. It's not a tourist spot. It's a residential area; someone who goes must have a legitimate reason or an identity there. Still… there is one route no one knows about— not even they do."

"How do you know about it?"

"It was meant to stay secret, but because you've come asking for help, I'll tell you on the trust you won't reveal it. If caught… or if you die, then so be it."

"Trust us— nothing we do will bring harm to your people," Owais said, gripping her shoulder and meeting her eyes.

"My brother used to fight with the Alliance. The wadi used to have a special underground passage— the tunnel runs from a sealed section of what looks like Zargam's fort, and opens into our adjacent house, which has been empty for a long time because its residents are all dead. The tunnel is a leftover from the days when Ahmad Shah's men fought the Russians. My brother told me about it. They once tried to destroy that route when they were moving in favour of Zargam, to prevent others using it, but it fell into enemy hands. The secret remained. I can get you in through that passage, but the responsibility to keep the secret falls to you."

"We give our word, sister— we will never speak of this." Safir pledged.

"Very well… come with me." She stepped out of the room and they followed.

Outside she led them to a staircase hidden against the neighbor's wall and lifted it into position. They climbed the makeshift ladder to the adjacent roof. Unlike their courtyard the next house had proper rooms, though ruined from above.

Owais moved the ladder to the other side as Maria instructed, so they could descend.

They moved across and down; in the dark Owais switched on a torch.

They reached a locked room door. Maria pulled the lock and a fixed bracket slid out— a ruse. The room within was empty; there was no way forward— only windows and the sealed hatch of a loft above, shut tight like a door long unused.

"Where's the way?" Safir asked Maria, summoning the torchlight.

"From there— the neighbouring room holds a big stool. Bring it." She pointed to the shuttered loft hatch.

Owais fetched the stool. Together they placed it and climbed; he and Safir hauled Maria up behind them. From above the adjoining structures looked like the toilet and bathroom roofs— a lower slab a few feet down, narrow and dusty, about four by twelve feet. The opening to enter was just at the edge; the far wall was exposed brick, unplastered — exactly where the shutter hid a passage so the plaster had never been done.

"Cover your faces— it's dusty." Maria warned and wrapped a scarf around her mouth.

They tied handkerchiefs over their faces as she advised and began clearing debris. At the far end the brickwork was loose; with Maria's direction they removed the bricks and found an opening. Steps led down rather than a jump. They descended a narrow stair to a blocked door— the outside showed no lock, but the mechanism could be worked from below.

"How will this open?" Owais asked.

"Look down— there are grooves. Push them up with your fingers. The clip will pop out; slide left and right. It's a slide bolt." Maria indicated two grooves at the base of the door.

He placed both hands and lifted; the bolt unclasped and the leaves slid aside. A dark passage opened.

"You told us how to get in— but how will we leave so that the door looks locked from outside when you're already gone?"

"I will go with you. I'll guide you to the place and wait until dawn for your return— if you manage to come back. If you can't, I'll close the route after your disappearance; I won't close it before knowing your fate." Maria walked ahead, leading them.

The tunnel was rudimentary but propped and shored. Air was stale; the passage was seldom used.

"The door we left in the courtyard was locked from outside. If you return and find it locked, push the latch out from the frame," she explained.

"It's possible they found the other mouth and permanently shut it."

"Had they done that, they would have come through the tunnel to this side."

They asked about her life. She explained that until Karzai's days life had been comparatively stable; corruption existed, but ordinary people were safer than in the times of Russian or Taliban rule. But the current collapse had brought religious extremism and economic ruin.

It took them half an hour to cross the tunnel… and eventually it came to an end at a thick sliding door of the same kind. Beyond it, they found themselves in what felt like a dry stepwell. There were round, spiral stairs there to go upward, and climbing along them, they emerged into a closed space resembling an attic, so cramped that there was not even enough room to stand. Sitting, they slipped out through its other opening, where a drum had been kept to climb down, and the heap of junk lying around made it clear that this place was used as a store. The door here did have a latch, that much was true, but it too was bolted from the other side.

"Don't speak loudly— your voice may reach them." Maria whispered.

"How do we get out of here?" Safir asked.

"Look at the top of the door frame— push the latch out with your finger."

Indeed, where the latch sat there was a straight bar which could be pushed out. Usually it was long and bolted, but Owais shoved it free and the door opened into a dusty, abandoned storeroom; a stair ascended at one end.

"Understand this— this is a sparsely inhabited wing of Zargam's house, mostly storage. From outside it looks like one big mansion but inside it's like ten or twelve houses combined, each housing his men. Not families, no women— only fighters and their weapons and ammunition. Some local women come to prepare their food, and to satisfy carnal needs they pull girls from surrounding settlements like us. Mostly men are sleeping now; you will pass stairs into a corridor that leads to an inner courtyard. Up those stairs you may find night sentries; be careful. On the third roof up there, you'll find Mustaqim. Speak to him and he can tell you about the girl."

"How many men are with him?"

"Seven usually live there but at night rarely more than three or four at a time."

"Now tell us— if we return after you leave, how will we close and make it look as if the door was locked from outside?"

Maria took a length of twine from a bundle nearby. She slid the door's leaf up into place and fixed the latch in its slot. Then she threaded the twine through the slot and hauled it so that the long bar, with latch attached, pulled into the hole and held. With a few tries she pulled the twine tight; from outside the door would appear locked.

"Got it," Owais said.

She withdrew the latch, opened the door and stepped out.

"I will wait here until morning for your return. If danger comes, I'll slip away. What you want is almost impossible— but if you can manage it, return via this same route. Escaping out into their ranks is not feasible. Try to come back this way, and beware of leaving any trace of your passage— if this path falls into their hands the blame will fall on us, too."

"All right. Keep the torch— you'll need it to find your way back. We have one more torch. Because the floor is dusty our footsteps will leave tracks; after you leave, brush up the dust so the prints settle." He passed her the torch and she nodded. And both of them took their Mausers back out of their bags and drew a knife each— tools that were invaluable in places where work had to be finished in complete silence. One last look at Maria and they headed for the stairwell with steady steps.

At last, the hour of action had come. A single misstep could cost them their lives. Muscles tightened and pulses quickened; eyes and ears strained to the utmost.

●●

Jabbar Shah was pacing restlessly in his chamber while two guards stood silent at the open doorway, heads bowed. This was a wing of the royal palace of Aramin— the residence of Sultan Rakshan Buzaglo's Grand Vizier, Jabbar Shah— and at the moment he looked as if he might tear a man to pieces. On the opposite side of the room stretched a broad arched opening through which the wind entered freely, carrying the scent of dusk. Outside, the light was fading and darkness was descending like a curtain.

Every few steps Jabbar Shah's fists clenched, his lips moved with inaudible muttering. Then, at the cry of a falcon, he stopped abruptly and strode to the window. His eyes lit up — the bird was gliding toward him with wings spread wide. Quickly he slipped a gloved hand into a leather gauntlet resting on the sill and held it out. The falcon folded its wings and settled neatly upon his arm.

"I have been waiting for you, Shuggū," Jabbar Shah murmured, stroking the bird's back.

Around its neck hung a small leather capsule. He detached it, placed the bird upon its wooden perch near the window, pulled off the glove, and set it aside. The capsule held a narrow slip of parchment— a message. As he read, lines of deep contemplation creased his brow. When he had finished, he folded the parchment, slipped it into his pocket, and turned toward the door.

He had barely stepped outside when he almost collided with Fardhan Buzaglo, striding down the corridor surrounded by his attendants. Jabbar Shah halted out of courtesy; Fardhan was the Sultan's half-brother— a man Jabbar despised but still had to honor. He was of small build, with a narrow face that carried an expression of cunning malice.

"Where are you hurrying off to, Shah? You never find time for me," Fardhan said with mock sweetness.

"Whenever you summon me, I shall come," Jabbar replied, outwardly respectful.

"I hear the empire is facing some troubles. What's going on? Surely you can let me in on it."

"Nothing of concern."

Fardhan kept his eyes fixed on Jabbar's face for a moment, then curled his lip in disdain and walked on. When he had gone, Jabbar Shah exhaled a long breath and continued in the direction he had been heading.

The royal palace was vast— almost a town unto itself. It took him some time to reach the Sultan. On the way he learned from an officer that the Sultan was in the Darbar-e-Khaas, conferring with his commanders on some grave matter. When Jabbar arrived, the meeting had just ended and the nobles were taking their leave.

He bowed deeply.

"Ah, Shah— we were just about to send for you," the Sultan said, motioning him to sit upon the diwaan before him.

"Sultan… the news is not good. We are in danger."

"What is it? Take a breath, tell me calmly— what calamity has come?"

"Sultan, the realms of Qazaar and Rakh'aan have set aside their disputes and joined forces against us. Their armies are already marching toward Aramin."

"What! But why?" The Sultan sprang to his feet; Jabbar rose with him.

"According to our spies, your stepbrother Fardhan is behind it. It's his doing— a game played so cleverly that we can do little to undo it now."

"What has he done?" The Sultan trembled with anger.

"You know he has long coveted the throne. He's bought off most of the Aramin generals. It was his collusion with them that forced us to dismiss Elman, yet the outside world never learned that Elman no longer serves us."

"Yes, but— what then did he do?"

"You remember Alesar Saidov, Rakh'aan's chief warlord who seized several of our territories. Fardhan sent Elman to eliminate him, pretending it was on your orders. Elman took his men, killed Saidov, but two of his comrades were captured. One was executed; the other escaped that very night with someone's help. Two days ago, the princess of Rakh'aan arrived in Almat with her entourage for pilgrimage, and coincidentally the princess of Qazaar was there as well. Elman's fugitive reached them, attempted to abduct the Qazaar princess, failed, poisoned her with Zahr-e-Al-Shet, and fled with the princess of Rakh'aan. Before he escaped, the Rakh'aan guards recognized him as one of Elman's men and informed both courts. Now Rakh,aan and Qazaar have allied against us and are marching in vengeance."

"I will have that traitor flayed alive!" venom dripped from the Sultan's tongue.

"The matter has gone beyond our hands, Majesty. Most of our commanders have already shifted allegiance. If we act openly against them now, a mutiny will erupt within our own ranks. In that case, they might even imprison you— and when the combined armies of Rakh'aan and Qazaar arrive, they will hand you over as the one responsible."

"And I learn all this only now?" The Sultan's eyes blazed.

"I've warned you many times of his intrigues, but you thought him merely a petulant child— you told me not to waste thought upon him."

"Hmm. We were mistaken indeed. We thought his tantrums harmless and that he'd tire of ambition soon. We were wrong, Shah… So, where is Elman now? Only he can prove our innocence."

"He's vanished. Our spies are hunting him."

"And how far have the Rakh'aan and Qazaar armies advanced?"

"By tonight they will reach Bashar-Pama. We must stop them there. It is the only terrain where, even with fewer numbers, we can hold them. If they cross Bashar-Pama, we will not withstand their combined might— defeat will be certain."

"Can we not seek aid from Shah Alam?"

"I tried, but some of his own nobles have rebelled. He is mired in civil strife; he cannot help us."

"Oh, Fardhan… you wretch— what have you done!" The Sultan sank onto his throne, rubbing his temples in despair. After a moment he looked up again— "Can we not parley with Sultan Zarir Lugasi and Sultan Alesar Attali? Perhaps they might listen."

"I doubt they will. Our enmity spans generations; we've raided each other's strongholds for years. This is the first time two foes have found cause to unite against us— they won't waste the chance, least of all the Rakh'aanis."

"But what will be the outcome? Will our army even fight, facing theirs together?"

"They're marching united, unaware perhaps that Fardhan is behind it. Stay ignorant of his treachery for now — stand beside him publicly, rally the troops, and command them to march toward Bashar-Pama as if to attack Rakh'aan. Once they are there, retreat will be impossible. We must first survive this storm. Then, Majesty, you may deal with your brother and the chaos he has sown."

"Very well. Summon all the commanders— including that snake. We ride tonight for Bashar-Pama. Prince Rayad will remain here to govern, and you, Shah, will guard him against Fardhan's plots."

"As you command, Sultan." Jabbar Shah bowed again, stepped back four paces, and withdrew.

The Sultan began pacing the chamber in restless thought.

●●

Morning had long broken. Birds were already at their work; leaves and blades of grass, wet with dew, looked up to the sun that now warmed them with a gentle light.

A mountain stream flowed between rocks— and along its course walked Rayyaan and Ghazal, hand in hand with the water's music. Rayyaan was Rayyaan as ever, but Ghazal wore the face of Saarah. They spoke as they walked. For breakfast, she had forced a few fruits into his hands, and now he was in his full playful mood.

"So, the old men— those who live two and a half centuries— leave their homes and settle in forests?" he asked.

"Yes. Once worldly duties end, they devote all energy and time to worship. It's our tradition— there's nothing wrong in it."

"And when will your father retire to a forest?"

"When he is relieved of his duty toward his daughter."

"And for daughters— when does that time come?"

"Never. Their final years of worship are always spent within their homes."

"Why— are women afraid to live in forests?"

"No, but our custom is simply that way."

"Okay… and how do your people have children then? I mean, you live such long lives— shouldn't your families grow enormous?"

"That too follows a pattern. No matter how long our lifespan, we have only two or three children, and that too during particular cycles— not any time like humans. And none becomes a father before a hundred years."

"Of course! Otherwise, if someone fathers a child at twenty-five, by the time he grows old he'd have great-grandchildren as old as his own sons. The houses would be overcrowded with ancients instead of children!"

"Right— that's part of maintaining balance."

The even ground ended and the path grew rough, but they kept climbing. Now they had to hold roots and hanging vines to pull themselves upward.

"Why do people choose such hard places for worship?"

"So that humans cannot intrude in our communion with the Divine."

Climbing higher, they reached a place where long vines dipped to touch the water below and a rock face rose before them. Beside the falling water ran a narrow ledge, barely wide enough for two people, ending after twenty paces in a cave. Holding each other's hands, they crossed the ledge and entered.

Inside, darkness prevailed, yet the light spilling in from outside softened it for several yards.

At the point where light completely vanished, the cave ended— and there sat an old man, draped entirely in white, hair and beard silver as frost. He sat cross-legged in the air— about two feet above the ground, supported by nothing visible. His eyes were closed, body motionless, as if in deep slumber.

"Baba…" Ghazal whispered softly.

The old man's eyes opened. The moment they rested on Ghazal, his face filled with affection; but as they turned to Rayyaan, lines of anger spread across his brow.

He thundered something in a language Rayyaan could not understand.

Ghazal immediately dropped to her knees and replied in the same tongue he had spoken— a language completely foreign to Rayyaan. He understood from her tone that she was recounting every detail of what had happened. Rayyaan kept studying the old man's face… sometimes surprise, sometimes disapproval, sometimes anger, and sometimes sorrow flickered across it. The old man spoke again, then Ghazal, then he, then she— and in this exchange nearly half an hour passed.

At last, the conversation ended. Ghazal stood, gestured to him, and they turned back.

Once they stepped out of the cave, Rayyaan exhaled deeply.

"Who was that venerable elder?"

"My elder uncle— Abba Huzoor's older brother. I've come here with him twice before. Otherwise, how would I know where in these wildernesses someone is immersed in worship?"

"And why did he get angry when he saw me?"

"Because you're a human. He's angry at the very sight of any human. Be thankful you were with me— otherwise God knows what he might have done to you. And when he heard about our marriage, he was even more furious. But once I reminded him of the prophecy, he calmed down, and he was forced to accept the marriage."

"Fine— tell me whether he could help at all?"

"He doesn't know where Baba Abdali's sanctuary is, but he told me about Baba Jabari— the one who used to guide people to Baba Abdali nearly three hundred years ago. He's still alive and at a very specific place. He can help us."

"And how do we reach him?"

"We'll have to travel a long distance toward Alkan, in the Nuristan province— and we must begin this journey now."

"And what if Shah Alam's forces block us? What if those Dozakhis stand in our way? How will we ever reach him… especially if it's a long journey?"

"We'll see."

"How?"

"If you stay quiet, I'll be able to think."

And he fell silent.

"By the way, he knew of you— not you personally, but your family and your lineage." After a few moments she broke the silence, looking at him.

"What do you mean? Why would he know us? I'm not anyone special. Yes, maybe I'm from a landowning family so humans consider it something, but what's special about me for the jinn?"

"Your grandfather— the one who founded your estate… he knew him. He knew the other estates of Karagal too. He says all the roots of the present-day chaos lie in your people."

"What? How?"

"By human reckoning, perhaps not— but by our reckoning, this is the civilized era of our world… which means that until barely a hundred to a hundred and fifty years ago, we jinn were spread out across countless small settlements and principalities over a region stretching roughly five to eight thousand kilometers. That is to say, one or two settlements of our people might perhaps be found almost anywhere in the world, but the main region is this very area. The most important reason for this is that this region also has human populations, because of which all the things we require are readily available to us; and also because this is where there are vast uninhabited and desolate tracts, where our people can live in large populations in such a way that there is no need to interact excessively with humans.

So, in that uncivilized era, there used to be the chieftain of a tribe— Hikmatyar Ghazavi— a very formidable jinn. No one knows from where he acquired such power that he became invincible, that is, impossible to defeat, for everyone. For the next hundred years he fought wars with people throughout this entire region, conquered them, bent them to his will, and forced them to come under his patronage… in this manner, Ghazavi conquered the whole of this region and established a great sultanate, which we know by the name of Altunia. It had four central points— that is, four centers of power in four different tracts, from where control over the surrounding areas was maintained. Among these centers, one is Aramin, which is settled in the deserts lying to the West of Al-Jiban in Oman. One is Rakh'aan, which is inhabited between Iraq and Syria. One is Qazaar, which is near Modar in Turkmenistan; and one is Panjshir, which lies in the area near Kabul in Afghanistan that is known in the human world as Panjshir as well. Although Panjshir, being a green region, is completely inhabited by humans, within those very mountains— meaning beneath the ground— our city is also settled, which we too call Panjshir.

Hikmatyar Ghazavi had appointed different governors in these regions, who would handle the entire surrounding area like local controllers. Thus, while Aramin was under the control of Rakshan Buzaglo, Rakh'aan was under Alesar Attali— Qazaar was in the hands of Zarir Lugasi, and the city of Panjshir was in the hands of Shahryar Isavi. For a long period after that, Altunia continued to flourish, but approximately thirty to thirty-two years ago, Hikmatyar Ghazavi suddenly disappeared at a time when his wife Imama was pregnant— a woman he loved more than anyone in the world. After his disappearance, his wife died while giving birth to a child, and he never returned… no one knows where Hikmatyar Ghazavi vanished so suddenly in this manner.

After this, his close and loyal companion Nazaar took control of the rule into his own hands— but he was not Ghazavi, such that people would fear him. Gradually, he began to lose control, and rebellions started erupting in different parts of the dominion. Seeing this, Nazaar sensed danger for Ghazavi's son, so he took the child with him and disappeared somewhere. Left behind, Altunia began to break apart… and the governors to whom Ghazavi had entrusted the four centers declared those centers independent principalities and proclaimed themselves their sultans. At first, when this newly acquired power came into their hands, they tried to attack one another's realms and conquer them as well, but when each proved to be more than a match for the other, sooner or later, upon realizing this, all four withdrew and confined themselves within their own sultanates. Even so, none of them lives in peace within his own dominion, because their control, too, is not like Ghazavi's. Just as people did not accept Nazaar as their master after Ghazavi, in the same way they do not accept these rulers either, and from time to time one chieftain or another keeps drawing his sword against them and continues to declare rebellion. Their entire lives are being spent struggling against these rebellions.

The rule of Panjshir came into the hands of Shahryar Isavi— who had an illegitimate son, Shah Alam… who himself had once been the chieftain of a tribe. Then, no one knows how, he managed to gain access to Baba Abdali and obtained from him such power that after that no jinn could defeat him, nor kill him… and after this he launched a rebellion against Shahryar. Now Isavi was already such a debauched man and of such a wretched character that people themselves were fed up with him. As a result, no one stood in Isavi's favor against Shah Alam, and Shah Alam conquered the sultanate. He killed his own father and his half-brothers, and kept his half-sisters in his harem. Now, since he is not different from Isavi but rather two steps ahead of him, no one is happy with him either, and from time to time some chieftain or another keeps rebelling against him. This is another matter that, thanks to the boon granted by Baba Abdali, no one's blade works against him, and most rebels are killed at his hands."

"Alright… but where do my grandfather or our estates come into this?" Rayyaan asked, thoroughly puzzled.

"Before Altunia was formed, Hikmatyar Ghazavi accomplished something major— and for that he needed the help of four humans. These were Abuzar Sadazoi, Khudabakhsh Hamaar, Araz Khasoor, and your grandfather Hassan Afridi. They were ordinary Pashtuns from Swat to Chitral— not landlords.

In return for their help, Ghazavi led them to an ancient treasure buried in Kandahar— from the era when that land was known as Bactria, conquered by Alexander. Perhaps hidden to protect it from plunder. Whatever the case, the treasure passed to those four men, and from that wealth they established the four principal estates of Karagal— Bagraat, Mahepora, Shahelaar, and Kaanwabeel.

At first, they had no enmity; they had accomplished a mission together. But something happened that turned them into enemies. And that part— you must tell me."

Rayyaan sighed— "I've heard fragments of this, but neither my father nor my grandfather ever confirmed anything. I thought they were rumours. Maybe it's true… maybe not. But yes, I know the feud began over land. Once the quarrels intensified, two families got entangled, then all four. Meanwhile, their children, our fathers— grew up. Bagraat's Abuzar Sadazoi had two sons, Jabir and Nabam, and a daughter Juwairiyah. Mahepora's Khudabakhsh Hamaar had three sons— Yasir, Huzaifa, and Shadan. Shahelaar's Araz Khasoor had one daughter Amziya and three sons Arzaan, Shahan, and Anas. And my grandfather Hassan Afridi of Kaanwabeel had two sons— my father Waqar and my uncle Waleed— and two daughters, Laiba and Alina.

Our tribes have a very old custom— the custom of winning a woman. It's not a crime, nor an outrage, but a measure of bravery. The woman understands the tradition; even if she is taken after the death of her own father or brothers, she accepts the new relationship and fulfils it with dignity. It's not slavery— the man gives her all rights and respect and keeps her like a queen. Anyway… However, at a very young age, Jabir Sadazoi of Bagraat fell in love with Laiba, the daughter of Afridi of Kaanwabeel, who was also my aunt, they must have asked my grandfather for her hand. But the feud had grown so bitter by then that he refused. Jabir got furious, revived the old custom, attacked Kaanwabeel, and carried Laiba away. My grandfather was killed in that attack.

That started the cycle… In that generation— Jabir Sadazoi took Laiba Hassan; Hassan Afridi was killed. Mahepora's Shadan Hamaar took my other aunt Alina; my uncle Waleed killed Khudabakhsh Hamaar in retaliation. Bagraat's Juwairiyah Abuzar was taken by Mahepora's Yasir Hamaar; Yasir's brother Shadan and Juwairiyah's brother Nabam were killed in the incident. Shahelaar's Amziya Araz — my mother was attempted to be taken by my uncle Waleed; he was killed by her brother Arzan. In revenge, my father Waqar Afridi killed Arzan and married my mother.

If one looks at it, because of all these farces, in the next — that is, our generation, everyone had formed some kind of relationship with one another, and this should not have been repeated; yet no one knows what kind of madness possessed everyone's heads that all this happened again in our generation as well. Nabam Sadazoi's son Umair tried to take Inaya Khasoor; Inaya's brother Rahil was killed. In revenge, Inaya's other brother Sohail, with his cousins Farrukh and Safir, attacked Bagraat, killed Umair, and took his sister Raika — whom Sohail married. Umair's brother Hanzla Sadazoi took Inaya; in that chaos, their grandfather Araz Khasoor was killed. Mahepora's Noman Hamaar tried to take my sister Zikra and was killed by my father. In retaliation, Noman's brother Rushan Hamaar killed my brother Shameel and took my other sister Iram. Maybe I would have gone to avenge that— but before I could, my father sent me away so I would not remain trapped in these tribal cycles."

Ghazal paused— "Bade Abbu says all this is not without reason. Whatever Hikmatyar Ghazavi accomplished with the help of those four humans— a curse was born from it. A curse that condemns all of you to endless feuds, to bloodshed, to destruction. That one day Altunia will collapse — and so will your estates.

He doesn't know how to break the curse. Maybe Baba Jabari does. He can help us reach the level of freeing ourselves and Panjshir— from Shah Alam. But beyond that destruction, he has no remedy."

"Oh… this conspiracy is getting more and more complicated," Rayyaan said, scratching his head.

"We can only deal with matters up to our own level— the rest is beyond us. There's just one hope— the curse born from that ancient act, performed jointly by humans and jinn, may only be undone through a human–jinn union. And perhaps… that union is ours. The prophecy— that I would marry a human and he would free the realm from Shah Alam — points towards exactly this."

"Hmm… so the story that began with my grandfather was meant to end with his grandson. But tell me— how did someone as stunning as you live in Mahepora without some desperate prince drooling over you?"

"I was very young when my mother died in an accident… and around that time, Mahepora's wealthy Nawaz Mangal lost his only daughter— Saarah to blood cancer. She was exactly my age. My father had a connection with Nawaz sahib. With my mother gone, raising me alone was difficult— and because of the prophecy, he wanted me to be raised in a human world. So he requested Nawaz sahab to bring me up.

They were drowning in grief and welcomed me instantly. By then, Abba had taught me enough control over my abilities to change my appearance— so I accepted becoming Saarah. Her death and burial had taken place in Islamabad, so people never knew... and I took her place. To this day, everyone believes I'm their real daughter Saarah.

I usually remain in her form, hidden behind a hijab. Only when I come to our home in Dera Jamal Khan do I live in my real form. Abba always came to see me in Mahepora, and occasionally he would bring me to the village on special occasions."

"And Nawaz sahib never had more children? I mean... parents can keep a secret, but siblings? Isn't that impossible?"

"Saarah had been sick from the beginning, so they had avoided more children. After her passing and my arrival, they had two kids— both nearly ten years younger than me. The boy is nine years younger, the girl eleven. They're now ten and eight. At this age, what would they understand? For them, their elder sister will simply marry the prince of Kaanwabeel and leave."

"Fair enough... but one more thing. Suppose everything goes right— a perfect happy ending— and we live a normal life. We'll have two or three kids, they'll grow up, we'll see their weddings... but your ageing and mine are worlds apart. Say I turn fifty— I'll be an old man. At seventy, eighty, I may die. But you... who knows when you'll even start ageing? So as time passes, our appearance gap will keep widening. How do I explain that? Why aren't you ageing? Why is your time frozen?"

"When Abba first told me about the prophecy— that I would marry a human, I had the exact same fear. I asked him. And he told me a very old story... Something like this had happened centuries ago too. A great turmoil had arisen, and a girl had been chosen to end it— she too had to marry a human. It's a law, perhaps... that if a human–jinn alliance creates a great fitna, only a human–jinn alliance can end it. And the one chosen for such a destiny— whether it's a boy or a girl from our kind— is chosen by fate itself. And they must bear that burden at any cost.

The girl chosen before me— she married a human man, had three children with him, ended the turmoil, and after spending a few beautiful years with him, once she had borne his three children, her second marriage was arranged… to a human woman.

A rumour was spread that she had a fatal illness and would die within five or ten years. Then as the gap in their appearances began to show, she took to bed… and finally, upon her own insistence, her husband announced her death. A funeral was even held. But that night, our people retrieved her from the grave.

For the human world, she died that day. In our world, she lived another hundred and fifty years. She could have married again— someone from our kind, but she remained devoted to the man she'd loved. So, she spent the rest of her life alone. Though until her husband's death, she continued to meet him secretly— something not difficult for us.

So, understand this well— this too is our destiny. We will pay for ending this turmoil… whatever the cost. You and I— both."

The thought struck something deep inside Rayyaan. A heaviness settled on him, and he fell silent.

They covered the rest of the journey in quiet, eventually reaching the same cave where they had spent the night. Perhaps the Dozakhis had entered behind them, but they had not harmed the horse. He was still there, wandering near the cave mouth, and neighed softly the moment he sensed Ghazal's presence.

"We need to cover great distance during the day— at night, we'll travel through the skies," she said, mounting the horse— "Just pray nothing obstructs our way."

Rayyaan climbed up behind her, holding her tightly, and the horse broke into a gallop— in a direction Rayyaan couldn't identify.

The rush of cold air hitting his face made speaking difficult. Ghazal remained quiet too. They travelled in silence. And though the horse had wings, he kept them folded and raced only on his legs— covering unknown distances by noon. A few human settlements flickered in the distance, but they avoided them carefully.

When the horse finally stopped, they were inside a plum orchard.

"There's fruit here— and water. Come down. Sleep well through the afternoon, otherwise you'll complain the whole night." She dismounted.

She was right. The long ride had shaken every bone in his body, and hunger gnawed at him. They let the horse graze and ate the fruit to their fill. Soon, exhaustion overpowered Rayyaan and he dozed off instantly. He didn't even know what Ghazal did afterward.

He woke up naturally— refreshed.

Ghazal was sleeping right beside him… but something else caught his eye. Across the orchard, instead of leaves, dozens of tiny dwarfs hung from the branches— staring at them with unblinking eyes, smiling with torn, grotesque lips.

A chill ran down his spine.

Had they stumbled into the same silk orchard where Ghazal had rescued him earlier?

His alarm stirred Ghazal awake. She looked at him, then around, and understood everything.

"Are we in the same orchard where I got trapped before?"

"Can't say. It doesn't stay in one place— it shifts around."

"But now… we'll have to deal with these things."

"It's not night yet— their powers are limited. Show them your strength."

"Okay." Rayyaan stood. She sat up too— "Alright, brothers— I really need to pee… give me two minutes, then we'll talk."

They said nothing. Rayyaan stepped aside.

"Sit down properly— and wash, or use a lump of clay. That's our rule!" one dwarf yelled from behind.

Ghazal had warned him of this too, so he obeyed. Once done, he returned.

"So… will you come one by one, or all at once?"

They found this hilarious and began laughing in shrill, twisted voices— chaos spreading across the orchard.

It wouldn't have stopped— if Rayyaan hadn't grabbed the nearest dwarf and slammed him against a tree. The creature let out a horrific scream and fell limp.

Silence.

Shock rippled across the orchard— then rage.

All of them attacked at once.

But since they had to fight Rayyaan on human metrics, they paid the price of their age and weakness. They shrieked, transformed into cats, lions, wolves, dogs, serpents— contorted their faces into monstrosities— but none of their tactics worked.

In barely twelve or thirteen minutes, most of them lay scattered across the orchard— some dead, some unconscious, some badly wounded. A few who still clung to the branches stared at him in terror. Rayyaan gestured for them to fight— but they did not budge.

"Let's go." Ghazal grabbed his arm.

They took the horse and left the orchard behind.

"Marvelous. My instinct was right— you were sent for Shah Alam's downfall. Had they attacked me, they would have fought on my terms— and even weak and old, they would have overwhelmed any jinn. We can handle two or three— not so many at once. But you… you know modern combat. That's why you defeated all of them alone.

This one news alone will shake the entire council. Everyone will be forced to believe you're the one chosen to end Shah Alam. And Shah Alam… he'll understand it too— and he will become even more dangerous now."

And then they mounted the horse again and left that phantom orchard behind.

●●

(To Be Continued in 'The Kingdom Written in Sand and Time — Part Two')

Acknowledgement

To every reader who walks into unknown worlds with an open heart— this journey exists because you believe in stories that breathe. My deepest gratitude to those who lend strength, inspiration, and silence when a writer needs it most.